MASTER
MANIPULATOR

NICOLE S. GOODIN

MASTER MANIPULATOR

A COCKY HERO WORLD NOVEL

NICOLE S. GOODIN

Paperback Edition
ISBN: 978-0-9951276-9-2

Master Manipulator
First published May 2020
Cover design by Nicole Goodin
Images purchased from Shutterstock
Editing by Spell Bound

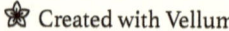 Created with Vellum

DISCLAIMER

This book is a work of fiction. All names, characters, places and incidents either are products of the author's imagination or are used fictitiously. Any resemblance to events, places, or persons, living or dead, is purely coincidental.

The author acknowledges all song titles, song lyrics, film titles, film characters, trademarked statuses and brands mentioned in this book are the property of, and belong to, their respective owners.

Nicole S. Goodin is in no way affiliated with any of the brands, songs, musicians or artists mentioned in this book.

To everyone who has ever had to fight for their happily ever after.

AUTHOR'S NOTE

Master Manipulator is a standalone story inspired by
Vi Keeland and Penelope Ward's Cocky Bastard It's
published as part of the Cocky Hero Club world, a
series of original works, written by various authors,
and inspired by Keeland and Ward's *New York Times*
bestselling series.

This book has been written using UK English and
may contain euphemisms and slang words that form
part of the New Zealand spoken word.
Please remember that the words are not misspelled.
They are slang terms and form part of everyday, New
Zealand vernacular.
I.e: I'm from New Zealand and sometimes we say
weird things down here... please try and be cool
about it.

1

Ky

MY STEP FALTERED as I laid eyes on the stunning blonde woman scanning the departures board, causing me to walk directly into the back of the irate-looking businessman in the line in front of me.

"Sorry," I mumbled, as I stepped around him, my eyes searching for the blonde once more.

Thick, golden waves hung past her narrow waist, almost down to her tight, perky ass, the mass of hair swaying gently as her head slowly moved side to side, reading each line carefully.

Her pouty lips pursed and relaxed, her teeth nibbling her bottom lip every so often.

She was living, breathing, perfection.

I stepped out of line, unsure where I was going, but knowing wherever it was, it involved her in one way or another. I'd always done well with thinking on my feet; I'd come up with something. First, I needed to get closer – check I wasn't imagining things.

It took me only a few moments to circle back, coming towards her from the opposite angle.

She cocked her head to the side, still reading the board with concentration that caused a small furrow in her forehead. I didn't know what she was looking for – a flight back to whatever planet she came from was my guess, because she sure as fuck didn't look like any woman from this world.

I slowed my walk and approached her from behind, hoping to catch a glance at anything that might tell me who this woman was and where she was going.

I might have finally been on my way back home, my travels over, but if she was headed to Mexico, I might have been able to muster a craving for tacos.

Something must have aligned in the stars for me in that moment, because her phone rang, startling her, and she dropped everything she was holding to the floor.

"Motherfucker," she muttered under her breath.

I grinned. Face like an angel, mouth like a sailor. Two of my most very favourite things in a woman.

Her passport, itinerary, *the works*, all tumbled to the ground at our feet. *My lucky day.* I crouched, scooping them up under the guise of chivalry, all the while ensuring that I got a good look at the information I needed to see.

Blake Vincent, travelling to Sydney, Australia.

I smirked to myself. Well, 'Blake headed for Australia', this was your lucky day. Actually, more accurately, it was *my* lucky day.

"And... no way in *hell* am I answering *that*," she muttered to herself as she turned, stuffing her phone back into her bag as she did.

Her eyes fell to the ground, looking for her stuff.

I stood back to my full height, which towered over hers, and held out my hand.

Her gaze travelled from the documents in my hand, up my arm until she finally reached my face. I didn't miss the sharp inhale of breath from her full, pink lips, or the whispered, "wow" that slipped past them.

"You really shouldn't leave important things lying around like that, blondie."

Her wide, bright eyes narrowed slightly. I'd never seen eyes like hers; one vibrant blue, one emerald green, so big, so fucking beautiful.

"Thanks for the tip," she replied, popping the 'p', her gaze dropping as she reached out to take her belongings back from me.

Australian.

I kept my grip a moment longer than necessary, forcing her eyes back to mine. She looked surprised, startled maybe by my insistence.

"You're welcome," I replied arrogantly, before I'd even given her the opportunity to express her gratitude.

She opened and closed her mouth like a goldfish,

unsure of how to reply, her frown growing by the second.

Blondie was flustered.

I took one last, lingering look at her, and turned, a smirk still playing on my lips as I disappeared through the crowd, heading back to the line for my flight, knowing full well this wouldn't be the last time I'd see her. We were going to be stuck together in a circular metal tube, thousands of feet in the air for the next fifteen hours, give or take, and I intended to do what I did best – make the situation work in my favour.

A plan formulated in my mind as the queue inched forward, one passenger at a time getting their boarding pass and checking in their luggage. That's one thing I wouldn't miss now that this adventure was all over – the airports, the waiting, the fucking around. I was sick to death of living out of a suitcase.

I caught sight of blondie joining my queue, about five people separating the two of us, but I didn't turn. I didn't need to; I could feel the daggers being thrown in my direction from all the way over here, even *with* my back turned.

There wasn't a lot of skills I possessed in this life but getting a reaction out of women was one of them. The other was taking risks and, more often than not, having those risks pay off, and as I stepped up to the check-in counter, I prepared to work my magic.

"Good morning, sir, travelling to Sydney today?"

American. Too easy.

There was something about American women

when you were an Australian male. Our accents drove them wild. One simple sentence could turn even the most sophisticated of women into coy, hair twirling, doe eyed, blushing, bimbos. I just had to hope that this particular female wasn't immune to my charms – or a lesbian.

"Morning," my eyes travelled down to the name badge pinned on her chest, "*Teresa*, and I most certainly am."

Teresa should probably have been used to any and all accents by now, given she worked in an airport that saw a crazy amount of flights leave to the land down under and the rest of the world each day, but if the sparkle in her eye and the way she pushed her chest out, just ever so slightly were anything to go by, I'd say she was quite the fan of a bit of Australian sausage.

"Heading home?" she questioned.

Small talk. Always a good sign.

"Something like that."

She let her eyes linger on mine a moment longer before glancing at the computer screen in front of her.

"Can I have your passport and booking number, please?"

I handed her the documents, leant my elbow on the desk, and began to lay the groundwork.

"You married, Teresa?" I asked as she punched my details into her keyboard.

She faltered, her eyes meeting mine. "N-n – no."

"Boyfriend?"

She nodded. "Been together three months."

"Congratulations. I just got married."

"Congratulations to you too then." She looked a tad deflated at the knowledge, but she'd come around. If there was one generalisation I was willing to make about women, it was that they were all romantics at heart.

"Thank you, wish I could say I'd gone more than five minutes without fucking it up, but that's the way my life seems to go." I shrugged.

She cocked her brow, her body leaning in closer to mine. "What do you mean?"

"She's furious with me already."

"Oh, I'm sure that's not true."

I glanced back over my shoulder, hoping that blondie wasn't about to let me down. I didn't need to worry. There she was, in all her pissed-off, sexy perfection, still pinning me with a look that could have killed.

"You see the beautiful blonde? The one trying to murder me with her eyes?"

I brought my focus back to Teresa. Her eyes darted in the direction mine had just been, searching for the woman in question.

"Oh *wow*, she really *does* look mad."

"That's an understatement."

"What did you do?" she asked, leaning closer again, now fully invested in my story.

"We got married yesterday, and I messed up the rings." I held up my hand to show her that I wasn't wearing one, "I got the sizing all wrong and they couldn't have them ready in time for the ceremony. So, we got married with no rings and now she's convinced it's a curse."

"Whoops."

"And then on top of that –" I baited her.

"Oh no, there's *more*?"

I restrained my smile. Poor, sweet, little Teresa was playing right into my hands and she didn't even know it yet.

"Afraid so. It was my job to book the honeymoon, and I messed up the flights, somehow managed to book us separately. We're not even sitting together. I'm going to have to figure out a way to get a glass of champagne or something delivered to her on the plane and hope like hell she'll be speaking to me by the time we land."

A slow smile crossed her face. "I can't do anything about the rings, but the seating arrangements... *that* I *can* help with."

"No? *Really*?" I feigned surprise.

"Give me two seconds."

She sat back at her desk, really settling into her work now as her fake fingernails click-clacked across the keyboard.

Click-clack.

Click-clack.

Click-clack.

"*Perfect*." She smiled triumphantly, the irritating sound coming to an immediate halt.

"You found us two seats together?" I prompted.

"I did you one better, I found two side by side... in *first class*."

"Oh, thank you, but our tickets are only –"

She held up her hand to stop me from speaking. "No extra charge."

Hook, line and sinker.

"I couldn't possibly..." I replied, playing my part to perfection. I was all the right things, shocked, surprised... grateful. I really had this bullshitting business locked down. I should have been on Broadway.

"Consider it a wedding gift. Happy wife, happy life, Mr. Bateman. That's what they say." She gave me a knowing smile.

"Well, if that's what they say, then who am I to argue?" I grinned.

"Exactly."

God, I sounded so cringey to my own ears, I wanted to give myself an uppercut, but Teresa was lapping it up.

"Thank you, I really appreciate it. I don't know what I can do to repay you."

"It's no big deal," she assured me.

I gave her my best appreciative smile and she ate it up.

"I know it's a lot to ask, but do you think you could do me one last favour? Don't tell her that it was anything to do with me. Pretend it's a random upgrade or something?"

She nodded at me knowingly. "*Of course*, she'll be

so surprised when she boards the plane and you're waiting for her."

I chuckled. *Oh, you have no idea.*

"I'll even request that the hostess bring you both a glass of champagne the minute she gets to her seat." She winked at me.

This was too easy; I should have pushed my luck further. Seems like Teresa here would have found a way to give me *whatever* I wanted.

"You've got no idea how much I appreciate this; you might have just saved my marriage."

Her cheeks coloured at my praise. "You're welcome. Now, I've got you all checked in, Mr. Bateman, I just need your wife's name and we'll be done here."

I glanced back at blondie, she caught my eye, scowled and then proceeded to look anywhere *except* in my direction.

No skin off my nose, beautiful, you're going to be seeing plenty of me.

"Blake," I said around a grin, "Her name is Blake Vincent."

2

Blake

I HADN'T PLANNED on getting into a sort-of argument with a drop-dead gorgeous, albeit *cocky*, stranger, but apparently it was going to be one of those days.

I risked another glance around the departure lounge, searching for him, but he was nowhere to be seen. Odd, considering he'd been in the line for the same flight as me, but hey, I wasn't about to look a gift horse in the mouth.

The last thing I needed was another run-in with him.

Not after how the first one went.

It could have been worse; he could have been more parts psycho than he was arrogant and taken off with my passport or something like that. That would have really been the cherry on top of the shit sundae that was my life.

I patted down my jacket pocket, checking for the hundredth time that my passport was still tucked safely in there. *Paranoid much?*

I needed to get on this plane. *Desperately*, like my life depended on it, because in a way, it kind of did.

My eyes swept the room of their own accord once more, but still nothing. I breathed a sigh of relief. He might have been pretty to look at, but that was where the appeal ended. That guy had his head so far up his own ass, I'd have been willing to bet that he didn't know night from day.

At least I'd be able to enjoy this upgrade without the worry that I might run into him again somewhere along the trip. Something made me believe that a guy like that would make it his mission to piss me off. I'd given him a reaction, albeit a subdued one by my standards, but a reaction nonetheless.

That cocky, self-assured smirk on his lips told me everything I needed to know about him – Mr. Tall, Dark and Ridiculously Handsome – within about two point five seconds. I had his MO all sewn up.

He was a player, in *every* sense of the word if I had to guess. He was one of those guys that made you stop and look twice, and the worst part about it was, the bastard knew it. He was used to getting what he wanted, and he didn't like to settle for anything less. I imagined him to be self-employed, not a CEO or businessman, he wasn't the type – a little too rough around the edges – but something that involved him having to take orders from nobody.

That was my assessment, and I didn't care if it was accurate or not, because with a little bit of luck, I was never going to be put in the position where I had to find out how right or wrong I was.

My phone rang again, pulling me from my favourite pastime – making judgemental assumptions about people I didn't know – and I closed my eyes in frustration.

Guilt.

Shame.

Disappointment.

I wasn't taking the call. Not now, probably not ever.

I didn't even glance at the name flashing across the screen, I just powered the phone down and tossed it into my overpriced handbag.

I'd have to get a new sim card when I got to Australia, and then hopefully, my phone might never ring again. Ever.

I glanced at the time on my watch, noting that it was nearly time to board.

I didn't know the procedure for first-class boarding, given that I'd never actually flown first class – I'd come to America in economy, and although luxury somehow surrounded me while I was here, I'd never gone anywhere by airplane since.

"Good morning, passengers travelling on flight number four, three, seven, seven to Sydney, Australia, we'd like to invite those of you travelling in first class to please make your way to the front, have your boarding passes ready, and your passport open to the photo ID page."

I guess that's me.

I stood, collected my carry-on and slowly made my way towards the departure tunnel.

"Thank you, have a nice flight."

"Travel safe."

"Enjoy your trip."

"Thank you for flying with us."

The pleasantries continued from passenger to passenger, the brightly smiling airhostess scanning each boarding pass and glancing at each photo as it was presented to her until it was my turn.

I handed her my boarding pass and she scanned it, her eyes lingering on her screen for a moment longer than with anybody else. She double-checked my passport and I waited, expecting her to tell me there was a problem with my newly acquired, first-class ticket, some type of computer malfunction or something.

She smiled wide, "I hope you have a *fantastic* flight, Blake."

She looked at me as though she knew something I didn't, but I wasn't about to hang around and find out what it was. I was heading straight to my cushy, first-class seat, and preparing myself to get some serious shut-eye.

"Thanks," I mumbled, taking my passport back from her. I followed the signs directing me towards the plane, trailing after the rich folk towards the aircraft door.

Once inside the plane, I was directed upstairs, and shown personally to my seat, if you could even call it a seat, it was more like a mini bed – think five-star hotel meets aircraft. It's a shame I was such a flake; this fancy, rich lifestyle really did suit me. I always thought I was born to have money, even though my new reality was a harsh contrast to a lavish lifestyle.

I didn't know what good karma I was afforded for this luxurious upgrade, but I was grateful.

I almost cried when I saw the leg room, not that I planned on spending much of the trip sitting vertical. I hated flying, especially long haul because sleep was like a drug to me, and right now, I needed a hit. A big one, straight into the vein.

I'd been sleeping like shit the past few weeks, probably the past few months if I was being honest, but being honest with myself wasn't really my speciality. No, I preferred to live in a state of delusion and then watch on with wide, disbelieving eyes as my life crumbled down around me. *That* was my style.

"Champagne?"

It was only ten in the morning, but no one in their right mind said no to champagne.

I turned around, looking for the bearer of gifts, and found myself face to face with a pretty, made-up-to-perfection, red-headed air hostess, holding not one, but two glasses of bubbles, with another full bottle behind her. *This day just keeps on getting better.*

"You have no idea how much I need that," I told her.

"I could take an educated guess." She smiled.

She handed me one of the glasses and sat the other down for my seat buddy, who was yet to make an appearance. Not that I cared who it was, it wasn't like I needed to stretch out to get enough space. I could put in my ear plugs, snuggle up under a blanket and not give another human being as much as a second thought for the next however many hours it was going to take to get my ass back to Australia. As long as it wasn't some old bird who wanted to tell me about every fucking grandchild she had, I'd be happy. I might have been a lot of things, but a bitch to old ladies wasn't one of them.

I downed the contents of my flute in one go, the fizzy liquid tickling my nose.

Perky red hadn't moved – must have been one of her 'educated guesses' that the glass wasn't going to last long as far as I was concerned.

She smiled, still polite as ever and took the glass back when I held it out, offering me another one.

"You know what? I think you and I are going to be fast friends. Thank you." I smiled gratefully.

"You just let me know if there's anything I can do for you. We want to make this a flight you'll never forget."

Weird, but whatever, lady.

Maybe being intensely helpful was a service they only offered up here.

"I'm good for now, thank you."

She pointed out where I could find my toiletries, pyjamas – *hello first class* – showers and the open bar.

This was crazy. I'd sell my soul to travel like this all the time. Actually, that's a lie; I'd had the opportunity to give a lot less than my soul for an even more luxurious life and look how that'd worked out for me.

I sat my new glass down on the arm rest – real glass too, no plastic cups like they give the peasants downstairs – and began my pre-flight ritual.

I located my eye mask, blanket, ear plugs, pillow and fluffy socks. I settled into my chair, tugged the eye mask over my eyes and turned out my reading light.

We still had to load the rest of the plane, but that didn't mean I couldn't get a head start on nap time. It'd also work in my favour, just in case a sweet little old lady *did* turn up – couldn't talk my ear off if I was out to it.

I got myself comfortable, more comfortable than should be legal on an aircraft, and crept my hand along the armrest, searching for my glass.

I'd down that, shove my ear plugs in my ears and be out for a solid eight hours, all going to plan.

I should have realised that I was *me*, and that *nothing* ever went to plan for me. Nothing. *Ever*. It had become a defining quality of my personality at this point, just ask my sister. *If there's something that can in no way go wrong, give it to Blake and she'll find a way to fuck it up.*

I slid my hand forward in search of the booze, felt around, but came up empty. Unless the glass had grown legs and hauled ass out of there, I should have found it already.

"Thirsty?" a deep, seductive, very male voice asked.

I froze, my fingers stilling.

It can't be.

That voice wasn't new to my ears, as much as I'd have liked it to be, it *wasn't*. I recognised it instantly.

It was him. Mr. Arrogant Prick.

I thought through my options in a flash, not that I had many to consider. The way I saw it, I could do one of two things. Pretend to be asleep – not particularly believable given he just saw me moving, but a possibility. *Or*, I could face him, send him packing and get on with my beauty sleep.

I chose the latter.

My eye mask was the first thing to go; if I was right, and I was about to come face to face with *that* man, I needed as many of my senses on alert as I could possibly have.

I slid it from my face and dropped it to my lap, before finally allowing my eyes to wander up his long legs, past his narrow waist, to his broad shoulders, leaving only his perfectly chiselled face.

Damn him.

"Hey, blondie."

The bastard had my glass of wine in his hand.

"*You*," I accused.

He chuckled, as though this whole thing was some type of joke, and then sat down in the seat right next to me.

"What are you doing?" I demanded.

"Sitting in my seat." He held his ticket out in my direction, and sure enough, clear as day, right there in black and white, was his seat number. Right next to mine.

My mind whirred, before coming up with the most obvious conclusion.

"*You* did this, didn't you?"

"I don't know what you're talking about."

He offered me my glass, and I snatched it from him, almost spilling the champagne. That would have been a rookie mistake, I needed it now more than I could have ever imagined possible.

He smirked, that arrogant, blood boiling smirk, and I brought the glass to my lips, sipping it.

I didn't know where my new best friend with the wine went, but I knew I needed her to get back here, stat.

I looked around for a call button, so I could ask for exactly that, when I heard him chuckle.

"Something funny?" I snapped.

"You have *no* idea."

Reluctantly, I met his gaze, struck again by just how dark his eyes were; brown, almost black irises flecked with tiny slivers of gold.

"What did you do?"

"Depends what you're referring to?"

"Cut the shit. It's no coincidence that we're both here, right next to each other. How'd you swing it?"

His lip twitched. *Amused.* The ass hat was *amused.* "I might have told a little white lie." He leaned across, and stage whispered, "If anyone asks, we're newly-weds on our honeymoon and you're pissed as hell at me."

"Newlyweds? *Honeymoon*? Are you high? There's only one part of that story I understood, and it's the part about being pissed. That was *incredibly* accurate."

He chuckled again, deep and throaty, and I hated the way it made butterflies flutter in my stomach.

"C'mon, blondie, this is such a special time in our lives, something to tell the grandkids one day, don't waste it being mad."

The captain had started speaking over the inter-com, but I couldn't focus on a word he said. No, my attention, *and* my rage, we're solely focused on the infuriatingly handsome stranger sitting next to me.

I brought my glass to my lips again, downed the contents and glared at him. "I'll tell you how this is going to go, I'm going to ignore you for the remainder of the flight," which given that the plane was only just pushing back, was going to be a very long time, " and *you* are going to do the same in return. I'm not inter-ested in playing your games, nor am I interested in being hit on, understood?"

He just laughed. Right in my face before leaning in even closer and sitting his jaw in his waiting hand. "You're welcome."

Jesus Christ. Not again.

My eyes narrowed, my frustration getting the better of me.

"What for this time?" I asked through clenched teeth.

"For the upgrade. The champagne. The company. The mind-blowing sex."

He was doing it again, that ridiculously cocky smirk. It made me want to reach over and wipe it off his face with the palm of my hand.

"The *what* now?" I hissed, registering what he'd said.

"I mean, the last part hasn't happened yet, but give it time." He chuckled, winked at me, leaned back in his seat and reached for his own glass.

Motherfucker.

I didn't know what the rules were concerning committing murder over international waters, but it was a long flight, and if he kept this up, there was a good chance I was going to find out.

3

Ky

I'D NEVER HEARD a woman huff so many times. She'd glared at me so long I thought I seriously might burst into flames before she turned away, giving me her back. It was adorable. She was sexy as fuck when she was mad.

I might have to keep her that way.

One of the air hostesses chose that moment to stroll down the aisle and crouch in the space next to me as pissed-off-blondie jammed her ear plugs into her ears.

"Mr. Bateman," she said, quiet enough that Blake would have to have strained to listen in. "My colleague filled me in on your..." her eyes darted to my 'wife', "*situation*, and I just wanted to let you know that if there is anything I can do to help you sweeten her up, just let me know."

I took in her tight up-do, her red hair shiny in the light. If it weren't for the woman next to me, I probably would have hit on... I glanced down at her name tag, *Leah*. She was hot, and I'd never had the opportunity to join the mile-high club, but given the semi I was sporting for blondie, and *blondie* only, I wasn't going to find out today. Not unless there was some drastic turn of events within the next fifteen hours that turned her apparent hatred for me into lust.

"Thank you, Leah, I appreciate that. I don't know what you have in the way of chocolate, but it's got me out of a situation or two in the past."

Blake could have been dairy intolerant for all I knew, or on some ridiculous carb-free diet, but hell, I had a sweet tooth and I'd be more than happy to take it off her hands.

Leah winked at me, straightened herself up and went in search of the sugar.

I relaxed back into my seat. Hell, even if this thing didn't come off in any way, shape or form, I'd still scored myself a free first-class upgrade. Not a bad day at the office.

I flicked through some of the movies on the screen, but my focus wandered back to blondie, she'd given up huffing and puffing like the little engine that could and had moved onto tossing and turning like she couldn't get comfortable. Which was obviously bullshit, given the ridiculous level of comfort surrounding us.

She was agitated, and it had nothing to do with the accommodation, and everything to do with me, if I had to guess.

I tapped her on the shoulder, and she dutifully ignored me.

"Blondie."

Still nothing.

"Blake."

"How do you know my name?" she snapped.

"So, you *can* hear me after all."

"I don't think they make earplugs effective enough to drown out your level of obnoxiousness."

"Is that so?"

She twisted her petite body to face me, her legs tucking underneath herself as she pulled out her ear plugs "*Look*, I get it, okay? You've got the whole, handsome, alluring, charming thing going for you, right? You smirk and women fall at your feet, correct?"

"Something like that." I gave her the exact smirk she was referring to.

She glared at me. "Well that's not going to work with me, you got it?"

Bullshit. I could see the truth in her eyes, no matter how hard she was trying to hide it. I got her all hot and bothered.

"Whatever you say, blondie."

"*Blondie*, really? Could you be any less original?"

I leaned across and tugged a strand of hair between my fingers. "Probably."

She swatted at my hand. "You may never call me that again."

"Oh, but I will."

"You're a jackass."

I chuckled, deep and low. This woman had more fire than a blazing inferno and here I was, running in headfirst without even suiting up. I was bound to get burnt, but I'd worry about that later.

"Your eyes are different colours."

"He's as sharp as he is handsome, ladies and gents," she drawled, the eyes in question never leaving mine.

"That's the second time you've called me handsome in the past sixty seconds, is that what you really think?"

Her eyes narrowed as her frustration grew. "I think you have selective hearing."

"I think you're attracted to me."

She was silent for a beat, then said, "I'm going to need you to stop talking before I seriously consider hurtling myself out the door and getting sucked into oblivion."

"We haven't taken off yet."

She briefly closed her eyes and shook her head. "You're seriously missing the point."

A slow smirk spread across my face. I didn't know if this was getting her motor running, but it was working for me. I was hanging on her every word. Our banter was turning me on, big time.

She let out a frustrated growl.

"You know what..." she stopped midsentence, scowled again and then raised her brows. "What's your name?"

I could have made her work for it, but honestly, I'd been dying to hear my name come from those soft, pink lips since the first moment she caught my eye.

"Ky."

"*Ky*? Are you some type of surfing hipster?"

I chuckled. This woman was oddly perceptive. "Matter of fact, I am."

"Figures." She rolled her eyes. "*Ky*... alright then."

It might have only been two letters, but it'd been a long time since I'd heard my name come from the mouth of a female with an Aussie accent, and it felt oddly like coming home.

"It's short for McKay."

"Yeah... so that's *not* a name."

"Tell me about it, I've been called MAC-KAY my entire life. I didn't think MAH-KY was that hard to figure out."

"Serves you right for having a name that's not really a name." She sighed. "Not that I can talk, I think my mum wanted a boy, giving me a guy's name and everything," she said, unimpressed.

"I think Blake is a sexy name."

If my comment surprised her, she didn't let it show.

"My middle name is Cameron."

I hadn't seen that, but I filed the information away for future reference.

"You might have a point."

She gave me a 'told you' tip of her head.

I wasn't completely sure when it happened, given

that my attention was elsewhere, but we were in the air now, the plane had levelled out and the seatbelt sign was off. *Huh.*

"So back to my original question, how exactly do you know my name?"

"Caught my eye when you were throwing your stuff all over the floor."

She arched a brow at me. "Oh, I bet it did."

I shrugged. If she was waiting for me to feel remorse for violating her personal information and then using it to manipulate a situation in my favour, she was going to be waiting a long time.

"Then what, hmm? You sweet talk the ticket chick? You must have some hidden charms I haven't been privy to viewing, getting us bumped to first class is no small feat."

"Who says I wasn't already in first class?"

"Oh, *please.* You're not the type."

"Are you saying I look like I belong in cattle class?"

This was too amusing. Every time she opened her mouth, I expected one thing and got something else entirely.

"If the assumption fits."

"You shouldn't make assumptions you know, it makes –"

"Yeah, yeah," she rolled her eyes, "An ass out of *you* and me, whatever. *Did you* have a first-class ticket?" She already knew the answer.

"Nope."

"So...?"

"So, *what*?" I asked, enjoying her frustration far more than was healthy.

"Jesus Christ, forget it. I'm not playing your games; I'm going to sleep."

Oh, but you already are playing, blondie. You have been all along.

I watched, amused, as she started up with the huffing and puffing again, shooting me daggers anytime our eyes met. I let her get as far as reaching for her eye mask before I spoke again.

"Like I said, I told her we were on our honeymoon..."

She stopped wriggling around but didn't look at me. I waited for her full attention. "I'm listening."

"Said that you were mad at me because I stuffed up our ring sizes and we didn't have them for the wedding, and then I topped it off by mentioning I'd made a mistake with the airline booking and we wouldn't get to sit together."

That got her attention. She glared at me and it only made me want her more.

"God, you're a pathological liar, aren't you?"

"Only when it's for a good cause." I grinned.

"So what? You just batted your lashes at her, and she waved her magic wand?"

"Pretty much."

"You better be careful you don't ever mess up that pretty face of yours, reality wouldn't be as kind if you were ugly."

I chuckled. More unexpected sass. This girl was too much.

"That's pretty rich coming from you, blondie."

"Oh please, I'm not the one flirting with strangers to get what I want."

"I wouldn't dream of flirting with *anyone* – not in front of my wife."

"You're ridiculous."

"Maybe, but you're falling in love with me already."

"Not only are you ridiculous, you're also a moron," she replied, not missing a beat.

We stared at one another, me grinning widely and her scowling.

I leaned across, my nose filling with her sweet, floral perfume.

"I don't mean to be rude, blondie, but could you stop talking my ear off now? I want to try and get some rest; it's a long flight."

"Mother of god," she muttered under her breath. "If I don't hurt you before we get off this thing, it'll be nothing short of a miracle."

I pointed towards the front of the plane. "We're airborne now if you'd still like to consider jumping out the door? I could ask the airhostess to put on the fasten seatbelt sign for the other passengers?"

She looked like she wanted to reply, but instead she bit her tongue, flipped me off and stuffed her ear plugs back into her ears.

4

Blake

INFURIATING WAS a word that sprang to mind. Arrogant was another.

Conceited.

Cocky.

Smug.

Sexy.

They all fit. Ky, in all his sun-kissed-skin glory, was as presumptuous as he was irresistible. Not that I was about to tell him that.

Ky Bateman – last name supplied by perky red, who'd returned with no wine, but a lot of chocolate as I pretended not to watch – was *trouble*. He may as well have had the word inked into his skin. He was also tall, toned and impossibly handsome, which didn't bode well for me and the situation I'd found myself in.

I *never* engaged in arguments with strangers, but I couldn't seem to help myself as far as he was concerned. It was as though he'd been handed the instruction manual for my make and model, and he'd studied *hard* – he knew exactly which buttons to press to get me wound up.

"Chocolate, wifey?" he offered.

I had my eyes shut tight and my ear plugs back in my ears, which were seemingly as effective as thin air, but he didn't need to be made aware of that fact. If I couldn't refrain from engaging in his games, I could ignore him entirely. It was only fifteen hours.

"C'mon, forgive your husband... have a chocolate."

I felt his finger prod my arm.

Should have brought sleeping pills.

"I'm not your wife, you're not my husband," I snapped. "We're going to get off this plane and never see one another, *ever again*."

I heard a gasp and my eyes flew open.

Perky red was staring at me like I was the most savage bitch she'd ever had the displeasure of meeting.

"She didn't mean it," Ky reassured her around a grin, before popping another chocolate into his mouth. "She's always had quite the temper."

Little did he know, I actually had the patience of a saint. I worked with children, and if I had a temper like a ticking time bomb, I'd never make it past morning break.

I guess I could forgive him, or anyone else watching this situation unfold for thinking I was on the brink of screaming, because I damn well was. There was just... *something* about him that made me rage like a wound-up bull that'd just spotted a red flag.

I needed to get a grip. I was usually unflappable, cool, calm and collected. I had to channel that Blake – she could handle him. After everything I'd been through lately, I wasn't going to let some handsome stranger be the thing to finally crack me.

"I'm sorry," I glanced at perky red apologetically, "but listen, he'll be back on the market soon enough, he's yours if you want him."

I think I'd just successfully ensured I wouldn't be fast friends with her after all, she looked shocked.

Well that makes two of us, honey.

"She's got a morbid sense of humour." Ky chuckled, looking thoroughly amused. "Don't take her too seriously."

Perky red nodded, her eyes bouncing between the two of us as she tried to figure out what on earth was going on. *Let me know if you do.* I sure as hell wasn't any closer to solving this puzzle.

"Thanks again for the chocolate. The endorphins should do the trick." He thanked her.

She smiled tightly at my pesky seat neighbour and disappeared down the aisle.

"Chocolate?" he offered again, unfazed.

"Can you stop? She thought I was a total bitch."

"You *are* a total bitch."

"If she stops bringing me wine, it's going to be all your fault."

He grinned widely then, like the idea pleased him.

"You have chocolate in your teeth," I grumbled as I reached out and snagged the tray of luxury chocolates from his grasp.

"What's your story, blondie? I can't quite figure you out."

"Maybe I like it that way," I replied. "Ever think of that?"

I tossed one in my mouth and moaned in appreciation. It was possibly the creamiest chocolate I'd ever tasted.

When he didn't respond, I glanced at him, finding him watching my mouth with rapt attention.

He blinked, once, twice and then shook his head. "What'd you say?"

It was my turn to smirk.

I raised a brow at him, and his lips turned up in a slow, unashamed grin. "Sorry, blondie, but if you're going to make sex noises, expect me to lose my train of thought."

"If you think *that* was an appropriate response to sex, you must not be very good at what you do."

A low, throaty chuckle slipped past his lips. I expected him to argue the point, but he didn't take the bait and somehow that arrogance only pissed me off more.

"C'mon, Blake, we've got nothing but time, tell me your story."

"Tempting, but I'm good."

I took my time, looking at each chocolate before making a choice.

"What are you running from?"

The winning chocolate slipped from my fingers, back into the tray.

"*Excuse me*?"

His dark eyes focused on mine. "You're running from something. What is it?"

"I don't know what you're talking about."

"An omission of truth if I've ever heard one." His grin was victorious. "Let's be real for a minute; no one in their right mind leaves California right before New Year's Eve unless they're running away."

"Well then, given that we're on the same flight, what are *you* running from?"

His forehead creased. "Me? *Nothing.*"

"Case and point." I raised my brows at him.

"I think you missed the 'in their right mind' part."

I couldn't argue with that. He was crazy. Taunting a strange woman in an airport, then manipulating people to get an upgrade to sit next to said woman was not normal behaviour.

Ky Bateman was likely a sociopath.

I should have requested my old seat back, that would have been the smart, self-preserving thing to do, but it was just so luxurious up here. It wasn't like he was going to be able to do anything too crazy to me in a plane filled with people. *Right?* Not that the old dude across the way who knocked back two glasses of scotch and a handful of pills before passing out was going to be a key eyewitness.

"You can think what you want, I'm just going back home to see my sister."

"Sister, huh?"

"I'm sure you're familiar with the concept of a female sibling," I deadpanned.

"You always such a smart ass?"

"I think you bring it out in me," I replied through gritted teeth as I selected my next calorie-filled victim.

"You're welcome for the chocolates by the way."

Jesus Christ, he was cruising for a bruising. I resisted the urge to fire back with the cutting remark on the tip of my tongue, instead deciding to thank him properly by eating each and every one of these things, even if it made me sick.

I swatted his hand away as he reached over to take one from the tray.

"Do you get Wi-Fi up here or what?" I asked around a mouthful of chocolatey goodness.

"This is first class, blondie, you could ask for a Brazilian model to bring you jello shots and they'd find a way to make it happen."

"I think I'll settle for the Wi-Fi."

I had my iPad with me in my bag. I hadn't planned to use it, given that my idea was sleep and then more sleep, but I hadn't anticipated *him*.

I doubted I could have slept right now if I'd tried.

"So why are you going to Sydney?" I asked,

already knowing I was falling into the trap he'd so carefully laid out for me. *Screw it*. He could pester me until he ran out of time and then I'd be rid of him.

"I grew up on the outskirts, haven't been back for years though."

"Why not, sparky, they refuse you entry into the country?" I questioned cheerily.

"Funny. You're funny." He pointed at me, his snug black t-shirt riding up his forearm, revealing more toned, delicious skin and the bottom of a tattoo I desperately wanted to see. "It was just time. I've been travelling around the US for years, the UK and Europe for a bit before that. I guess I'm just sick of living out of a suitcase."

"That sounds fair. Do your parents live in Sydney?"

He shook his head. "My dad is in Brisbane but we're not close."

He didn't mention his mum or any siblings and I didn't ask; there was something about his expression that told me he wasn't comfortable talking about it, and even though he'd pulled me right out of my comfort zone, this felt different. I knew all about the concept of not speaking about family.

"Have you got friends in Sydney?"

"My cousin, Chance. I was actually meant to go and stay with him in Cali while I was there, but he moved to Australia about six months ago with his wife and kids. More room for the goat."

"The *what* now?"

"Don't ask."

"Yeah... too late."

"His wife Aubrey is kinda into rescuing stray animals. This one has some kind of sentimental value or something, so they brought him with them when they moved."

"Right. *Weird*."

"You've got no idea. Anyway... They've got a place a little way out of Sydney now, so I'm going to go and stay with them for a bit until I decide what I want to do."

"Sounds like you've got it all figured out."

I wished I had even half of the plan he did, but that was my reality. I was a hot mess.

"Older sister?" he prompted me.

I nodded.

"How long since you've seen her?"

"About a year."

"I bet she'll be happy to catch up."

I would have been willing to bet that she was going to be royally pissed, but that was a story for another day – preferably one that would never come.

"I'm from Sydney originally, so I guess once I get settled back in and find a job, I'll get myself a place again." I shrugged.

"You were a long way from home, blondie."

"Sure was."

"What brought you to California?"

"A guy." The words were out of my mouth before I could filter them.

My heart thumped at my unintentional revelation.

He chuckled. "You don't strike me as the kind of girl who follows a man halfway around the world."

That got my back up for no other reason than the fact he was absolutely spot on. I wasn't that girl.

"You're hardly qualified to make assumptions about what kind of girl I am."

"Pot, kettle, black," he drawled, no doubt referencing my earlier assumptions about him.

"Touché."

"You're a real mystery, Blake Vincent."

He looked at me in a way that made me feel uneasy; soft eyes, a smile tugging at his lips – his gaze never releasing its hold on me. I wasn't sure where the hell he had come from, but if he didn't go back soon, something terrible was going to happen – I could feel it.

"And you're a real problem, Ky Bateman," I mumbled to myself.

5

Ky

"No thank you, I don't eat airline food."

I looked at her like she was crazy. "Blondie, this isn't some crappy plane food, this is a luxury three-course meal," I argued.

"I'm good."

I turned back to the airhostess whose name I hadn't bothered to learn. "She'll have it."

"I think you need a hearing aid," Blake snapped at me.

The airhostess's eyes bulged as I ignored my lovely 'wife' and proceeded to take the offered food.

This was the best meal I'd had in weeks; I wasn't about to turn down another serving – not even if it meant getting chewed out about it.

The hostess was a brunette this time, and she

scurried away as soon as I had it all, no doubt to go back to wherever all those perfectly made-up women hung out, to talk about the bitch in seat ten, D.

I chuckled thinking about it as I tried to make room to squeeze in the second plate.

"Give me that."

"You just said you didn't want it."

"That was before I saw how much you wanted it; all of a sudden, I'm hungry," she replied smugly.

I couldn't even be mad, she was good. I was being beaten at my own game more often than not since boarding this plane, and I was okay with that. It was refreshing to have a woman push back for once.

"Hope you're not a vegan," I quipped as I passed her the plate housing the finest cut of steak I'd probably ever seen.

"I think I'd eat that bad boy even if I was." She licked her lips as she sliced into the juicy cut of meat.

I moaned as another mouthful made it past my lips. I didn't know if they had a fancy chef held hostage in the baggage hold or what, but it was some seriously good food.

I snuck a look at Blake as she ate. She was so fucking hot, even in the airline pyjamas she'd changed into an hour or so ago.

She'd piled all those unruly blonde waves into a messy bun on the top of her head, with only a few soft tendrils floating down around her pretty face.

She sat cross-legged on the generous seat, her legs tucked up underneath her.

"Stop staring."

"I'm just mourning the loss of my second dinner."

She smirked, sassy as shit.

"I didn't think you'd have space after all those chocolates."

"Are you trying to say I'm fat?" Her brow was raised, her fork full of food paused on its way to her mouth.

"Oh yeah, you're a real whale."

"The correct answer to that question is always 'no', just for future reference."

"Noted."

"No seriously, pay attention. I'd hate for your future wife to get past all of this bullshit arrogance you put forward, and love you anyway, only to have you fall short when you don't know the correct answer to the fat question."

"Should I be taking notes? Are you going to quiz me on this later?"

She rolled her eyes, and I waited for her to take another bite before she answered. "Trust me, sparky, if there was a test, you'd already have failed."

I scowled at her. "What's that meant to mean? We've been on this plane for hours now and you haven't killed me yet."

"I think that says more about my self-control than it does about your ability to test it."

"You're a tiny little savage, you know that?"

"Noted," she mimicked.

I couldn't help grinning. She was too much, too quick, too drop-dead fucking gorgeous.

"Will you have a drink with me, blondie?" I asked, more genuinely this time.

She must have sensed the change in my vibe because she swallowed slowly, her unique eyes darting glances at my face.

"What do you mean?"

"I mean, we're sitting here, having a good time – seems like the perfect time for our first date. Have a drink with me."

Her brows shot up. "You and I seem to have different understandings of the word 'good', and it most certainly is *not* a date, but I need some alcohol if I'm going to survive the remainder of this trip, so yeah, sure. I'll humour you."

"All I heard was the 'yes' part."

"*Of course* you did."

I flagged down the hostess before realising I didn't know what Blake liked to drink.

"Do you want some fruity cocktail or something?"

She looked offended.

"Gin?"

Her face told me no.

"More champagne?"

She looked past me. "I'll have a whiskey, neat, please."

I really *should* have been taking notes. At the very least I should have been deciding on the answer I thought was correct, and then going with the complete opposite – that probably would have been closer to right.

"Make it two," I told the hostess.

Blake waited until she was gone before speaking. "You're not very good at this, sparky."

"It would appear that you're correct." I chuckled. "But hey, I got you here, I can figure out the rest as I go."

She leaned across, her legs sliding to the side and the v neck of her pyjamas falling open slightly as she rested her elbow on the arm rest. "What exactly *were* you hoping for when you messed with fate and forced us together?"

"This feels like a trick question."

"How?"

"If I tell you what I was hoping for, you'll probably slap me and call me a pig." I smirked knowingly.

"I figured as much."

I'd never seen a woman roll her eyes so many times in such a short space of time. Must have been another of my charms.

"So, you act like a prick in the airport, get us sitting together, and then what? Next thing we're in the mile-high club?"

"I mean, if you're offering."

"You're a pig."

"I told you you'd say that."

She cracked a smile. "Not funny."

"C'mon, it's a little bit funny."

Our drinks arrived courtesy of the brunette, who I was certain this time was taking far longer than necessary in our area just so she could listen longer.

I passed one of the solid tumblers to Blake.

"Cheers to us."

"Cheers to me not having thrown you from the aircraft yet," she replied cheerily.

I huffed out a laugh. "I guess I'll drink to that."

"But there's still plenty of day left yet," she muttered.

She downed the contents in one go, and I'd have been lying if I said I wasn't a little impressed by everything about her.

I watched her carefully as I sipped my own drink. She yawned widely.

"You should get some sleep."

"What a novel idea, can't imagine why I didn't think of it myself. Maybe if you stopped talking for more than thirty-five seconds, I might have had a chance."

I grinned, then began counting to forty in my head.

She frowned, a little crease appearing across her forehead as she watched me sit there silently.

"Thirty-six, thirty-seven, thirty-eight, thirty-nine, forty," I announced. "Look at that, you're still awake, blondie."

She shook her head, amusement still playing on her lips no matter how hard she tried to bite it down.

"Is your occupation driving people crazy for a living by any chance? Because you're awfully fucking talented at it."

"Nope."

"Well what is it then?" she pressed, her curiosity getting the better of her. "If I'm going to be stuck here with you, I figure I should at least know one real thing about you."

"I'll tell you mine if you tell me yours," I bargained.

I watched as she internally debated before giving me a half-grin, half-grimace. "Now you've made me want to keep it a secret."

I chuckled. "I really bring out your mature side, don't I?"

"I'd say the same back, but I'm not sure you ever had a mature side to begin with."

All sass, this woman.

"Guess."

"Alright. Do you work for yourself?"

I thought about it for a moment. "In a way, I guess. Yeah."

"Do you –"

"Don't I get a turn?" I interrupted her, eyeing her up and down. "Since you're all about withholding information all of a sudden."

She gestured for me to go ahead.

"Model?"

She snort-laughed. "I'm five foot four. That's a cute attempt at flattery but try again."

"Nurse?"

She shook her head. "Not a big fan of needles."

"That's too bad, I was just picturing you in a slutty nurse costume."

"You know what?" she replied quickly, biting down a grin. "I think it's time to watch a movie."

"Perfect; our second date. What are we watching?"

She breathed out deeply. "Have you got an off switch by any chance?"

I grinned wide. "Don't believe I do."

She huffed out a breath. "Do you have any idea how sleep deprived I am right now? I'm not sure I can keep up this relentless banter much longer. Fair warning, I might stab you – and the cutlery is real up here remember."

"I'll take my chances."

"I wouldn't. You don't know how badly I need my eight hours."

"Do you like action movies? What about a thriller?" I asked, ignoring her jibes as I flicked through the options available.

"Ew, no blood and guts. I prefer those things *inside* bodies."

I grinned to myself; she might not have realised it, but she'd just given the green light to date number two.

Another member of the cabin crew came and took away all our dishes, and I took a moment to get more comfortable, stretching my long legs out further. I was confident she was kidding about stabbing me, but I wasn't sorry to see the knives go, just in case.

"Rom-com?" I offered.

"Why don't *you* watch anything you'd like, and *I* get some sleep?"

She started moulding her pillow and slipping down lower in her seat.

"Don't kid yourself, blondie, you'll never be able to sleep with all this sexual tension swirling between us."

She yawned. "You have an overactive imagination, did anyone ever tell you that?"

"Might have heard it once before."

We fell into a comfortable silence, her drifting to sleep and me still looking for a movie to fill in the hour or two that I was willing to let her rest. I wasn't a total asshole – I'd let her have a *short* nap.

A movie caught my eye. I nudged her leg. "Look, blondie, have you seen this one?"

She didn't open her eyes. "What's it going to take for you to let me get some sleep?" she grumbled.

I grinned to myself at her obvious irritation.

"Meet me in the bathroom in two minutes?" I joked.

"Fuck off, sparky." She lifted her hand and flipped me off. *Again.* "Not even if the plane was going down," she quipped. But her lips told a different story. Blake could deny it all she liked, but there was something brewing between us and I wasn't going to give it up until I knew exactly what that was.

6

Blake

I KNEW I hadn't slept long, but given the company I was keeping, I was grateful I got any shut-eye at all.

I peeked over at him. He was engrossed in a movie, his stupid, sexy mouth stretched wide as he laughed.

I groaned softly. God, I hated the way that sound made my belly flip.

I was in a real serious situation here. I still had several hours in Ky's company, and then we'd land and go our separate ways forever. I didn't know which part of that situation I was more worried about, and that scared me, because as much as I hated to admit it, he was right – we *did* have chemistry.

"Welcome back, blondie," he said, his eyes not even leaving the screen.

"Have you been watching me sleep or something?"

"Nope. The snoring stopping was a dead give-away," he replied as he slipped off his headphones.

My eyes bulged.

He turned away from his screen and chuckled as he took in my expression.

"I *don't* snore."

"You sure about that?"

Nope. I wasn't sure about that at all, but one thing I was sure of was a subject change. I yawned and stretched out my arms, my eyes falling to the empty ice cream bowl in front of him. "You had ice cream and didn't get me any?"

"There was brownie too."

I scowled.

"Look, Miss 'I don't eat airline food', you slept through our second date, I don't think you're in a position to throw stones."

"Poor little pet, you're a slow learner, aren't you? Let me make it simple for you. *You and* I," I gestured between the two of us, "are *not* dating."

"Are you sure? Because it feels like we're dating. Mood lighting, top shelf drinks, good food..."

"You're impossible."

"I'm *right*."

"Pesky accountant?" I asked, even though I was certain it was wrong.

He shook his head. "Dancer?"

"Like a pole dancer?" I raised a brow.

He groaned. "I was thinking ballet, but now I'm

imagining you wrapped around a pole and I have to say, I like where this conversation is going."

I leaned across the small divider between us and lightly shoved his shoulder. "I wasn't born with rhythm, so no, to the ballet *and* the pole."

"That's a crying shame."

"You *would* think that."

He reached under his seat and pulled out his bag, taking an iPad from the front pocket.

"Asshole lawyer?" I tried again.

He shook his head, grinning as he powered on his tablet. "Do you plan to insult every profession during this little guessing game?"

"In my defence, the asshole part was only directed at you specifically, not the profession as a whole."

"Well you're wrong, about the lawyer, *and* the asshole part."

I pouted.

"You ever bet on a horse race, blondie?"

I shook my head.

He held the iPad up in my direction, showing me the live feed of a race meet in Australia. "Want to try?"

"So, you're a gambler. Why does that not surprise me?"

"You in?"

I shrugged a shoulder. "I guess so, but I haven't got any money on me."

"Doesn't matter. We'll make our own wager."

That sounded like a terrible idea if I'd ever heard

one. I had a pretty strong feeling that making any kind of bet with a man like Ky was comparable to making a deal with the devil, but I was stubborn – shying away from a challenge wasn't in my nature.

"What did you have in mind?" I asked warily.

"What do you want?"

Loaded question.

"To know what you do for a job?" I offered with a shrug.

He smirked. "Not high enough stakes. Try again."

I huffed out a breath. "Sleep. I want sleep."

He nodded, thinking it through. "Alright, your horse wins, and I'll leave you alone for the entire rest of the flight, you can sleep till your little heart's content."

"And if *you* win?" I questioned, knowing full well that deal would no doubt be stacked in his favour.

He drummed his fingers on the corner of his device. "If *I* win, you come with me when we land – there's something I want to show you."

I balked. "You *can't* be serious?"

"Oh, I'm dead serious, blondie."

"Didn't your parents ever teach you about stranger danger? It's like survival one, oh, one."

"We're not strangers."

"On what planet are we anything *other* than strangers? I've known you all of about six hours."

"You wound me, blondie, acting like you don't know me when we're due to start our third date."

I arched a brow at him. I wasn't even going to dignify that with a response.

His lips stretched into a wide grin. "You know enough to know I'm not going to strangle you and dump your body in the woods."

"*Do I*?" I challenged. "I don't even know what you do for a job."

"Fine, I'll sweeten the deal. If I win – you come with me, and I'll throw in my job as a bonus point."

Bad idea, my brain screamed at me. This was more than a bad idea; it was a momentous, epically stupid fucking idea.

Stupid, stupid, stupid.

It was still a terrible idea as I extended my hand for him to shake. "Alright, sparky, you got yourself a deal."

A devilish grin slid onto his face as he took my hand in his. I tried to ignore the way tingles raced up and down my spine at his touch, but it was impossible. The mysterious Ky Bateman affected me in a way no man had managed to do before. He got under my skin and each glance, every smirk, only pushed him deeper.

He rested his elbow next to mine and set up the tablet between us so we could both see.

"You're going to have to help me out here, I have no idea what any of these numbers mean," I admitted.

He spent the next ten minutes explaining how it all worked; the favourite in the field, the pay-outs for winning and placing, the starting gates, the jockey's records, the horses last several places, and the track conditions. It was a lot to take in.

"So that one highlighted right there, that's the favourite?"

He nodded. "Hot favourite too, it's barely making a profit for a bet on the win."

I replied, "Mmm," in agreement, as though I knew what that meant when really I had absolutely no clue.

He chuckled, seeing right through me.

"Let's do this thing then, I want that one, *Blue Eyed Princess*, she looks good for the win."

I was way out of my depth here, but she was the favourite, and that seemed like a good enough bet in my eyes – it was like using the 'ask the audience' feature on a game show.

He clapped his hands together slowly. "Very convincing, blondie."

I poked my tongue out at him.

"You *sure* that's the one you want?"

"She's the favourite for a reason. Why don't *you* just worry about picking *your* own horse and *I'll* worry about *me*," I snapped.

"Sure thing. I'll take *Just Sassy*. Reminds me of someone I know."

Clever, very fucking clever.

"Are *you* sure, sparky? Doesn't look like great odds to me."

"Is that your expert opinion?"

"Matter of fact, it is."

He smirked and went back to looking at the screen. "Why don't you just worry about picking your own horse and I'll worry about me," he mimicked.

I double-checked the numbers, and with only one minute left until start time, my horse was still the clear favourite. Ky's was somewhere towards the back of the field. Maybe I'd listened to the instructions wrong, but it seemed like a lousy pick to me.

"Here we go, Blake; may the best better win."

I hated the way my heart raced when he said my name. I also hated how nervous I was about this stupid race, but I needed to win – there was no way I wanted to get in a car with him when we got off this plane.

They loaded the last horse into the starting gates, and I couldn't for the life of me figure out why there was a small part of my brain that didn't think it would be the worst thing ever if I lost.

"What happens if neither of us wins?" I asked quickly.

"First to cross the line," he murmured, his attention on the screen.

The horses burst out of the gates and my hand shook.

My horse went to the front, taking an early lead and I cheered.

I heard Ky chuckle, but I didn't look at him. I couldn't take my eyes off the brown horse with the pink and white clothed jockey on its back.

"C'mon, number ten, go you good thing!" I cheered as my horse took an early lead.

"You're making a scene."

"I don't care, I'm *winning*," I gloated.

"You're winning... *for now*, blondie."

I scowled but shut my mouth. I didn't know the first thing about horse racing, but *surely* I couldn't lose from here, I had metres on the others.

The horses spread out as they came around the corner and into the final straight, thundering towards the finish line.

C'mon, c'mon, c'mon.

Ky's hand landed on mine and squeezed, and my breath hitched.

"There she goes," I heard him mutter. I watched on in dismay as his horse, number two, came flying out of nowhere, passing mine so easily you could be forgiven for thinking *Blue Eyed Princess* was just out for a Sunday stroll.

"*No*," I breathed as three other horses caught up and overtook mine as well.

I dropped my head onto his hand – the one that was still covering mine – when a close up of the finish line showed his horse coming in as the clear winner.

My donkey trotted over in fifth, which might have been okay in the world of racing, but in the world of making bets with handsome strangers, if it wasn't first, it may as well have been last.

"Bad luck, blondie." His sexy voice teased me, his tone amused.

"Fuck off, asshole."

"Don't be like that." He chuckled.

"Why do I feel like I just got played?"

There was silence for a few beats.

"Have you ever heard of a bookie?"

I sat up to look at him. He still had my hand

trapped, but frankly, that was the least of my worries right now.

"What, like those dodgy old guys from the movies who take people's money and provoke them to make lousy bets?"

"That's not exactly how it works."

"Explain."

"Punters – the people betting – go to a bookie to place their bets, usually on sports, horses, dogs, football... that kind of thing. The bookie takes the money, and if he thinks it's a good bet, he places it. If he thinks it's a bad bet – he doesn't. If the punter wins, the bookie pays him."

"What happens if the bookie doesn't place the bet, but the punter wins?"

"Then the bookie loses. He's out of pocket. A good bookie knows everything about the field. He knows a good bet from a bad one."

It clicked into place in my head. I snatched my hand from his. "Oh, you asshole! You're a bookie?"

He grinned, cocky as shit. "I think it's a blessing they've cleared away the cutlery after all."

"I think that's the most honest thing I've heard come out of your mouth all day."

"I'd say I'm sorry, but I don't want to start lying so early into our relationship."

"You played me."

"That's the way the cookie crumbles, sweetheart."

"You knew your horse was going to win."

"I had a pretty good idea."

"You are a master manipulator, Ky Bateman," I said with a shake of my head.

"I'm going to take that as a compliment, blondie, and because I'm *such* a good guy, I'm even going to give you a few minutes to let it really sink in while I go take a leak."

I glared at him as he slid from his seat and stretched his arms above his head, showing off a slither of rock-hard abs and giving me a glimpse of another patch of ink on his side.

Fuck. My. Life.

He took a step, paused and glanced at me over his shoulder. "Secretary?" he guessed.

"Nope."

"Lucky I've just bought myself some more time to guess." He was smug as fuck.

Shit. Shit. Shit.

I just ensured that.

I'd lost the bet. It might not have exactly been fair and square, but a loss was a loss and I had to deal with what I was going to do about it.

Crap. Play stupid games, win stupid prizes.

There was only one thing for it. I took out my phone and connected to the Wi-Fi before opening my emails.

I still addressed my letters to Ida, even though I knew damn well I was sending them to a woman named Soraya, but I was weird like that – old habits were hard to break.

I'd been writing into the 'Ask Ida' column for years. If there was so much as a slight inconvenience in my life, I wrote in – I wasn't necessarily looking for an answer, which was lucky because I rarely got one, but writing the question was therapeutic for me.

But one day, I got not only a response, but a brutally honest one from Ida's assistant at the time, Soraya. After that, I wrote to Soraya personally, and she replied with the kind of honesty only a stranger can give you. I kept writing to her, even after she quit her job and had children with her husband Graham, and she still took the time out of her day to reply – said something about the whole thing having senti-mental value to her.

I took a deep breath and tapped out my question.

Dear Ida,

I've been on a plane with an infuriatingly sexy man sitting next to me for the past fourteen hours, and long story short, we made a bet. I lost. He won. The wager? That I have to go with him when we land so he can 'show me something'. He's a total stranger... should I go?

-Indecisive Pansy, Miles High.

I glanced down the aisle, hoping that I'd caught Soraya at a good time. I needed answers and I needed them *now* – even though I knew deep down that I'd never asked a question that I didn't already know the answer to. Thankfully for me, her reply arrived quickly.

Dear Indecisive Pansy,

How sexy are we talking? Because when a strange man wants you to follow him into a carpark

to show you something, it's usually his penis. Scratch that, it's ALWAYS his penis.

If you think he'd have a nice one, I say put on your big girl pants and go for it.

-S x

As amusing and totally unhelpful as always, but as per usual – the push I needed.

7

Ky

I LOOKED over at Blake as the wheels touched down on the tarmac at Sydney airport. She'd been quieter ever since she lost the bet, and I didn't blame her, hell, I wouldn't have blamed her if she took off running the minute her feet hit solid ground, but I hoped she didn't.

I wasn't ready to say goodbye to her yet – sitting next to her was the sweetest kind of torture. I wanted her, *so badly* – more than I could justify in my head given she'd only breezed into my life less than twenty-four hours before. She was sexy, sassy and sweet. The perfect blend of the three. She had a smart mouth, wasn't afraid to bite back, yet she was good to the core – I could tell.

"Back on home soil, blondie, how does it feel?"

She'd changed back into her clothes and freshened up earlier, her soft lips now a deliciously tempting shade of pink.

"It feels like I'm about to walk into the lion's den if I'm being completely honest with you."

I chuckled. "I won't bite, Scout's honour."

"Coming from a pathological liar, that doesn't mean much."

"Speaking of lies, you up for one last show? I'd hate the hardworking staff to feel like they failed at getting us back together."

"What did you have in mind?" she asked as she collected her belongings and I followed suit.

"You could take me up on that bathroom offer?" I smirked. "We're not mile high, but I think it still counts."

"Hard pass."

"Worth a shot."

The look on her face assured me that it was not.

I thought for a moment. "Do you trust me?"

"Not in the slightest," she quipped.

Liar.

I ignored her. "Just follow my lead."

I got to my feet and held out my hand for her to take.

She glanced at it apprehensively.

"It's just a hand, blondie."

She rolled her eyes and placed her palm delicately in mine.

I led her down the aisle, pausing when I heard

the two air hostesses bidding farewell to the other passengers.

I had her pressed against the wall, her bag falling to the floor before she even registered what was happening.

My arms caged her in as she gasped, looking up at me with those big, beautiful eyes.

"Don't knee me in the balls," I murmured at her ear before my lips found purchase on her skin.

She trembled, and I swear to god, I was instantly hard. This might have started out being for show, but there was nothing make-believe about how badly I wanted her right now.

One day soon, I was going to kiss this woman for real and she was going to enjoy every god damn second of it.

I brushed my lips against her throat, and she hummed, her head dropping back against the wall as her hands gripped the front of my t-shirt.

"Well, I see the two of you made up," a voice came from behind me, and I smiled against blondie's neck. "Sorry to interrupt, but we need you to disembark the aircraft so the other passengers can do the same."

"No problem," I replied, straightening up and locking eyes with Blake. "We can finish this in private."

Her cheeks heated.

I chuckled – knowing full well that I was playing the arrogant prick role like a pro – scooped up her bag and took her hand in mine, towing her past the red head, the brunette, and down the stairs.

"You're such a tool," she hissed at me as she tried and failed to tug her hand back.

"C'mon, blondie, that was fun. You know it was."

"That was *humiliating*."

"Who cares, you're never going to see them again."

She didn't reply, which I was learning meant she'd realised I was right, but she was too stubborn to admit it.

We did the airport rigmarole, and surprisingly, she didn't leave my side the entire time.

"I've been expecting you to bolt," I confessed.

"Can't... I haven't got my bag yet." She smirked.

She had an answer for everything. I took her hand in mine again as we watched the conveyor belt go around and around and this time she didn't protest.

"That's mine." She pointed to a black leather duffel bag.

Mine was not far behind hers, and not much smaller either. I was surprised at her choice of luggage. She seemed a little high maintenance, I was expecting her to have a giant pink suitcase filled with hair products and heels or something, but this was going to make my life a hell of a lot easier if I did manage to keep her from ditching me. I hadn't anticipated a second passenger when I planned out my ride.

I hadn't anticipated carrying on our little white lie to every member of airport security who'd listen to me either, but it was fun, and it made Blake squirm, so here we were.

"That's it?" I questioned her.

She tried to take it from me, and I dodged her, swinging both of our bags over my shoulder together.

"I can take it."

"And run away from me? I don't think so."

She pouted. "I was *kidding*. A deal's a deal. You can trust me." She batted her lashes, but I wasn't buying it.

"I'm being a gentleman," I insisted as I nudged her in the direction of the exit.

"I call bullshit."

"Humour me."

We walked side by side through the airport and out into the stifling hot Australian heat. "Welcome home," I muttered, wiping at the sweat already forming on my brow.

I wouldn't say it was cold in Cali, even though they were in winter right now, but it certainly wasn't an Australian summer.

"It's hot as balls out here."

I laughed – full-on laughed at her choice of words.

"Can we get this over with already?" she pleaded.

Sweet, sassy, Blake had no idea what she was in for. My money was on her thinking I'd booked us an uber and was going to take her to some nearby café or something and then send her on her merry way. She couldn't have been more wrong.

"Follow me."

I weaved through the crowds and headed out towards the parking garage where I was expecting to find my ride. "Wait here," I told her as I ducked into the small on-site office to collect my keys.

I smirked at her as we walked past row after row of cars, all lined up one after the other. "Which one of these is yours?" she finally asked.

"Which one do you think is mine?"

I caught her eye and she tipped her head side to side, thinking it through. "Considering that bet you made on the plane, I think you've got a pretty good eye. I think business is probably going well for you."

Point to Blake. Business was very good to me these past few years.

I slowed my pace and she did the same.

"Maybe the BMW?" she pointed to a flashy, brand new BMW.

"Nope."

"Audi?" she asked hopefully, pointing to another.

"Wrong again."

"Land Rover?"

"You're not very good at this."

"Why don't you just put me out of my misery?"

I let her get ahead of me, and slid in behind her, my free arm coming up at her side to point. "*That's* mine."

She gasped at the contact before her eyes found my ride. "You're *kidding* me?"

"Not even a little bit. Bought that bad boy in an online auction and had the guy bring it out here for me."

She spun around to glare at me. "So, let me get this straight, not only do you expect me to get on the back of that death trap, but you want me to do that, knowing that you haven't even ridden it before?"

I swallowed deeply, my pulse racing as I stepped closer to her again. "Do you really think I'd put you in any danger?" It was meant to be playful, but it came out husky, honest.

Her retort was lost on her lips as she searched my expression, her chin tipped up to look at my face.

"I don't know," she whispered – allowing herself to show vulnerability for the very first time since we met.

I reached up and gripped her chin between my thumb and fingers. "I would *never* put you in harm's way. I promise you, Blake. Take a chance? Trust me?"

"I don't have clothes for a bike," she whispered.

"I have a spare jacket in my bag. Your jeans are fine."

She nodded, letting me lead her closer to the bike.

I grabbed out the jackets and handed her one. She shrugged it on, and I found myself sporting a semi again. That woman was irresistible enough on her own, but wearing my jacket, she was overwhelmingly tempting.

"Shit," I breathed as I distracted myself with strapping our bags to the back of the bike and undoing the lock holding the helmets.

I was playing with fire again. A raging fucking fire, but it was too late to run. I was invested, hooked on every part of this woman. I wanted more, no, I *needed* it.

"*Blondie.*"

Her eyes met mine.

"Are you ready?"

8

Blake

MY DAD always used to say that at any given time, you were only ever three seconds away from making a decision that could change the rest of your life.

Time slowed down as he swung his leg over the seat of the powerful bike.

One Mississippi.

He held out a helmet for me to take.

Two Mississippi.

His smirk, the one that kept making my knees weak, graced his perfect face.

Three Mississippi.

I could tell him no, break my word and run, but I wasn't that kind of girl. A deal was a deal and I needed to see it through. More than needed, I *wanted* to.

It wasn't wise, it wasn't safe, and it certainly wasn't what I needed in my life right now, but Ky didn't care about any of that. He didn't follow the rules – he was smart but reckless – and I had a feeling there was no way in hell he was ever going to take no for answer anyway.

Screw it.

I took the helmet, clipped it up and climbed on the back of his bike.

"That's my girl," I heard him say as I clamped my legs tightly against his back and weaved my arms around his rock-hard middle.

"We crash and die, and I'll kill you."

"Seems counterproductive, blondie, since I'd already be dead."

Smart prick laughed, his addictive, alluring laugh again as the engine roared to life and the huge bike vibrated beneath me.

I squeezed him tighter, pressing the side of my face into his back.

I felt his laughter this time, rather than heard it, as he lifted his feet from the ground. We took off and he weaved effortlessly through the streets of central Sydney.

It took a little while, but then we were out of the city and onto the open road, heading south, and he was lucky that we couldn't talk, because I would have demanded to know where we were going well before this moment if I'd had the chance. I wasn't expecting him to take me out of the main city.

God only knows where we're going.

I watched the countryside slip past us, the ocean in the distance, and I hoped like hell that I hadn't made a mistake putting my life in this man's hands. He could have been a serial killer for all I knew.

This was so unlike me; I'd had my wild side in check for years – I wasn't that girl anymore – the kind to hop on a stranger's motorcycle with absolutely no idea of the destination, yet here I was and it was too late to back out now unless I felt like hurtling myself towards the asphalt at one hundred kilometres an hour, which I did *not*.

We stayed on the bike for what felt like forever, but in reality, was probably about two hours, going through numerous little towns before slowing down and finally turning off in a town called *Kiama*.

Ky drove us to the very edge of the coast, and stopped the bike, killing the engine.

My muscles were so tense from holding on tightly for so long, that I almost couldn't let go of him to climb off.

"We're here, blondie," he prompted me.

I stretched and unwrapped myself from his body on shaky legs, tugging off my now sweaty helmet.

"Where exactly is *here*?" I questioned, looking around, my gaze lingering on the tall, white light-house. Wherever we were, it was pretty, I'd give him that.

"I thought you were meant to be a local?"

He pulled off his helmet and shook out his sexy, dark hair.

"I'm a local... to *Sydney*. I'm a city girl; I've never been this far south."

He shrugged off his jacket and I did the same.

"Why doesn't that surprise me?"

"What are you implying, sparky?" I sat my hands on my hips, pinning him with my stare.

Bastard just laughed and held his hand out for mine.

I must have slipped into another dimension while I rode on the back of his bike, into one where I'd lost my mind, because my hand was in his before I even had the chance to think about whether I really wanted it there or not. He was like a magnet and all of a sudden, I was apparently made of tin.

"We used to come here when I was a kid. It's one of my favourite spots in the world."

I could see why; it was beautiful. I liked that he'd brought me here, to a place that meant something to him.

"You came here a lot?"

He nodded – if I didn't know better, I'd have thought he might have been nervous.

"What are all those people looking at?" I inclined my head towards a viewing platform where people were standing around, cameras at the ready.

"That's what I came here to show you." He pulled me in that direction and muttered something about the swell running south east – whatever the hell that meant.

We were only halfway across when a huge wave rolled into the shore and sent a massive spurt of water flying in the air right in front of us, showering half of its audience.

"Oh my god! A blowhole?" I asked excitedly. I'd always wanted to see one, ever since I watched that movie, *Fools Gold*. I was a sucker for Mathew McConaughey. "That is *so* cool."

I pulled on his hand, eager to get closer, but he tugged me back, halting my progress and spinning me into him.

I looked up at those intense dark eyes and my pulse spiked. He was staring at me with such a sweet, tender expression it was hard to remember how I'd ever thought he was irritating. I swallowed the lump in my throat. "*What*?"

He shook his head. "Nothing, I'm just glad you're here."

So am I. The thought surprised me, but I realised it was true. I was happy to be here, *with him*. As crazy as it was, I couldn't imagine being anywhere else in this moment.

Not with my sister, not in America. Nowhere else but *here*.

I gave him a shy smile and pulled his hand.

He chuckled and let me get my way, coming up beside me and slinging his arm around my shoulders.

"Please tell me we get to see that again?"

"The current is running perfectly for it, so yeah... next set should be a good one, second wave is the biggest."

"You sound like you know what you're talking about."

"Hipster surfer, remember? Plus, I've been here so many times when I was younger that it's burned into my memory forever. Mum always said I should have run tour guides."

"She live around here?"

He'd mentioned his dad living in Brisbane, and that he was re-married, but this was the first I'd heard of his mother.

He didn't reply for two long seconds. "She died when I was twelve."

"I'm so sorry."

I knew what it was like to lose a parent, and it wasn't something I'd wish on an adult, let alone a twelve-year-old boy.

"Me too, blondie."

"How did she die?"

"Breast cancer. They found it too late."

"That can't have been easy for you."

My mum didn't die, but she left, never to be seen again, so as far as I was concerned, she was dead. That was twenty-years ago, and it still formed a ball in the pit of my stomach when I thought about it, so I couldn't imagine how he must have felt when he thought about losing his mother.

"It wasn't. Then Dad moved on three months after she died, and things between us have been strained ever since."

I didn't know what to say. There was nothing I could have said that could possibly make him feel better about a situation like that.

"Ky, I…"

"I know, blondie, I know," he said, his eyes on the horizon.

Another wave rolled in, and the spurt of water shot up again, but not as big this time.

We were close enough to get sprayed, and the cool water felt refreshing against the sticky, summer air that was clinging to my skin. Ky's arm around me was doing nothing to help cool me down; I felt like my skin was burning hot where it met his.

"My mum left when I was eight," I blurted out. "Never came back."

He tightened his grip as we stood side by side, watching the next wave approach the shore. He was right, it *was* the biggest of the set.

"That's really shitty," he replied.

"It was just me, Dad and Carmen after that."

"Single guy, raising two girls couldn't have been easy."

The water smashed violently against the shore, and the blowhole didn't disappoint, sending water rocketing up into the air, showering us again.

I laughed as I shook out my arms and tried to wipe the moisture from my face. "That's *incredible*."

Ky turned me towards him, draping his other damp arm around my shoulders.

It was anyone's guess what had come over me, but I followed his lead and wrapped my arms around his middle, pulling him closer. He was so much taller than me, the top of my head only reaching his shoulders.

"He re-marry?" Ky murmured.

I shook my head. "Eternal bachelor."

"That's too bad."

I blinked back the tears springing to my eyes and nodded in agreement. "He'd have been a good husband."

His hand left my back and then I felt his fingers on my chin. He tipped my face up from where I'd dropped it to hide from him. "So... what now, Blake?"

What a weighted question.

I knew what he meant. I'd gotten on the back of his bike against my better judgement, and now I'd found myself in yet another predicament, out here, hours from where I'd planned to be, with no real idea of what was going to happen next.

"I don't know," I admitted.

His eyes searched mine. "Tell me what's going on in that pretty little head of yours."

Asking what *wasn't* going on in there would have been a far shorter list.

"I didn't know you were going to take me for a ride two hours into the middle of nowhere. You've kind of screwed me."

"Is that so? Maybe you should have been more specific about the rules." His tone was playful.

I rolled my eyes.

"Come with me, blondie." He oozed sincerity.

"Come with you where?" I breathed, even though I already knew what he meant.

"To my cousin's. I don't know what's going on here, but I'm not ready for it to be over yet. I know you feel the same way."

"Ky... I... I don't know."

Damn him and those gorgeous dark eyes... that sexy smile... I *did* know. I wasn't ready for it to be over yet either.

He asked me the question of the century. "You got somewhere else you'd rather be?"

Did I? Honestly, I couldn't think of a single place. I guess there was no need to *Ask Ida* about this one. I'd figured it out on my own. I wanted to be wherever he was.

"Truth is, as much as it pains me, I *don't*."

He smiled so wide it stole the air right out of my lungs.

It was clear for anyone to see that my answer pleased him just as much as it terrified me.

"You're not a serial killer, are you?"

He pretended to think for a second. "At what point does a murderer become a serial killer?"

"I believe it's when the body count reaches three or more."

"Then no." He grinned. "We're good."

I knew he was joking, but I'd seen that Ted Bundy documentary one too many times.

He chuckled, his stare pinning me. "You can trust me, blondie... in fact, I think you already do."

Damn him.

"Fine," I breathed. "I'll come."

He pulled me close and I lost myself in him, the feel of his body against mine, his scent... and the steady thump of his heart.

What have I gotten myself into?

9

Ky

WHEN I PULLED into the gateway of Chance and Aubrey's property, I was a bundle of nerves. My heart was racing, and my palms were sweating like crazy.

I'd never taken a woman home to meet my father, and I was a hell of a lot closer with Chance than I'd ever be with my dad, so bringing her here was a big deal.

Her grip had tightened around my middle, and I realised she must have been feeling nervous too. I didn't blame her.

The chick had a serious set of balls – getting on a bike with a guy she barely knew and going to stay with people she not only didn't know but had barely heard a thing about. That took guts – Blake was bad ass.

I rode the bike slowly up the drive, taking in the sprawling property. It was elevated, not right on the beach like I'd expected from Chance, but I guess a boxed-in little section by the sea wasn't ideal goat-keeping conditions.

I slowed the bike to a stop and shut off the engine. "Here we are, blondie."

We were greeted by two gorgeous little children that I'd been watching grow in pictures and on face time. It'd been years since I'd seen Chance and Aubrey – Bree was only a newborn when I last stayed with them.

"You weren't kidding about the goat." Blake giggled as Pixy, the ridiculous fainting goat, barrelled out after the kids.

"Uncle Ky!" Bree yelled as I climbed off the bike and held my arms out for her to throw herself into.

I may not have spent much time with them in person, but I loved these kids like they were my own, and I felt incredibly guilty about never having made this happen sooner. That was all going to change now, though. I was here and I had no plans to go anywhere anytime soon.

"Why aren't you in school?" I demanded as CJ joined the hug.

"I'm only three, silly." Bree beamed, her auburn hair bouncing. She looked just like her mother.

"I'm starting next year." Five-year-old CJ beamed at me.

"That's awesome, bud."

"Who's the pretty lady?" Bree asked as they let me go and Pixy bounded up to Blake.

Blondie smiled so wide at the stupid goat; I was jealous of him. I was even more jealous as she crouched down to pat his dopey-looking head.

"Bree, CJ, this is Blake."

"That's Pixy," Bree informed Blake, right as the stupid bloody thing fainted, dropping to its side and falling to the ground.

Blake gasped. "Oh my god, what did I do?"

Bree giggled hysterically.

"Oh, ya bugger!" I heard Chance yell. "Princess, the damn goat's fainting again."

"I swear, I barely even touched her," Blake replied, her tone panicked.

"He's a boy," CJ piped up.

"He faints allllll the time," Bree added. She wandered over to Blake and rested her hand on her arm. "You're *really* pretty."

Blake's gaze bounced between me, Bree, CJ and the goat before coming back to rest on Bree. "He really does this all the time?"

Bree nodded; her green eyes wide as she stared up at Blake adoringly.

"He'll be okay?"

Damn. Looked like I wasn't the only one besotted with blondie.

"Yup." Bree reached for Blake's long hair and smiled at her.

Chance jogged over, his shaggy hair falling in his eyes as Aubrey appeared behind him out of the house. "Mate, you made it." He grinned at me. "I was starting to think you'd got lost."

He pulled me into a hug, clapping me on the back.

"We took a detour, wanted to show Blake the blowhole, plus, you live in the middle of bum-fuck nowhere."

"Tell me about it, mate, I imagined something more central, but I just do what I'm told these days."

He released me and turned his attention to blondie, who had gotten to her feet, and now had Bree's hand in hers.

Kid works fast. I'd have to get some pointers.

"Chance, this is Blake, a friend of mine."

"Hello there, little lady, he didn't kidnap you, did he?"

"No." Blake pouted. "I lost a bet."

Chance laughed, his whole frame shaking. "Figured you couldn't get a woman that pretty to go anywhere with you of her own free will."

I flipped him off. *Smug bastard.*

Aubrey chose that moment to join us, brushing past me and heading straight for Blake.

"Princess, this is Blake – Ky's hostage," Chance told her.

I ran my hand through my hair and groaned. "She came willingly. Give me a break."

Blake arched a brow at me as Aubrey pulled her into a hug, one-handed from Blake since it seemed Bree wasn't about to let go of her hand anytime soon.

The embracing carried on until everyone had

been properly introduced, and somewhere in between, Pixy got back to his feet and started nibbling on a plant as though he hadn't just flaked out.

"Are you Uncle Ky's girlfriend?" Bree asked Blake.

Blake's eyes flitted to me, before going back to the little girl.

I chuckled. I wasn't about to throw her a lifeline.

"We're friends," she explained.

"You're a girl and you're his friend. *Girl-friend*." CJ sniggered. "I had *two* in America."

I shook my head at him in amusement. "Aren't you still meant to think girls have cooties or something?"

"Uncle Ky, I do *not* have cooties," Bree argued.

They had cute accents – a weird mix of Australian from their dad and American from their mum.

"Of course not, baby, you're made of sugar and spice and all things nice."

She giggled. "Then what is CJ made of?"

"Slugs and snails and puppy dog's tails," I recited the poem.

She smiled so wide, it hurt my heart. She was seriously gorgeous. CJ seemed like a pretty good kid too, but this little girl, I could tell she was going to have me wrapped around her little finger with no more than a batt of her lashes.

I tickled her and she laughed, a big belly laugh.

I caught Blake's eye as I stood tall – she was looking at me with an emotion I couldn't place.

"C'mon, I want to show you my room." Bree tugged on Blake's hand.

Blondie looked to me for help.

"You going to give me back my girl, BB?" I teased. I'd called her BB in our weekly video chats for most of her life – it stood for Baby Bree.

"No," she said as she skipped along, pulling on Blake's hand, Pixy right in behind the two of them.

"You're on your own, blondie," I called after them.

"Can you please go and make sure your sister doesn't keep Blake in there all day?" Aubrey asked CJ.

He nodded and took off after them into the house.

I breathed in a deep breath, finally feeling like I was home, even though I'd never been here in my life.

"I missed you guys."

"We missed you too, mate," Chance replied, slinging his arm over Aubrey's shoulders.

"So..." Aubrey said, her eyes sparkling, "we didn't know you were bringing company."

I ran my hand through my hair. "Sorry, I probably should have called or something. It wasn't exactly planned..."

"She's more than welcome. Unless you really did kidnap her?" Aubrey's brow furrowed. "She *did* come here willingly, right?"

"For the most part." I smirked.

"Exactly how long have you known that woman?" she asked, her green eyes pinning me.

"Flight was fifteen hours, three-hour drive... so... let's just say about twenty hours."

That surprised them both.

"We just let a total stranger go into the house, *alone* with our children?"

"*Shit.*" I took a step forward – not that I was worried, I trusted Blake already – but that didn't mean Chance and Aubrey did. "I didn't think, I'm sorry."

Chance chuckled and nudged his wife. "You're so mean."

Aubrey grinned. "Relax, lover boy – I saw everything I needed to know when she was worried about Pixy. She's a good one."

"*Really?*"

"Of course, I'm an excellent judge of character." She waved away my concerns.

"Must be. She knew she liked me the moment she met me," Chance bragged.

"Well... I'm not sure I'd go *that* far."

They made cute little faces at one another that made me want to hurl. They were ridiculously sweet and in love.

Couple goals, right here.

"I don't know what it is about her, but I can't get enough. I saw her in the airport, and I knew I needed to find out more," I admitted.

"Awww."

"Don't encourage him," Chance grumbled good-naturedly.

"I think it's sweet."

"You would, princess."

The three of us stood there, grinning at one another. God, it was good to be back in the company of people I loved.

"It's a beautiful bedroom – I wish mine was as pretty."

I glanced up at the sound of her voice and I couldn't help the smile that crossed my face at the sight of her. Bree had managed to score a piggy-back ride now – the kid was good.

"Looks like you're not the only one who likes her." Aubrey giggled.

Chance jogged over, snagged Bree off Blake's back and tossed her up in the air as she squealed and laughed.

"You all good?" I asked as I took Blake's hand and tugged her into my side.

She looked up at me with those big eyes of hers and nodded. "She's a sweetie."

"She sure is."

"You have a beautiful home." Blake turned her attention to Aubrey.

"Thank you, you know, I wasn't *entirely* convinced when he first suggested the move over here, but Chance really wanted to give the kids an Australian upbringing, and I have to admit, it is beautiful here. Plus, I got the house I wanted, so win-win."

The girls made small talk about the house for a few minutes while I watched Chance running around with Bree, and then CJ and Pixy too.

"I can't believe you brought that goat halfway around the world." I chuckled.

"He's family. And besides, I talked the guy into giving us a really good deal on the rate."

"Of course, you did." I smirked.

If there was one thing Aubrey was particularly skilled at, it was negotiating a deal. I guess that was the attorney in her.

"Let's get you settled in." She clapped her hands together. "Are those seriously the only bags you have?" She gestured to the motorcycle. "And what is it with you Bateman men and your aversion to vehicles with four wheels?"

"We just know how you ladies love the bikes," Chance chimed in.

I grinned. I swore Blake and Aubrey rolled their eyes simultaneously.

"I hope you don't mind sharing a room, the other spare bedroom is kind of a mess..." Aubrey rambled on.

"Thank you so much for the offer, but I don't want to impose on family time, I can just go and find a hotel or something," Blake cut her off.

"Nonsense. You're more than welcome to stay here with us."

I could have kissed Aubrey. She clearly wanted Blake to stay, so she would be staying. Blondie didn't know it yet, but Aubrey always got her way. *Always*.

"It's not a problem, honestly."

"It's the busy season, everywhere is all booked up."

I didn't know if Aubrey was full of it or not, but I was here for it.

"I didn't think of that," Blake murmured. "Are you sure it's okay? I'd hate to impose."

Aubrey looped her arm through Blake's and tugged her away from me. "I'd love to have you stay. I haven't made many friends out here yet; I've been missing girl talk." She turned and looked back over her shoulder at me. "I'm going to show Blake around. You can bring the bags in."

I shook my head, chuckling. "Your woman is a slave driver, Chance."

"You're telling me." He grinned a goofy grin that made it obvious he wasn't in the least bit unhappy about it.

"Cocky, show Ky where he can park that death trap," Aubrey called over her shoulder.

"Yes, ma'am." He saluted her.

I didn't know where the hell my head was at, what on earth I was doing, or what my endgame was, but I knew one thing for certain; I couldn't let Blake go – the rest would have to figure itself out later.

10

_____

Blake

I WAITED, my belly fluttering nervously, for my sister to answer my call.

"Hey, where the heck are you? I thought you would have been here hours ago."

She'd offered to pick me up from the airport when my flight got in, but I'd declined – told her I'd find my own way. I wasn't sure if that had been my best idea now, given the circumstances.

"Hey, I –"

"Was your flight delayed?" she interrupted me.

"No, it was on time..."

"So where are you then?"

I blew out a deep breath and paced the room again – the room I'd be sharing with Ky. "I'm with an old friend I ran into at the airport. I know I said I was coming to stay, but... plans have changed. I'm in Pretty Beach."

"*Pretty Beach?*"

"Yeah."

I glanced out the window, the view of the ocean in the distance was so beautiful; Pretty Beach sure was pretty.

"Isn't that in the middle of nowhere?"

"Um... kind of?"

"You don't have any friends out of the city. Who are you with?"

"Her name is Aubrey. I knew her in school." The lie fell a little too easily off my tongue.

She was silent for a few beats.

"Okay... so you're not coming here at all, or..."

"I'm not really sure."

More silence.

"What the hell is going on with you, Blake?"

Wasn't that the question of the century?

Carmen and I hadn't been particularly close for years now, even less so for the past six months, but she was still my sister and she still knew when I was making a mess of things.

Pointing out my faults had always been her favourite pastime.

"I'm just taking a break," I whispered.

"Is that what you're calling it?"

"What's that meant to mean?"

"You know exactly what I'm saying. Your life is a mess, Blake. You need to sort yourself out."

No shit, Sherlock.

"I didn't call you for a lecture, Carmen, I called to tell you that I wouldn't be coming to stay at the moment. That's it; can't you just cut me some slack?"

"Fine." She huffed out a breath. "Is this your number?"

"No." I shook my head. "It's Aubrey's." *Not a lie.* "I haven't got a new sim yet and I'm not sure when I will. Some time off the grid might be good for me."

"Might make it harder for you to face reality, you mean."

I ignored her.

"Text me the address so I know where to find you and this mystery friend I've never heard of. That way when you show up murdered, I can tell the police where to start looking."

"Okay," I said with a roll of my eyes.

Carmen would have lost the plot if I told her the real story about who I was with and what I was doing, and that was exactly why I *wouldn't* be telling her anything more than I had to. She could have the address and that would have to satisfy her.

"I'll send it now."

"Alright. Well, let me know if you decide to come back to the city."

"Will do."

We hung up, neither of us bothered with pleasantries, and I did as promised and texted her the address of Aubrey and Chance's house.

"Everything alright, blondie?"

My head shot up, and there he was, in all his glorious perfection, watching me closely.

"It was my sister." I held up the phone. "Just letting her know that I wouldn't be turning up on her doorstep after all."

He pushed off the door frame and prowled towards me. "She pissed I stole you away?"

I shook my head. "I think she'll cope."

He smirked and dropped down next to me, so close our sides pressed together when the mattress dipped.

"I can take the couch tonight; you have the bed." He tipped his head backwards, gesturing to the bed.

"Don't be stupid, we're both adults – we can share a bed."

"You think you'll be able to keep your hands off me?" That cheeky smile graced his face again.

"It'll be a real effort, but I think I'll manage."

"I look forward to proving you wrong."

"Challenge accepted," I agreed.

"What do you want to do today?"

"Sleep?" I suggested hopefully.

He chuckled. "I'm not sure that's going to happen with the kids bouncing around."

"Don't forget the goat. What's the deal with that thing? I thought I'd killed it."

I shook my head, reliving the moment I thought the damn thing had dropped dead at my feet.

He chuckled, my body shaking along with his.

"I remember the first time the bloody thing did that to me, Aubrey and Chance had shot out to pick something up and left me goat sitting. I tried to give him CPR."

"You gave a goat mouth-to-mouth?" I tried to bite down my laugh.

"You bet I did. Aubrey is scary when she's mad, and I thought I'd killed her freakin' goat. She would have strung me up by my balls. She loves that thing."

"He *is* pretty cute."

"His breath isn't, I can tell you that for nothing." He shuddered. "I had my bags half packed to make a run for it, then the bugger just strolled into my room like I hadn't just virtually had my tongue down his throat."

I laughed, real genuine laughter. I hadn't laughed like that in months.

"Yeah, go ahead, laugh it up."

"You made out with a goat, it's funny," I choked out between breaths.

"*Blondie*, I did *not* make out with a goat."

"I think you did."

He moved so fast, I didn't even see it coming, he pinned me flat against the mattress, his arms caging me on either side of my head.

My breath caught in my throat, my laughter dying off.

"You're so fucking beautiful when you laugh, Blake."

He was going to kiss me. I could feel it. He lowered his head, closing the gap between us.

I wanted it – my lips against his – but I was conflicted... torn... scared... *confused*.

"So beautiful," he murmured, his hand coming up to my face to sweep the hair from my eyes.

I couldn't speak, could barely breathe.

He lowered his lips closer and I felt myself tremble with anticipation.

This was *it* – the moment that we would kiss for the first time. I could imagine what his mouth would feel like – how good he would taste. This moment had been brewing from the first moment we locked eyes.

He came closer still, and I could feel his warm breath on my skin.

"Ewww! Are you two *kissing*?"

Just like that, the moment was gone. Ky groaned and gave me one last, smouldering stare before pressing up to glare at the intruder.

My face had turned scarlet as I followed his lead, sitting up.

CJ stood in the doorway, a disgusted look on his face.

"Dude, I thought you had two girlfriends?"

"I don't *kiss* them," he replied quickly, clearly outraged by the idea.

"Neither do I, apparently," Ky muttered under his breath.

"Dad said to come and ask if you want to come to the beach. We're going swimming."

Ky turned to look at me. "You wanna go, blondie?"

Did I? Ky shirtless, dripping wet from the salty ocean water... If it meant I might finally get to see that tattoo in its entirety, I was in.

"I don't see why not."

"Good, hurry up and get your stuff. We're missing the good waves."

CJ took off again and Ky shook his head. "Cockblocked by a five-year-old. *Unbelievable.*"

As much as I wanted to kiss him, I was kind of glad that CJ had come in when he did. I needed to get my head on straight. Kissing Ky wasn't smart. I had enough going on in my life right now – as my sister had so lovingly pointed out – without complicating things further with a man I barely knew.

I needed to use my head and not let the butterflies in my stomach cloud my judgement. Ky Bateman was hot – there was no denying that, but that didn't mean I had to jump him. We could have fun together – with our clothes *on.*

He jumped off the bed and held his hands out to me to pull me to my feet.

I tried to ignore the tingles down my back that always seemed to make themselves known when our skin met, but when he tugged me hard, and brought my body crashing against his, I lost all rational thought. He was all lean, hard planes and sexy smirks. The bastard knew how irresistible he was.

"You look a little flushed, blondie." His hands found their way to my waist, skimming lightly up and down my sides.

"I was just thinking about the fact that I don't have a bikini with me. Are you allowed to go topless around here?"

It was his turn to look a little hot under the collar now.

"*Ky*," I whispered, my voice breathless.

"Mmm?" His lust-filled eyes didn't leave mine for a second.

"You look a little flushed."

It took a moment for my words to register, and another moment for him to regain control; when he did, he chuckled, ran his hand through his hair in that sexy way he had down pat, and grinned wide at me, showing off his pearly white teeth.

"That's how you're going to be, huh?" he asked as he stepped away, giving us both some much-needed space.

The sexual tension was so thick in this room, I was worried he was going to get me knocked-up with nothing more than a crook of his lips.

"Depends."

"On?" he prompted.

"On how many more times you plan on trying to seduce me."

He reached down, picked up my bag and threw it onto the bed for me.

"Always at least once more, blondie," he said with a grin.

11

Ky

"I'D LIKE it stated for the record that I saw it coming," Chance said as he sat down in the sand next to me, shaking his wet hair out and showering me with saltwater.

"Saw what coming?"

He nodded towards where Blake, Aubrey, CJ and Bree were running around on the sand with Pixy.

Most people weren't even batting an eyelid at the fact that there was a goat on the beach, so that made me think that he was a regular down here already.

"You and Blake, I think you might be endgame."

I shook my head, a smile on my lips.

I liked Blake, she was sexy, fun – she gave as good as she got, and she didn't fall for my charms as easily as other women. She was different and I liked that about her, but endgame wasn't even on my mind. I was looking for a bit of fun, nothing more.

"Nah, mate, I only met her yesterday. We're just hanging out."

He laughed at me.

"*What*?"

"You're totally fucked, and you don't even know it yet."

"Are you trying to gaslight me?"

"I'm not lighting anything; I'm just calling it how I see it. You've got it bad for that girl and for some reason I'll never understand, she seems to like you too."

I checked him with my shoulder, my gaze wandering back to the five of them.

Blake shrieked as CJ kicked water at her and she ran up the sand, Pixy hot on her heels.

Jesus Christ, I'd thought she was smokin' hot in a pair of jeans, but that tiny green bikini she'd bought on the way down here left next to nothing to the imagination.

I'd never got as hard on sight as I did when she stepped out wearing that fucking thing. I'd been talking down a hard-on for at least two hours and it was showing no signs of letting up either.

"I think you're confusing lust with love."

"You can want to screw a woman sideways *and* keep her forever at the same time, *trust me*."

I didn't really want to hear about his sex life, but Chance virtually never listened, and his oversharing knew no bounds, so I didn't bother trying to shut him up.

"Like me and Aubrey... I wanted to fuck that woman's brains out from the first moment I laid eyes on her. She was being a bitch, but I still wanted her."

"That's... *nice.*"

Aubrey had become like a sister to me over the years, and the last thing anyone wanted to discuss was their sister having sex.

He chuckled. "Point is, I fell for her along the way and it was the best thing that ever happened to me."

Blake's eyes met mine across the beach and she smiled wide. I couldn't help it, my mouth curved up the same way. She waved her hand, and I returned it with a wave of my own.

"Definitely screwed," Chance commented.

"Shut up." I jumped to my feet and brushed the sand off my hands.

"I'm not saying it's a bad thing, but one day when the two of you are shacking up, I'll be saying *I told you so,*" he called after me.

Whatever you say, mate.

Blake's eyes lit up as I came closer, and I could have punched my dipshit cousin for putting this crap in my head, because now that he'd pointed it out, I could see it. I could see myself falling hard for this woman, even though it was never meant to be on the cards.

"You look like you're having fun, blondie."

"I am." She beamed as Bree grabbed her hand.

"Uncle Ky, swing me!"

"It'll cost ya, BB."

She giggled. "How much?"

I crouched down before her. "One big kiss right here." I pointed to one of my cheeks, "and another one here." I pointed to the other cheek.

She giggled again before throwing herself forwards and planting two big kisses on my cheeks.

"Payment received." I grinned.

She placed her hand in mine and her other back in Blake's.

"Hey, where's my payment?" Blake pouted.

I leaned across, Bree between us and swept her damp hair off her neck before bringing my lips to the soft skin just below her jaw.

Her breath hitched and her eyes fluttered closed for a few seconds.

"That's your cut of the profit," I rasped at her ear.

Her teeth sunk into her bottom lip as I pulled away, Bree tugging at our hands.

"Swing me!"

"Yes, Ma'am," Blake replied, looking flushed.

We strolled down the beach, shooting each other looks and flirty smiles as we swung Bree into the air between us before she finally announced that she was hungry and ditched us to race back along the sand to where Aubrey had set up a blanket with a picnic lunch.

Blake smiled after her.

I gestured to the golden sand and we sat, side by side, not close enough to touch, but close enough that I could feel the warmth from her bare skin on mine.

"Hairdresser?" I questioned.

"*What*?" She laughed.

"I'm still guessing your job. Are you a hairdresser?"

"I cut myself a fringe once when I was about eight, does that count?"

I chuckled. "I don't think so."

We sat in a comfortable silence. "They're really great. Such a beautiful family." She'd been watching Chance, Aubrey and the kids.

"They are," I agreed. "You want kids?"

"Someday, I'd love a family."

I nodded my head in agreement but didn't say anything further.

"Have you ever been in love, sparky?"

Her question surprised me, and I wondered for a second if she'd somehow managed to overhear the conversation between me and Chance, but she couldn't have.

"Nope. Not even close."

She frowned. "What do you mean, *not even close*?"

"Exactly what I said. I've never met anyone I've been willing to risk giving my heart to."

"You make it sound so scary."

"Letting someone own a piece of you seems pretty scary to me."

Those insanely vibrant eyes of hers looked at me like maybe she'd never thought about it that way before.

"What about you, blondie, *you* ever been in love?" I asked, turning the focus away from me.

"Yeah." She sighed. "I mean, I think I have..."

"I sense a story."

"Not one I'm willing to tell right now."

I'd pushed her a lot in the hours since we'd met – because that's all it had been at this point, a matter of hours, even though it felt like forever – but something in her tone made it clear that this wasn't up for negotiation.

"What's the stupidest thing you ever broke up with a guy for?"

"What makes you think I broke up with guys for stupid reasons?" She arched a brow at me.

"C'mon, blondie, we've all done it. I'll even go first."

She gave me a 'go ahead' look.

"I wouldn't say *broke up*, but I didn't call her back after our first date because she ate her spaghetti by putting one end in her mouth and sucking it up like those dogs on that stupid movie."

She tried and failed to swallow her laughter and the sound made my breath come quicker. It warmed me from the inside the same way the sun was warming me from the outside.

"Seriously? Like one bit, or the whole bowl?"

"The whole damn bowl. No shit."

"You could have just avoided places that served pasta." She giggled.

"True, but some things you just can't unsee." I mock shuddered.

She cracked her knuckles. "Alright, sparky, I think I can one up you there. I broke up with my boyfriend of six months because he borrowed one of my books and folded down the corners to mark his page."

I chuckled. "I had one who cut her toenails in the kitchen sink."

She made a gagging gesture. "That's not only odd, it's unsanitary."

"Hit me with another one." I grinned.

"He snored."

"She only ever ate half of a piece of fruit and threw the rest away."

"Picked his nose and ate it."

I had to laugh at that one. "Were you dating a two-year-old?"

She shook her head, her smile creeping in again. "Nope, but I tell you what, you see a grown man eating his snot and there's just no coming back from that."

"What kind of guys have you been dating?" I chuckled.

"You can talk, sounds like you haven't had such a hot run either."

"Truer words have never been spoken... and you wonder why I haven't fallen in love with any of them."

"If you'd led with the toenail story, it would have made a lot more sense."

I chuckled.

I didn't know if it was the jetlag, or her company,

but I felt sated, like I could have sat here on this beach with her for days and never got tired of it.

"Personal trainer?" I said after a few moments of silence.

She shook her head.

"Chef?"

"God no, I'm a terrible cook."

"Lucky I'm a whizz in the kitchen then."

"Why is that lucky?" she bumped her knee against mine as her fingers trailed through the warm sand, raking patterns and then smoothing them back out.

"Because one of us will have to teach our children to cook."

She huffed out a laugh. "I think you might be getting ahead of yourself, sparky, like way, *way* ahead of yourself. I still haven't decided if I can tolerate being around you for more than twenty-four hours."

"If you say so."

"It's true. I'm not myself right now; I'm running on no sleep and too much champagne. I'm practically delirious."

"You're a terrible liar, blondie. I'll have to teach our daughter to be more convincing."

"Oh, we have a daughter now, do we?"

"Two girls and a boy."

I might have only been playing around, but thanks to Chance and his stupid mind games, I could see this with her too. She'd be an amazing mother; she was so good with Bree and CJ.

"Teacher," I blurted out as it clicked into place. "You're a teacher."

Her smile grew. "Finally got there, sparky."

"Yeah?"

"Mmm hmm, I'm a Kindergarten teacher."

"That's really cool."

"It's probably the only reason I can relate so well to all of your immature tendencies."

"She's a joker too, ladies and gents." I slow clapped.

She poked her tongue out at me.

"And you're calling *me* immature," I teased.

"I tell you what I am, *exhausted*."

"Me too. You want to head back?"

"Only if I'm allowed to drive." She grinned and pushed herself up to her feet.

I reached out my hand for her to pull me up and then held onto it tight when she tried to pull it back. Chance and Aubrey were already talking about the two of us, I figured I may as well give them something to talk about. She fought me on it for a few steps before sighing and giving in.

"You got a licence, blondie?"

"Of course I do, who doesn't have a licence?"

"Thought you might have been more of an uber kind of girl."

"Can you stop implying I'm some kind of high maintenance, city girl?"

"Can you stop implying I'm insulting you by just breathing?"

She laughed. "You're not insulting me by breathing, sparky." I tightened the grip on her hand as I waited for the rest of her jibe. "That privilege is reserved for when you speak."

There it is.

"You've done it now," I warned her.

She shook off my hand, shrieked and hightailed it down the beach as fast as she could.

I gave her a three-second head start before I took off after her, catching her easily and tossing her over my shoulder.

Bree spotted us and started cheering, her and Pixy joining us in the shallows as I waded into the sea.

"Ky Bateman, don't you dare –"

I didn't hear the rest of her threat; she was too busy being under water.

12

Blake

"Has Ky told you how Chance and I got together?"

I took another sip of my wine and shook my head. "Honestly? We haven't exactly had the time to talk about much at all." I felt my cheeks pink. She must have thought I was crazy, coming here on a whim like this with him. Maybe I *was* crazy. I certainly felt out of control. "It all happened pretty fast... and now here I am."

"I know that feeling," she replied, a smile playing on her lips.

The kids had gone to bed – crashed out about an hour ago, and even though I was shattered, I knew I'd get over the jetlag faster if I stayed up until a reasonable time and then did my best to sleep through the night.

Ky and Chance had gone out to the shed to look at surf boards or something, so it was just me and Aubrey, sitting by the outdoor fireplace, drinking wine. It felt oddly comfortable.

"Chance and I went on a road trip as total strangers."

That made me sit up straighter.

"I was in the middle of Nebraska, headed to California with about twenty hours ahead of me. His bike broke down, and I needed someone to change my tyre, so we made a deal that if he fixed my tyre, he could catch a ride with me. He drove me crazy, and I was a total bitch to him, but somewhere along the way... things changed. I guess he wore me down."

"She went down on me." Chance's voice came from behind me.

Aubrey looked over her shoulder at her husband. "What did you say?"

"I said you grew on me," he replied.

I bit down my laugh. He had a cocky grin on his face and I could see why; that wasn't what he said at all, but Aubrey either didn't notice or didn't care because she carried on with her story as Chance joined her on her seat, pulling her into his lap.

"Anyway, we found this guy along the way," she pointed to the goat sleeping on the ground in front of my seat, "yelled 'cunt' into the Grand Canyon, got fake married in Vegas and as they say, the rest is history."

"Wow... that's... that's some story."

"The way you and Ky are with one another

reminds me of the two of us," she said, shocking me further.

"Nah, I'm way better looking than Ky." Chance smirked.

I didn't bother telling him he was wrong.

"Course you are, cocky. But seriously, the teasing, the chemistry... I see it."

"I don't know about that," I argued. "Maybe it worked out for the two of you, but I can't see us adopting a stray animal, let alone getting married and having kids."

"Oh, I wouldn't say it exactly worked out for us... not right away. This guy made a pretty thorough attempt at screwing it up first."

Chance ran a hand through his hair. "Really, princess? You gotta spill the tea to everyone we meet?"

She ignored him, shooting me a look that said he got absolutely no say in the matter. "So, we go on this road trip, I'm falling head over heels for this cocky bastard, and what does he do? Runs out on me in Vegas right after we've slept together."

I gaped at her.

"You know what? I think I might just go find Ky." Chance tried to stand but was shoved back down by his wife.

"Sit your ass down."

He muttered something under his breath that I didn't catch.

"So anyway, he leaves me in Vegas, goes to *jail* for two years and then one day he just shows back up –

looking every bit as irresistible as the moment he left, albeit a little more stalkerish in his tendencies."

"And long story short, I won her over again and here we are," Chance finished for her, clearly trying to wrap up this little trip down memory lane.

"Bet you didn't know you were staying with an ex con, did ya, blondie?"

I'd been paying such close attention to Chance and Aubrey, I hadn't heard Ky sneak up behind me. I jumped, then smacked him playfully on the arm as he leaned over me.

"Can you *not*?"

He smirked, rounded the outdoor sofa and squeezed himself into the space behind me.

"By all means, make yourself comfortable."

"Will do."

He took even more space before slinging his arm around my shoulder and pulling my back against his front.

I could feel his heart thumping against my spine, and I was glad he couldn't see my face, because I'm sure it would have been obvious how he was affecting me.

Chance and Aubrey exchanged knowing glances, and I frowned.

They might have met on some type of fluke, and it worked out for them, but that wasn't what was happening here, *was it*? It couldn't be. The timing was all wrong. Ky had been right when he'd accused me of running from something; I *was*. I was running from reality.

"Can you sit still?" I demanded as he continued to wiggle around, almost pulling me into his lap.

"Sorry, I've still got a lot of nervous energy built up from the drive home from the beach.

"You, shhhh," I hissed.

Aubrey eyed us curiously.

Ky was just stirring shit. He'd let me drive Chance's ute home – reluctantly – but still, and then he'd spent the whole time with either his foot on the invisible break or his hand clenched on the 'oh shit' handle.

"She drove your truck like she stole it," he piped up.

"He's being dramatic."

"I'm being *honest*. It's lucky Pixy didn't ride with us, he would have fainted. You drive like a fucking slap happy loon."

I rolled my eyes. "You were perfectly safe the entire time, precious."

"Oh, I fucking respectfully disagree."

"I'm not confident that you understand what the word 'respectfully' means."

"Fine, then I *disrespectfully* agree."

He was doing it again. Getting me all wound up. *And turned on*. As much as I hated to admit it.

He'd been flirting all day, and after our almost kiss this morning, I'd been expecting him to try again – but he hadn't. I was glad in a way, if I was ever going to kiss Ky, I wanted to be on the top of my game, not tired and confused.

"Drama queen," I muttered.

He chuckled as Chance and Aubrey just watched on in amusement.

"Are you from Sydney, Chance?" I asked, changing the subject.

"Melbourne actually, but California was my home for a long time."

"What do you do for a job?"

I'd been wondering all day. I wasn't sure if he had the day off to be here with Ky, or if his day-to-day consisted of being at home with his family.

"Yeah, Chance, what *do* you do for a living?" Ky chimed in, amusement in his tone.

Chance smiled wide, dimples forming in his cheeks. He was gorgeous. I could see why Aubrey agreed to let him into her drive and drive across the USA. Men like Chance and Ky wielded their good looks like some kind of voodoo magic that made smart girls stupid. Girls like me.

"Well, little lady, I'm in the ass-modelling business."

I'd just taken a sip of wine, and it almost came back out at his answer.

I swallowed, trying not to choke as Ky shook with laughter, putting my entire body on high alert.

"I'm sorry, did you say you're an *ass model*?"

He chuckled. "Sure did. I was a professional soccer player back in the day. That didn't work out, but apparently my looks have held, right, princess? I actually make furniture too, but I thought you'd be more interested in the former."

He thought right.

"I'm definitely googling you later," I told him.

"I did the same thing!" Aubrey exclaimed.

I liked Aubrey. She was sweet but didn't take any shit. She reminded me of myself, minus the stupid decision-making. I liked Chance too; he was cocky, but good-natured. Ky was like him in a lot of ways.

"I'd been doing a bit of coaching in Cali before we left too, plus Aubrey had the shelter, so that kept us pretty busy."

"I went to visit while I was out there." Ky's fingers trailed up my bare arm as he spoke. "Eddie is doing a good job with it."

"Who's Eddie?" I questioned.

"My old cellmate," Chance answered. "He got out not so long ago. Came to stay with us and liked it so much he bought our place when we left."

I was almost too scared to ask what he'd been in for. I thought he'd tell me if I did ask – Chance seemed like a pretty open book, but I decided I'd save it for my Google search – that way I didn't have to try and play it cool to his face when I found out what he'd done.

"Eddie's cool, I liked him," Ky commented.

"You just like that he let you crash in his spare room," Chance joked.

"Certainly didn't lose him any points."

"We ran an animal shelter in Hermosa Beach," Aubrey explained, looking at me – my expression must have been as bewildered as I felt. "We had all kinds of animals there, and honestly, I wanted to bring them all with me here, but thankfully, Eddie turned up. He was great with them and he was happy to take over, so we decided only Pixy would make the trip."

"He's your only pet?"

Aubrey grinned and Chance groaned.

"I'm getting two piglets tomorrow."

"Seriously?"

"They're just babies – their mum is refusing to feed them, so I said I'd take them and hand-rear them."

"It took her all of five minutes to inform the *entire* community that we were open to strays," Chance complained.

"We've also got a duck that can't fly, three roosters and a sheep," Aubrey announced proudly. "But Pixy is the only one allowed in the house."

"We've barely unpacked the boxes, and this place is already a zoo."

"You wouldn't have it any other way and you know it." Aubrey grinned.

"I'd have you on your knees."

"*What*?" she asked, trying to glance at his face over her shoulder.

"I said, I aim to please," he bullshitted.

Ky laughed again.

I shook my head in amusement at the two of them. They were so in love. It hurt my heart to think about someone loving me the way Chance loved Aubrey.

I suddenly felt like I needed some space.

"I think I might hit the hay," I announced.

Ky reluctantly let go of me. "Speaking of hay, blondie, you can help me stack the barn in the morning."

I had absolutely no idea what stacking a barn with hay entailed, but I'd give it a go.

"Sure." I nodded. "I can do that."

Ky took one look at my unsure expression and cracked up laughing. "You're such a city girl."

13

Ky

BLAKE WAS STILL SLEEPING when I woke up, her chest rising and falling with each shallow breath.

It gave me a chance to watch her without getting caught. A chance I'd been dying to get again ever since I watched her nap on the plane.

She was a beautiful woman. Flawless, elegant kind of beauty. I'd never seen something so perfect.

I'd been certain she was kidding about us sharing a bed, but she'd been dead serious. I didn't push my luck by touching her; sleeping next to her was more than enough – for now at least.

Her lips pursed and relaxed as I watched her sleep and I wanted nothing more than to lean over and press my lips against hers, but I couldn't have our first kiss go that way – when it happened, I wanted her to remember every second of it. She couldn't deny it that way – this thing between us. Not that I would have believed her anyway, there was no denying our chemistry. It was electric; a blind man could have seen it.

I couldn't get my head around it. We met by total chance – our paths weren't destined to cross, yet here I was... completely hooked on her. I'd never been in love before, but I had to wonder if this was how it happened. Slowly, yet all at once.

She yawned and her lids fluttered before finally opening.

"It's creepy to watch people sleep, sparky," she said as her eyes found focus and she saw me lying on my side, facing her.

"I don't care."

"Well I do. I'm probably a mess."

Her hair was wild, framing her unmade-up face. She wasn't the same woman I first laid eyes on – she was better.

"I think you look perfect."

Those startling eyes searched mine, looking for my regular teasing bullshit, but came up empty. I was dead serious.

"You're not so bad yourself," she finally replied.

It wasn't exactly a glowing compliment, but the look on her face told the real story, so I'd let her lie with her words – this time.

"How's the jetlag?"

"I feel rested."

"You ready for a day's work, city girl?"

"Oh yay, the piglets!" She sat up, the sheet falling below her waist and I groaned.

Jesus Christ. This woman was trying to kill me. She'd gotten into bed after me, when the light was out, so this was the first time I was seeing the thin, white singlet she'd slept in. Forget a wet t-shirt contest, this thing was already see-through enough.

"Blondie, you're killing me."

She followed my line of sight to her chest where her hard nipples were poking against the sheer fabric.

She crossed her arms quickly, covering herself. "Sorry, I didn't really have anything to sleep in."

I let my head fall back against the pillow and stared at the ceiling while I asked the obvious question, "What do you normally sleep in?"

I was almost afraid of the answer.

"Ah... I sleep naked."

A strangled growl made its way from my throat. There it was. She was *definitely* trying to kill me. I couldn't think about her naked, not with Bree and CJ in the rooms either side of this one.

"I'll find something else to put on." I felt the bed move as she got up, and I must have lost a few brain cells, because I tortured myself by looking after her.

She was bent over, rummaging through her bag, nothing but a pair of skimpy black lace panties covering her delectable ass.

"Fuck," I whispered.

I tugged my t-shirt over my head and threw it

across the room at her. "For the love of god, put that on before I start something you'll regret."

She turned around and picked up my shirt. "Stop looking!"

"A man only has so much self-control, blondie, you can't walk around looking like that and expect me not to notice."

Knowing that I'd been sleeping next to her all night while she wore sweet fuck all, was doing some crazy shit to my body. I'd woken up with a semi, but that was well and truly erect now – she'd made sure of that.

She pulled my t-shirt over her head and watched as it fell to her midthigh. "Better?"

I was in so much trouble. It was worse. So, *so* much worse.

The sexy, mussed-up bed hair, wide eyes and pouty lips combined with her wearing my shirt and I was well and truly fucked.

I felt more than lust for this woman. Sure, there was plenty of that – I felt red-hot desire in spades every time I looked at her, but it was more than that. I craved her smile, her sassy backchat... I wanted to look into those crazy, unique eyes of hers for as long as she'd let me.

"Ky?" she asked, her tone timid.

"Yeah, blondie?" My voice sounded like gravel.

"You okay?"

I shook my head. "Not with you looking like that... wearing my shirt... *shit*."

"I'm sorry." Her face turned pink.

"Don't be sorry, just put some clothes on."

"Out you go then."

"No can do."

"What? *Why*?"

"I'm pitching a tent... if you know what I mean, so unless you want to stay and help me take care of it..."

Her lips formed a small 'o'. "I'm just going to take some stuff to the bathroom," she announced quickly.

"Good idea, blondie."

She scooped up a few things and rushed from the room.

I let my back hit the pillows again as I chuckled. Chance was right – I was in a world of trouble with this one.

I thought about rubbing one out to thoughts of her ass, bent over in front of me, but I couldn't do it. I would come so hard for her, and when I did, I wanted to be buried deep inside her tight little body.

I groaned, got up and got dressed, all the while chanting at my dick to chill the fuck out.

Blake didn't come back, so when I'd finally coached myself into a state that was acceptable for human interaction, I wandered the house in search of her. I found her in the kitchen, sitting at the table with Aubrey and Bree. Bree was standing on a chair behind Blake, brushing her hair.

"Morning." My voice came out raspy as I locked eyes with blondie.

She held my gaze for a few long beats before blushing and looking away. I knew she was thinking about my dick and whether I'd given in and pleasured myself or not.

I smirked. I liked sassy Blake a whole hell of a lot, but I had to admit, blushing Blake was pretty fucking sexy too.

"Good morning, Uncle Ky."

"How are you today, BB?"

I crossed the room and dropped a kiss to the top of Bree's head. "I'm good, Blake is letting me be her hairdresser."

"That sounds like fun, want me to get you some scissors?"

"Ky Bateman, don't even joke," Blake growled.

Bree giggled.

"Where's your daddy?" I asked her.

"I've got him getting the barn out back ready for the piglets," Aubrey informed me.

"I'm so excited!" Bree shrieked.

"Inside voice, baby."

Bree gave her mum a 'whoops' look and then carried on dragging the brush through all of Blake's long, golden hair.

"You want some coffee, sparky?" Blake offered.

I shook my head. "Can't stand the stuff, blondie, sometimes it's like you don't know me at all."

"Probably because I *don't* know you at all." She laughed. "But seriously, no coffee? How do you have so much energy to drive me insane?"

"It's pure natural ability. No caffeine required," I replied as I pushed the door open and stepped outside, going in search of Chance.

I needed some air.

I was feeling all sorts of crazy shit in there watching Blake with Bree. She was so sweet with her. Patient, kind and loving. She was nothing short of incredible. She'd slotted into my world effortlessly.

I was falling. Too hard, too fast, too... *everything.*

"Chance?" I yelled out when I reached the barn.

"In here, mate."

I found him in a small penned-off area, where he was laying down hay – presumably for the new arrivals.

"I can't believe you're getting pigs."

"Neither can I, but I gave up arguing with that woman a long time ago, she always wins anyway."

"You two seem happy out here."

He stopped messing around with the pen and stood up to face me. "We are. Best thing we ever did. I love America, but I wanted my kids to grow up with the childhood we had. You remember when we used to spend day after day down at the beach, or out on the McIntyre's farm riding the bikes? My kids hadn't even seen a roo with their own eyes until we got here."

"I remember the McIntyre's." I smiled fondly at the memory. After Mum died and shit turned bad with Dad, I spent all my school holidays with Chance and Adele. Watching horse races with their mum is what got me hooked on racing in the first place – not that I ever anticipated making a career out of it. "I think this is a pretty awesome place to bring up kids."

"And it doesn't hurt that some pretty decent surf breaks are right around the corner."

I chuckled. "Can't imagine it would."

"Chuck me that rake."

I passed it over, then took a look around the rest of the barn. "You got a lot of room for strays in here, man."

"Tell me about it. It scares me, but fuck it – she's happier when she's surrounded by animals. Even demented ones like that bugger."

Chance pointed at Pixy, and he bleated, as if on cue.

"You ventured out to Archer Racecourse? I'm thinking of taking Blake tomorrow, there's a big meet on."

"Nope. I think I missed out on the gambling gene. I'm a lousy bet."

I'd forgotten about that. He'd always been more likely to pick the horse coming in last than he was the one coming in for the win.

"What's the situation with you two? You know you're welcome to stay as long as you like – *both of you*, but have you talked about what happens next?"

"I haven't even kissed her, let alone had a deep and meaningful about our future," I admitted.

"For real? I figured you two were fucking."

"Give it time; I've only known her five seconds."

"Only took Aubrey a few days to fall for me," he replied smugly.

"Yeah good for you, but I don't plan on disappearing for two years without a word when I do get the girl."

I didn't blame Chance for doing what he did and finding himself behind bars, but I did blame him for not just being honest with Aubrey in the first place. She would have waited for him and they both would have endured a hell of a lot less heart break.

"Yeah, well that's hindsight for you," he grumbled.

I smirked. "Don't you worry yourself with my love life anyway, I've got it covered."

"Ky?" I heard Blake call out.

I grinned. "In here, blondie."

"You really like her, don't you?" Chance said, all trace of giving me shit gone.

"I think I might."

He watched me, a grin spreading across his face. "Welcome to the love club, mate."

14

Blake

So, it turned out manual labour wasn't for me after all, but that didn't mean I couldn't enjoy watching Ky sling bales of hay, sweat glistening on his bare, bronzed chest.

I'd been right about that tattoo; it was a work of art. That might have been as much of a credit to the canvas as it was to the artist, but either way, it was stupid amounts of sexy. Same with the other one he had on his side. I'd never really given much thought to whether I was a fan of ink or not, but on Ky, I could confirm I definitely was.

He'd been going for hours, and I'd been wiping drool from my chin the entire time. Every defined, lean muscle on his body was working overtime, and my god, it made for good watching.

Chance was in there too, and as beautiful as he was, I only had eyes for his cousin.

Ky turned, caught me staring again and smirked. Fuck I hated that smirk – I loved it too, but that wasn't the point. I wanted to wipe that cocky grin right off his face.

He was driving me wild.

I wasn't in a position to want a man like this, but my traitorous body was betraying me more and more as the minutes ticked by.

"Books or movies, blondie?" he called out, making me smile. This had been our game for the past hour or so.

"Books," I replied.

"Movies," was his answer.

I could have sworn he was picking the opposite of everything I said, just to bait me.

"Have a little imagination, sparky."

"Oh, trust me, blondie, I'm imagining *plenty* right now." The inuendo fell from his lips effortlessly. His eyes were sinfully dark, his body unfairly sexy as he stood before me. It wasn't okay – *I* wasn't okay.

My breath hitched and he didn't miss it.

Bastard.

He grabbed another bale, his biceps bulging as he threw it up against the barn wall, on the top of the pile.

"Dark chocolate or milk?" I asked, trying to change the subject.

"Milk."

"Me too."

He winked at me and I clenched my thighs together to try and fend off the building pressure at my apex.

I was the worst person in the world for feeling this way about him – given the mess I'd left behind in my wake, but I couldn't help it. Something deep inside of him spoke to something deep inside of me. I wasn't in control of it, but I needed to be.

He went back to his work and I went back to my ogling.

I needed advice, even though I knew what I should be doing – *running*... leaving Ky Bateman in my rear-view mirror – but I didn't know how. Hell, I didn't even know what I was doing here in the first place. All rational thought went out the window when I was faced with this man and his sexy smirk.

I pulled out my phone, still without a sim card and typed in the Wi-Fi password that Aubrey had given me this morning.

I pulled up my email account and typed out my question.

Dear Ida,

Am I a terrible person for wanting to rip off a stranger's clothes and have a literal roll in the hay with him?

-Morally Fucked, Middle Of Bum Fuck Nowhere.

I snapped a picture of Ky's bare, sweaty back as he hoisted a bale of hay above his head and attached it to the email.

"Cats or dogs?" he asked without turning.

"You can't make me choose."

"*Choose*, blondie."

"I refuse. I want both."

"Rulebreaker." He chuckled, his eyes flitting to mine.

I raised a brow, waiting for him to give me his answer.

"Cats."

His choice surprised me. I was expecting him to be more of a dog kind of guy.

"Really? I thought cats and their attitudes would be too much for a guy like you."

"I've got a weakness for sass and pussy; you should have figured that out by now."

I wasn't sure if I was being insulted or complimented, but I definitely knew I was blushing.

My phone pinged with an email and I grinned.

Dear Morally Fucked,

You went with him! Good for you, how's his penis? And yes, you're going to hell – I'll see you there.

S x

I had to laugh. She was nothing if not brutally honest.

She'd added a picture of her smiling baby; it was one cute kid.

I sighed, tucked my phone into my pocket and jumped off the bench I'd parked my ass on.

"When is Aubrey picking up the pigs?" I asked Chance.

"Oh no, little lady, she managed to convince the

bloke to deliver them and everything. My Aubrey always gets things her way. They should be here in about an hour."

I liked her more and more by the day.

One of the kids yelled out to Chance then and he stopped what he was doing and left the barn to investigate.

I watched him go, my curiosity growing.

"What's on your mind, blondie?"

Ky had stopped working and was sitting on a bale of hay, an ice-cold water bottle in his hand and sweat dripping down his chest.

God, he was perfection.

"What makes you think something's on my mind?"

"That little crease between your eyebrows. Come, sit." He patted the spot next to him.

My frown deepened. It worried me that he could read me so easily. I thought I'd been doing a pretty good job of keeping my guard up – but maybe I needed to re-assess.

I closed the gap between us and sat myself down as far away from him as possible. Not because he was sweaty and stinky, but because I didn't trust myself to keep my hands off him.

My self-control was waning – big time.

"I told myself it didn't matter, but I'm dying to know... what did Chance do to spend two years in prison?"

I glanced at him out of the corner of my eye and he was grinning, a knowing half-smirk.

"I've been wondering when you were going to ask me that."

"He didn't kill anyone did he? I like the guy; I'd really hate to think he was capable of that."

He shook his head, his expression turning slightly more solemn. "He didn't kill the guy, but he did do some serious damage."

"Why?" I breathed. "He's so chill. I can't imagine him getting worked up about anything."

"There's only one thing in the world that can make Chance see red, and that's if somebody hurts someone he loves."

That made sense – it fit with the man I'd been slowly getting to know.

"The man he attacked was his sister Adele's crack-head boyfriend. He beat him for an address – of where he could find the man who raped her."

I heard myself gasp. "*No*. Is she okay?"

He smiled a sweet, genuine smile with absolutely no hint of his usual cocky demeanour. "Yeah. She's doing great now."

"I'm glad."

I didn't know Adele – never met her, had no idea what she even looked like, but Ky cared a great deal for her, that was obvious, and that was enough for me.

"*That's* why he left Aubrey in Vegas," I thought aloud.

"Stupid bugger should have just been honest with her." He sighed, running a hand through his dark, inky hair. "Would have saved them both a lot of heartache.

A ball formed in the pit of my stomach. *Could I save myself some heartache?*

I knew I should have been honest with Ky, told him the series of events that led me to that airport in California, but I was scared. I didn't like the person I'd become, and I was worried that he wouldn't either.

I wasn't even sure why I cared. This little trip couldn't last forever, but I liked the way he looked at me – the softness in his eyes when I spoke – it was addictive, and I wanted to enjoy it while it lasted.

He had that look in his eye now as he watched me process, and I was struck yet again by how dark his eyes really were – the gold flecks mesmerising me.

"I guess some people are scared to be honest," I breathed.

"The truth always comes out in the end, blondie."

Was it hot in here? It felt hot. Like I had a burning temperature. I wasn't sick, and it wasn't any warmer out now than it was an hour ago, but my skin felt flushed. It must have been the Ky Bateman effect.

He reached over slowly and took my hand in his, playing with my fingers and not saying a word.

It was too welcome, too comfortable. *Shit.* I was in *big* trouble.

The tension between us built and I could tell he was thinking about kissing me.

I was thinking about kissing him too.

"Blake!" Aubrey yelled from somewhere outside the barn. "Hurry up, the pigs are here!"

He sighed.

I shot him a rueful glance as I got to my feet.

He didn't give up my hand, instead letting me get as far away as my arm could stretch before pulling me back to him.

I gasped as he tugged me right into his lap. "Why do I feel like they're all working together to keep me from kissing you?" he growled.

"Do you want to kiss me, sparky?" I tried to keep my tone light and fun, but I failed miserably. I couldn't hide how worked up I was. I was in his lap, for fuck's sake. He was sweaty and hot and unbelievably sexy.

"I've wanted to kiss you since the moment I first laid eyes on you." His confession made my heart race.

"What's stopping you?" I whispered as his face inched closer to mine.

"Blake! They're so cute!" Bree yelled before she came flying into the barn.

"The universe," Ky muttered. He rested his brow against mine, his eyes smouldering intense.

"Ewwww!" Bree giggled.

Ky leaned in, brushed his salty lips against mine just once and leant back. "I *will* kiss you, Blake Vincent, then I'll do so much more. That's a promise."

I was going to hold him to that.

I walked out of the barn on shaky legs, Bree's hand in mine as she blabbered on and on about how cute the new piglets were and what she was going to call them.

I barely heard a word, my mind was too scattered from the tall, dark and handsome man who had just promised he'd have his way with me.

I hoped he was right.

15

Ky

I WATCHED her drink her morning coffee with all the interest of a starving man looking at a plate piled high with food.

I'd formulated a plan after we got interrupted, yet again, yesterday. I needed to get her alone. I needed to show her how good we could be together.

The tension between us was at an all-time high, I knew she'd been expecting me to kiss her when we found ourselves alone in our room last night, but I'd been the perfect gentleman. *Didn't know I had it in me.*

Now that I'd imagined how I wanted it to go, I wasn't willing to settle for anything less.

I was probably making a big deal out of nothing, but you only got one first kiss and I wanted it to be one she'd never forget. Something in my brain told me that every moment with her was precious, that *she* was precious. Different. *Special.*

God, I sounded like a pussy. If one of my mates said this shit to me, I'd have told them they just needed to get laid. I *did* need to get laid, but there was only one woman who was going to be able to scratch this particular itch, and that meant putting in the groundwork. A girl like Blake didn't just give herself away without a little effort.

"We're going out today," I announced.

Her eyes bounced from me, to Aubrey, then to Chance.

"Nope, just you and me."

Her brows shot up in surprise.

I chuckled. "Don't look so afraid."

"I'm not scared of you, sparky," she challenged.

"No? You should be."

She rolled her eyes – the gesture making my dick twitch.

"Go get ready," I instructed.

"What if I don't want to go?"

She wanted to go, but she just *had* to challenge me at every step of the way.

"Got a better offer?"

"Maybe I do... Peppa and George *are* pretty cute."

"So, I'm below pigs now, wonderful."

Chance chuckled. Aubrey watched on like we were some television drama she couldn't get enough of.

"They give less lip." She smirked.

"Get ready," I demanded. "Dress nice."

She sat her cup down in the sink and took a step towards me. "Are you saying I don't always look nice?"

"Jesus Christ, just put on a dress, do your hair and meet me out here in thirty minutes."

She clicked her tongue at me. "So bossy."

I caught her as she tried to breeze past me. "You have no fucking idea how bossy I can be, blondie."

She didn't need further explanation to read my intentions.

Her breath came in fast pants as those eyes, *those damn eyes*, the ones that featured in every one of my daydreams, widened at me.

"Try me, Blake, you know you want to," I murmured.

"Maybe I do." Her teeth sunk into her bottom lip as she battled for composure.

"I can't wait," I promised, releasing her from both my hand and my eyes.

I watched her walk away, her hips swaying, totally fucking unsure of who'd just won that round.

"Woah, it just got *hot* in here." Aubrey fanned her face dramatically.

"Shut up," I grumbled.

"No can do, Romeo, you're really pulling out all the stops for this girl."

"I like her."

"You don't say."

"Don't know how an ugly mug like you managed to get her, but I like her too," Chance chimed in.

"She's *so* pretty," Aubrey agreed with him.

"Too pretty for him."

"No way, Ky is hot."

"Princess, don't call my cousin hot."

"You've got eyes, *Mr. Bastardo*, you can see he's hot."

"Uh, you know I'm still here, right?" I asked.

Aubrey waved me away dismissively. "Whatever, I'm just saying. She's gorgeous, you're gorgeous – don't fuck it up."

"I'll try my best," I replied dryly, making a hasty exit.

I waited until I heard Blake move from the bedroom to the bathroom before slipping into the room and changing into a black shirt and dark jeans.

I glanced at my watch. It had been forty minutes, and she was still showing no signs of emerging from the bathroom.

I rapped my knuckles against the door. "You ready?"

I tugged on my collar. Nerves fluttered in my stomach.

"Nearly," she replied. "Give me five minutes."

I leaned against the wall, waiting like a chump for the woman who stole my breath every time she looked at me.

She was obviously really fucking bad with time, because I waited there for another *fifteen* minutes, growing more and more impatient with every second that ticked by.

"We're going to be late," I grumbled as I reached for the handle.

The door swung open before my fingers found purchase.

The sight before me was one of absolute god damn wonder.

"Fuck me, blondie, I said *nice*, not sexy as hell," I choked out.

Nothing in my life had ever looked as good as Blake Vincent did right now.

Her sexy little body was covered in a form-fitting, white dress that hugged her *everywhere*.

She was higher up than I was used to, the sky-high heels on her feet bringing her forehead level with my mouth.

I couldn't help myself, I needed to taste her skin. I stepped forward and brought my lips to her forehead, kissing her once.

"Is it okay?" she asked nervously, tugging at the fabric on her hips.

"It's more than fucking okay, babe, you look... *Jesus*, there aren't words, Blake."

She lowered her thick lashes, coated in black, and her cheeks coloured. "Thank you."

I hooked a finger under her chin and sought out eye contact. "You're perfect."

Her fingers skimmed the collar of my shirt. "You look good all dressed up, sparky."

I looked like a mug next to her, but I didn't care. She was with me – that was the main thing.

"You ready?"

She nodded.

I took her hand in mine and led her out, through

the living room, past the cat calls and wolf whistles from my moron cousin and his shit-stirring wife and out to Chance's ute.

"I don't get to drive?" She pouted as I held open the passenger door for her.

"No way in fucking hell."

"Buzz kill."

"You're a bad enough driver *without* those shoes."

She glanced down at her feet. "You don't like my shoes?"

Quite the fucking opposite, actually.

I helped her into the vehicle. "I like the shoes, blondie, I can picture you wearing only them while I fuck you senseless."

Her jaw dropped. "Did you really just say that?"

I bit back laughter as I rounded the hood and climbed in.

"What happened to the innuendoes?" she demanded. "You're just coming straight out with that shit now?"

"Thought we were due a moment of pure honesty." I winked at her. "I'll be sure to go back to sexually suggestive comments from here on out."

She muttered away to herself as I pulled out of the property and onto the main road.

"Where are we going anyway? You never told me."

I peeked a glance at her. "The horse races. There's a big meet happening. I thought you might be up for a little rematch?"

She grinned wickedly. "I didn't lose that bet, you *played* me."

"Maybe I did, what's going to stop me doing it again?"

"Nobody fools me twice," she replied smugly.

I didn't know what was going on in her head, but my girl looked like she had a plan. She didn't need a plan, she *owned* me – she could bring me to my knees any time she wanted. All she had to do was say the words.

I flicked on the radio and music filled the cab.

I'd been singing along to a song I liked before her hand shot out and lowered the volume.

"You realise those aren't the words, right?"

"Aren't they?"

"Not even a little bit."

I shrugged. "Sounds like the words to me."

"Are you the full ticket?" she demanded, earning a grin from me. "You really think Jefferson Starship sang, *we built this city on sausage rolls*?"

"Girl knows her ninety's pop rock artists."

"And you know your pastry snacks, apparently."

I chuckled. *Always a clap back for everything.*

"Who died and made you the lyrical queen?"

"Probably the same person who crowned you king of destroying the classics."

"Touché, blondie, touché."

I grinned as the next song came on, I knew damn well what the words were this time too, but I wasn't above fucking with her. I turned it up louder.

Kings of Leon, *This Sex is on Fire*. Impossible to get wrong.

She groaned as I joined in the chorus. "You're taking the piss now."

I laughed, my eyes leaving the road for a moment to take in her expression before finding their way back.

"Did you seriously just say, *dyslexics on fire*?"

"No?" I mock frowned. "Is that what you heard? *Weird*."

"You're a moron."

"Some say moron, some say stud muffin."

"*Stud muffin?*" She bit back a laugh. "Nineteen eighty called, it wants its term of endearment back."

I'd never tire of seeing and hearing her laugh. It hit me square in the chest every single time.

"What can I say, I'm just an old-fashioned gentleman."

She scrunched up her nose at me before poking out her tongue.

"Pop or rock, blondie?"

"Pop."

"I'm more of a rock man, myself."

"Of course, you are." Another roll of her eyes. If she didn't watch herself, I was going to have to go all Christian Grey on her ass.

"Summer or winter?" I asked when silence enveloped us.

"Summer. I love the heat, the feel of a warm breeze in the evening... the beach... Summer is the best time of year."

"It's virtually summer all year round here."

"I might have to move." She sighed wistfully.

Me too. With you.

I needed to find my internal handbrake and rip that sucker up. My mind was about one hundred steps ahead of my reality.

"You?" she prompted, pulling me back to the present.

"Hmm?"

"Summer or winter?"

"Summer. Always."

"Look at that, we finally agree on something." She looked pleased about it.

"It's all sunshine and milk chocolate in our future."

I could tell that me remembering her answers pleased her, even though she'd never admit it.

She pulled her phone out of her bag, glanced at it and stuffed it back in.

"You expecting a call?"

She shook her head. "Nope. And even if I was, no sim."

"You can borrow mine if you want?"

"I'm good thanks, sparky, the only person I want to talk to is right here next to me."

I was fucking glad to hear it, but I couldn't help but wonder what she'd left behind in Cali. Surely she had friends, work colleagues... *someone* that wanted to check in with her.

I wasn't going to push her, that was her business, and frankly, if she wanted to give me all her attention, I wasn't going to say no.

"Did you just give me a compliment?"

She smiled and shook her head at me. "I did no such thing."

"I think you *did*."

"You can't prove anything; it's my word against yours."

We bantered back and forth for the next hour until we reached the racecourse. I learnt that she preferred CrossFit to running, oranges to apples, heels to flats and horses to cows.

I killed the engine and turned in my seat to face her. "Here we are, blondie."

She glanced out the windscreen at the sea of cars in the carpark. "Woah. Exactly what am I getting myself into here?"

I took her hand in mind. "Now that would be telling."

16

Blake

"YOU KNOW, something has been bugging me."

"Other than me, you mean?"

"Other than you," I confirmed with a smile.

He led me through a flashy area filled with well-dressed men and women, his hand pressed firmly to the small of my back until we reached a small table on the opposite side of the room.

"Hit me with it, blondie."

"Okay, so maybe this is a stupid question, but *why* would anyone use a bookie? Why not just place their own bets?"

He glanced around to see if anyone was listening to our conversation, a sheepish expression on his face.

"What?" I asked, leaning closer.

"Just keep your voice down, being a bookie isn't exactly legal."

Well, that was news to me, but not exactly shocking – Ky Bateman was a rule breaker.

"You're breaking the law?"

"Not right this minute." He winked.

I raised my brows at him and waited for him to give me a straight answer.

"It's a dying profession," he explained. "Back in the day, the only way to bet was in person, so punters couldn't always get to race meets to place their bet. The easiest way to get it done, was to place a bet through a bookie."

I nodded. "Okay, that makes sense, but surely they have an app for that now?"

"Exactly. There's still a handful of old guys that stick with what they know, but mostly, technology has made that aspect of the job redundant... but the other reason someone uses a bookie is for credit."

"You let them make bets with money they don't have?" I raised a brow.

He shrugs a shoulder. "Sometimes."

"And *that's* the illegal part." I nodded in under-standing.

"Correct."

"What's the most someone has ever owed you?"

"Fifty thousand," he replied without batting an eyelid.

"Fifty thousand, what? *Dollars*?" I demanded.

"No, *seashells*," he replied dryly, "yes, *dollars*."

I couldn't believe what I was hearing. I also

couldn't decide if this new information made me like him more or less.

"Did you get your money?"

He huffed out a laugh. "I *always* get my money."

The look in his eye told me he meant it.

"Are you like some d-low mobster offspring? Because if you are, now would be the time to tell me."

He laughed. "You're safe there, blondie."

Thank god.

"I'm kind of speechless."

"That must be a first." He smirked.

I scowled at him.

"America is filled with guys who bet beyond their means, you just have to know where to find them."

"That feels... *manipulative*."

"It probably is." He nodded.

"And you're okay with that?"

He shrugged his shoulders, his gaze wandering out the tall, glass window to the horses trotting around beyond. "A fool and his money are soon parted, blondie. And besides, if it wasn't me, it would have been someone else. At least I didn't turn up to their homes and terrorise their families or any of that shit. Never had to give anyone the beat-down like the other guys did."

"Sounds like you kept some charming company."

"Sometimes. Anyway, since it's a dying business and all, I adapted, moved on from it as much as I could."

I eyed him curiously. "If you tell me you're a drug dealer, I'm out."

He laughed again, his head falling back as his whole body shook. "I'm not a drug dealer, fuck, you're hilarious.'

"I'm glad you're amused."

"I gamble. Okay? I guess you could say I'm a professional gambler."

I'd heard of professional poker players, guys counting cards and all that, but this seemed ridiculous. They were animals and humans – there were less than no guarantees in horse betting.

"On *horses*?"

"Mostly. Sometimes I dabble in the dogs, but I prefer to stick to what I know best."

"So, let me get this straight, you make a living betting on horses?"

He nodded and winked. "Don't forget the part where I swindle vulnerable old men out of their life savings and then come after them with my gang of goons."

"Oh, ha, ha. You're so funny."

"Sarcasm. Very nice."

"What happens if you lose?" I demanded. The more I heard about this, the more ridiculous it seemed, but the more intrigued I became.

"I *do* lose." He shrugged. "Not often and usually not a lot of money, but *sometimes*. It's all part of it. What I do is a risk, but you can't get reward without risk."

"I want to see you in action."

"I bet you do." He waggled his brows suggestively.

I rolled my eyes. "Seriously. I want to watch. Show me how it's done, double M."

"Double M?"

"*Master Manipulator.*"

"Cute."

"I thought so."

He picked up the race book he'd grabbed on his way in and studied it carefully before moving to the small screen a few steps away and watching that for a few long moments. He pulled out his phone, messed around for a bit and then came back to my side. "Alright, go and put three hundred for the win on number six."

He held out a stack of cash for me to take.

"What? Why me?"

"You're my lucky charm." He pressed the money into my hand and took me by the shoulders, steering me towards the short line for the betting booth.

"*Three hundred*? Are you sure?"

He smirked. "I'm sure. Race starts in two minutes, get a move on."

"That's a lot of money," I reasoned with him when it was my turn to bet.

His eyes shone with amusement. "You're holding up the queue, blondie."

I stepped forward and held out the money to the white-haired man behind the glass. "Three hundred for the win on horse six, please."

"Fixed odds," Ky added in.

"Fixed odds," I repeated.

I had no idea what that meant, but the man behind the counter seemed to understand just fine.

He took the money from me and pushed a few buttons. "Three hundred on number six for the win, fixed odds paying out at a forty-five dollar and sixty cent return."

I took the ticket from him, my jaw falling lax. "I might be new to this, but if a horse is paying forty-five dollars to win a race, doesn't that mean it's not very good?"

Ky chuckled, took the ticket in one hand, my hand in the other and ushered me away. "Guess we're about to find out."

I followed behind him, as he slipped through the crowds until we were near the front, in perfect view of the course.

I could see the horses being loaded into the starting gates over the far side of the huge oval.

I was nervous. I didn't know why, given it wasn't my money we were betting with and Ky seemed so laid back about it he was practically horizontal, but butterflies had gone crazy in my stomach ever since I'd placed that bet.

Gambling is a rush.

"Show time," Ky said with a wink.

I watched on apprehensively as the horses were released from the huge metal gates and went flying out onto the track.

"Oh no, it's trying to go to the front," I hissed, jabbing him in the ribs with my elbow.

"It's all good, blondie."

"No, it's not! When my horse went to the front, it got smoked!"

"This isn't your horse though, it's *mine*." He grinned at me as our eyes locked, before he turned back to watch his horse.

It had started the race in about fifth, but now had made its way into third and it didn't look like it was slowing down any time soon.

"Let her run," I heard him murmur as the cheers picked up around us.

People were on their feet now, screaming and cheering for the horse they'd put their hard-earned money on.

I pushed up to my tip-toes, trying to see over the heads of the crowd when the horses came thundering down the home straight.

I might not have been able to see shit, but this was a rush like nothing I'd ever experienced. I was high on the atmosphere.

He fist-pumped the air silently as the race ended.

No... it couldn't have...

"Crossing in first is Alizay's Pride by two lengths, second is..."

No way.

The announcement faded out as I grabbed for the ticket in his hand to make sure I wasn't imagining things, but it was right there in black and white. Three hundred for the win on number six; Alizay's Pride.

"Holy shit."

"I told you that you were my lucky charm." He

155

picked me up and swung me around as I continued to stare at the ticket in shock.

I still couldn't form words as he led me back to our small table and pressed my shoulders down to get me to sit.

"You won?" I finally managed to ask.

He just smirked.

"Oh my god."

"You really didn't have any faith, did you, blondie?"

"I'm not going to lie to you, I had *none*. That paid over forty-five dollars for the win, Ky... that's..."

He looked smug as fuck, and honestly, I didn't blame him. He'd just made bank in about two minutes flat.

"That's like *thirteen hundred*..." I frowned as I tried to make the numbers work in my mind. "*Jesus*, sparky, that's over thirteen *thousand* dollars."

"Look out, rain man. You keep up that quick mathematics and they'll have to ban you from the casinos."

I sat my hands on my hips. "You just won close to fourteen k and you've still got nothing better to do than give me crap?"

"Wouldn't want to let the money go to my head now, would I?"

I studied him carefully. He was excited, no doubt, but his excitement seemed to be tied to me – not the fact that he'd just won that sum of money. The ticket was sitting lazily on the table between us, not clutched in his hand like a prized possession.

Realisation dawned on me. "This isn't a big deal to you, is it?"

He lifted one shoulder before letting it drop again.

"How much do you win?" I demanded.

A sly grin spread across his face.

"A lady never tells."

"You're not a lady."

"Same principles apply."

"How much, Ky?"

He thought for a moment, before answering, "I won close to one hundred thousand on a race last year."

"A hundred grand? On a *horse* race? How much did you bet?"

"Five thousand."

I was lost for words. Who in their right mind dropped five thousand dollars on a *bet*? This solidified it for me – Ky Bateman was mentally unstable.

"It wasn't that big of a deal, blondie. I took a hundred-dollar bet – turned it into five thousand, then bet that five thousand. All I stood to lose that day way a lousy hundred."

"That logic is fucked up." I laughed, borderline hysterical. "You're *insane*. I don't know if I'm intimidated or turned on."

His gaze turned hot, heavy and seductive. "I'd prefer the latter."

"How?" I demanded.

He frowned. "How are you turned on... or?"

I shook my head at him. "No, you pervert, *how* do you know which horse to bet on?"

"That's like asking a magician to reveal his secrets."

"Reveal them, magic man."

He'd tell me. I'd make sure of it.

"It's a lot of things; a good eye, knowledge of the course, the horses, the jockey, the trainer. There are a lot of factors."

"Tell me why you picked number six."

It was an outsider – it was never destined to be the winner, *clearly*, but somehow, he'd picked it anyway.

"That one was easy. It's a two-year-old, only two races under its belt and totally untried at this distance."

That didn't sound like a good reason to throw money at it at all. I opened my mouth to argue, but he held up his finger to stop me.

"I looked at the breeding. Alizay's Pride was sired from Dreams of Alizay – one of the top racehorses in Australia during its short career. Most people haven't heard of it because it was put into early retirement, but shit, when that horse was on the track, it was unbeatable at this distance. Then there's the jockey, he might not be the best in his profession anymore, but he's renowned for his placings on the shorter tracks – he knows how to get the best out of a horse at this distance."

"You knew all that?"

"The information is right there if you know what you're looking for."

"*Huh.*"

"Then I watch the pay-outs, the fluctuation, the rises, the decreases." He leaned in closer like he was telling me an inside secret. "There's a science to it, an algorithm, you know what you're looking for and you can pick up on it."

Most of this was like gibberish to me, but I was hooked on his every hushed word as though it was a secret I'd take to my grave.

"Anyone in the know – trainers, buyers, breeders, big-time gamblers – they wait until right before the race to place their bets. They don't want to give away any tips that would cause mass betting on the horse they think will win. More bets on a horse causes its pay-out to drop and its rank as favourite to rise, so they wait until as late as they can to ensure the best return. It's risky for me, leaving a bet late – sometimes I miss it – but if I can spot the fluctuation, usually combined with some type of knowledge – like the sire and the jockey in this case – then I can see it's probably a good bet."

"You're really smart, aren't you?"

A slow grin crossed his face. "I'm alright."

He was being modest. This was a lot. He wasn't just gambling – he was making educated bets, following formulas, assessing the field. I was seriously impressed.

Just when I'd thought he couldn't get any more attractive.

"There's always error in this business, Blake, especially with so much human involvement, but if you bet smart, you can come out on top when it matters."

"I can see that." My gaze flitted to his winning ticket.

He chuckled, stood up and slung his arm around my shoulders. "C'mon, blondie. You look like you could use a drink... my shout."

17

Ky

I'D TAKEN HOME A MUCH BIGGER pay day than the one in my pocket right now, but this one was the one I was never going to forget.

Because of her.

Everything was better when it was with her. She got excited over her ten-dollar bet coming in; it was adorable.

We'd decided to ditch the fancy shit and had opted instead to watch the last race of the day from the carpark.

Blake had kicked off her heels and had a bottle of beer dangling from her left hand as she strolled around. Not the cocktail-sipping, high-maintenance chick I'd pegged her to be at all.

This woman kept surprising me at every turn;

each time I thought I'd figured her out, she said or did something that made me do a double take, like right now as she twirled around barefoot in the long grass before skipping towards the barrier fence and climbing up on the concrete edge.

She looked over her shoulder to see if I was following her. "Ky, c'mon!"

I took a sip of my own beer, lazily watching her as she clung to the linked chain fence, her ass the picture of perfection in that dress.

"I could slap that ass."

"What?"

"I said, they need to cut the grass."

She narrowed her eyes at me. "Oh no you don't, sparky, your cousin might get away with it, but if you want to make sexually inappropriate comments to me, you can do it to my face."

I chuckled. "No problem." I looked right at her. "I'd like to see my handprint on your ass, Blake, watch that creamy skin pink up under my palm."

She blushed but didn't reply as she pushed up to her toes again, trying to see further out onto the track, I could see what my words did to her though – the same thing hers did to me.

"What's the matter, blondie, can't see?"

I came up behind her, and she grinned. She wasn't drunk, but she'd had a couple of beers and they'd loosened her up.

She spun around so she was facing me, her arms draping over my shoulders at the same time that mine found her waist.

She was almost at my height, with help from the ledge she was perched on.

"I can see just fine, thank you very much. It's about to start."

"Good. Then let's make a bet."

"How are you going to do that without your race stats, huh, hotshot?"

The corner of my mouth twitched. "Good old-fashioned luck I guess."

"Alright then." She agreed, never once taking her eyes from me. "I want the one with the green jockey."

"Orange," I replied without looking at the horse.

I slid my hands around to her back and down to her butt, my empty bottle falling to the grass.

"Your hands are on my ass," she whispered.

"Huh. So they are... how'd that happen?"

She tried not to smile as she shook her head in exasperation.

"What's the bet, sparky?"

I cocked my head to the side. "If you win, you can have half of my winnings from today."

She rolled her eyes. "I don't want your money."

"It's a good bet, you should take it," I insisted, stepping closer so we were pressed together.

"You drive me *insane*," she grumbled. She hated how much she liked that fact – I could tell.

"I think that might be the point," I replied, my voice husky.

Her eyes looked at me longingly. "So, for argument's sake, let's say I agree. What do you get if you win?"

I was silent for a few beats.

"I get you."

"*Me*?" she breathed, leaning into me.

"*You*."

The commentator's voice started, the race under-way, but our eyes remained glued to one another's.

"We got a deal, blondie?"

She shook her head, one small shake.

"No?"

I heard the thunder of hooves as the horses flew past us, but still, I didn't look.

"No," she confirmed.

My heart sank. I was so sure she felt it too.

"You can't win something you already own."

Her words sunk in, and I heard myself growl, the sound so primal and possessive it shocked me. My mouth was on hers in a flash, hot and demanding.

Her fingers weaved into my hair, her bottle joining mine on the ground as I pressed my tongue against her lips and she opened up for me, giving me access.

My cock hardened painfully against the seam of my jeans as she gave up control to me, letting me claim her mouth the way I'd been dying to for days.

She tasted of long summer days and even longer nights.

This wasn't just a kiss; it was a promise of more to come. It spoke of tangled sheets, breathless moans and endless possibilities.

"Ky." She whimpered against my lips as I sucked in a breath of air.

"*Jesus*," I grunted, my grip on her ass unrelenting.

She was pressed up so close to me, I was going crazy. My body, my mind... she had me all fucked up.

"Ky, that was..."

"*Life altering* springs to mind," I finished for her; my grin cocky as my brow rested against hers.

She dipped her head, her lips making contact with my neck, and I physically shuddered. The things this woman could do to me defied common sense.

I reached for her chin, gripping it between my fingers as I brought her lips back to mine. I wanted – no fuck that – I *needed* another taste. She sighed, the sound breathless, and I was a complete and utter goner.

This is it. This is what love feels like.

I knew it was crazy. We'd only met a few days earlier, but I didn't care. Blake wasn't just some girl I met in an airport; she was more important than oxygen at this point.

My body needed hers more than I needed my next breath.

"*Blake*?" I whispered, my heart hammering in my chest as she dragged in a breath.

"Mmm?"

"Will you be my date for New Year's Eve?"

Her eyes met mine, so unusual, so fucking striking, the smart clapback I'd be willing to bet was on her lips died, and for once, she gave me nothing but pure honesty. "I'd love nothing more."

Thank fuck for that.

I ran the tip of my nose up and down the length of hers, doing nothing but breathing her in.

"We didn't see who won."

"Me," I replied quickly as I lifted her off the ledge. "I've already got my trophy."

She giggled, her silky hair tickling my face. I let her down, her body sliding deliciously down mine until her feet found the ground.

"Then why do I feel like *I'm* the one who got the prize?" Her delicate fingers fiddled with the button on the front of my shirt as she peeked up at me through her lashes.

Fuck, I was no prize. I was *nothing* compared to her.

I leaned down, dipping my head to meet hers – now that we were back on even footing – and brushed my lips against hers, just once, in the softest, sweetest kiss of my life.

It was right there on my lips – my feelings for her. I could have opened my mouth and spilled it, but I held back. Blake wasn't some thirty-second race, she was a long-distance event. I needed to take my time, do things properly.

We made the entire drive back hand in hand, both of us drunk on the other. I couldn't speak for her, but I wasn't just drunk on her – I was blackout wasted. I had to coach myself to shut up and drive, every time I saw a rest stop or a motel, all I wanted to do was pull in and have my way with her.

Blake didn't deserve that, some quickie in the back of a ute, or some seedy room – she deserved the best, and I'd find a way to give it to her. Even if it meant exercising my diminishing patience.

I wasn't a particularly patient man to begin with, but I was no fool either and I knew some things were worth waiting for.

18

Blake

"You know, I never get tired of watching him out there."

I lolled my head to the side, towards where Aubrey was reclined next to me on the warm golden sand.

Her eyes were focused behind the breaking waves, where Chance and Ky were sitting, each of them on a surfboard.

We'd been down here for hours. Bree and CJ were making a castle, CJ's discarded board on the sand next to me.

He'd been out with the guys earlier, but Chance made the call to bring him in when the sets started to pick up.

I let my gaze wander back to the man who was

slowly stealing my heart – or what was left of it anyway.

"He comes out here nearly every day," she carried on. "I think time stands still when he's in the ocean. He can tell me he'll be gone for an hour and then six hours later he comes back... his hair dripping wet and a goofy smile on his face."

I could tell by the way she spoke that she wasn't bothered by her husband disappearing for hours on end.

"Sometimes I bring the kids down and just watch him do his thing. It's incredible. It's like he was born from the sea or something."

I knew what she meant; I'd felt the same way watching Ky glide effortlessly through the water when he caught a wave. It was so natural, so right. It felt like the wave just opened up and welcomed him in.

"Ky really likes you," she surprised me by saying.

"Did he say something to you?" I asked, looking at her again.

She shook her head. "No. he didn't have to. I've never seen him like this with a woman; sweet, attentive – playful. You bring out the best in him."

"I think he brings out the worst in me," I admitted sheepishly.

"All the best ones do." She smiled knowingly. "I'd never met such a cocky bastard in my life when I met that man." She tipped her head in the direction of her husband. "But he turned out to be so much more than that."

"There're things Ky doesn't know about me," I admitted, even though it terrified me to do so.

"I'm sure there're things you don't know about him too, but that's the beauty of communicating, you can just open your mouth and let it all out. He looks at you like you hung the moon, Blake, I can't imagine that's just going to change."

I nodded, thoughtful.

She was right, I knew that. I needed to talk to Ky, but I was afraid. Today had been the perfect day, and I didn't want to ruin it by telling him the details of my past. He didn't just look at me like I hung the moon, but all the stars too – I wasn't blind, I saw it.

I watched as he rode a wave right into the beach, before jumping off his board, tucking it under his arm and jogging up the sand towards me.

"Um... wow," I whispered.

He was picture perfect; his sexy arms, shoulders... lickable tattoos... his tight, defined abs... and to top it off, he was drenched, the water running from his hair, down his body.

"I feel your pain," Aubrey murmured. "Those Bateman men sure have a good gene pool."

I grabbed my phone off the towel next to me and snapped a pic.

That one is going straight to the wank bank.

It was also going to Soraya. I tapped out a quick email to send her when I got back to the WiFi.

Dear Ida,

Why is a man so insanely hot when he's dripping wet?

-Drooling Idiot, Pretty Beach

I grinned to myself as I attached the photo and hit send.

She was in for a treat when that went on its way.

Ky's eyes found mine and locked on as he strolled up the beach looking like a freakin' male model.

He smiled – not his usual cocky smirk, but a real smile, one filled with complete happiness.

Everything else disappeared when he looked at me like that. We could have been the only two people on this beach for all I knew, I didn't see anyone, hear anything else. Only him. Only me. Only *us*.

He stopped short of me, drove his board into the sand and dropped to a crouch. "You miss me, blondie?"

I nodded, unable to form words as every defined inch of him tempted me.

He chuckled. "Do you know how hard I get when you look at me like that? It's taking all of my self-control, Blake, not to fuck you right here on the beach."

That shocked me back to reality, I turned, ready to tell Aubrey I was sorry for the visual I was sure she didn't need, but she was gone, down the sand with her husband and children.

"No one likes sand in those places," I pointed out.

He reached out, his cool fingers sending shivers down my spine as he made contact with my jaw.

He turned my face back to his. "I'm really glad you're here."

I'd never heard him sound so sincere.

"I'm glad I'm here too," I whispered.

Even though I shouldn't be.

Even though I'm a terrible person.

Even though I'm bound to hurt you in the end.

I couldn't speak for him, but I think if someone offered me the choice of having him, knowing it was going to end in heartbreak in the end, or not having him at all – I think I'd choose the heartbreak. I just had to hope he felt the same way, and that once I told him the reality of my life, that he'd understand.

I might have acted like I hated him on sight, but if he really did end up hating me for real, I think it would crush me.

Ky was cocky, arrogant, and crass, but he was also kind, gentle and thoughtful.

He was a perfect blend of angel and devil, and I hated the universe for bringing him to me now – at a time where I couldn't have deserved him less.

"Can I buy you dinner?"

I nodded. He could have offered to make me a knuckle sandwich and I probably still would have said yes. I was a goner.

"You okay?" His eyebrows pulled together.

No.

Yes.

Not even a little bit.

Never been better.

I couldn't decide on an answer, so I gave him the only thing I could think of that wasn't a lie.

I reached out, my hand snaking behind his neck, and dragged him on top of me, his big, wet body pressing me into the sand as our mouths met, the kiss hungry, passionate and filled with emotion.

I took him by surprise, but it was short-lived, his reactions quickly catching up and taking over – his inner alpha coming out as he took control.

I'd never been kissed like this before, and I'd been kissed plenty. No one had ever made me feel like I was precious glass and sexy as sin in the very same moment.

Ky's eyes were gentle, but his hands were firm.

He looked at me like he had every intention of treasuring me, but his body told a different story. He flexed his hips, his erection pressing against my stomach.

I knew we were going down this path, but now that we were here, right on the verge of sleeping together, I was scared.

I didn't know how I was meant to walk away after that. I didn't know how he was meant to survive unscathed.

"I can't get enough of you, Blake," he murmured against my lips.

I felt the same way.

God, I felt *everything*. I was a terrible person... the worst.

I was going straight to hell.

"You make me crazy," I replied.

"Good," he growled before nipping at my bottom lip with his teeth.

I gave back just as good as I got, our lips, tongues and hands duelling for control.

He won. I think he always would.

"I think we better get off this beach," I panted when he finally released my mouth.

"You not up for a little public display, blondie?" He grinned as he rolled off me and pulled me up with him.

"That *was* a 'little' PDA," I informed him. "I'm worried that the locals might not feel the same way if we let it go much further."

He chuckled. "Killjoy."

I raised a brow at him. "You a closet exhibitionist all of a sudden?"

"When it comes to you, I'm a lot of things and none of them are particularly smart."

I swallowed deeply, his words hitting home. If only he understood just exactly how stupid letting me in was.

"Let's go, blondie, I'm not ready for today to be over yet."

I smiled, nodded and took his hand.

He drove us home and I giggled as I got a response from Soraya.

Dear Drooling Idiot,

I'll send you some bibs. Hell, I think I might need one too.

S x

Ky gave me a questioning look as I laughed at the screen of my phone, but I waved him off. This was girl talk and he was most certainly not a girl.

After he'd showered and changed, he drove us to a little place downtown that Aubrey insisted we go to.

We were just driving down the street – him behind the wheel because apparently, I couldn't be trusted anymore – when a kangaroo jumped out into the street and hopped across the road.

"Holy shit, did you see that?" I demanded.

"The roo?" he questioned, confused.

"Yes, *the kangaroo*, what the hell is it doing here?"

"You're such a city girl." He laughed.

"You're damn right I am, and where I come from, kangaroos don't hop across the street like pedestrians."

He pulled up in a vacant park and killed the engine. "Well Bree tells me that it's a common occurrence here."

I glanced out the window again, but it was long gone. "That's wild."

"I think it's pretty cool."

"You really like it here, don't you?"

He nodded. "I'm falling in love with the place."

I'm falling in love with you.

"It's pretty incredible."

He unclicked his belt and leaned back against his seat. "What about you, blondie? Could you see yourself living somewhere like this?"

His tone was casual, but the intensity in his dark eyes was undeniable.

It was a weighted question, one that scared me shitless.

We hadn't spoken a word about what the hell we were doing here, or how long it might last. We'd gone nowhere near the topic of what might happen next, and I for one was grateful. I couldn't give him anything more than right now, and even that I had my reservations about. He deserved someone who would give him their all – their honesty, their future.

I wasn't sure what the hell my future was.

My life was a mess. *I* was a mess.

"Honestly... I have no idea what my next move is, sparky. I love it here, it's beautiful, but I don't even know where I'll be next week."

He nodded slowly, his Adam's apple bobbing on a swallow. I doubted it was the answer he was hoping to hear, but I needed to start being honest sometime, and this seemed like a good place to start.

"I'm just taking every day as it comes – enjoying myself... as much as it pains me to give you a compliment."

That earnt me a grin.

He didn't push me for anything more the entire rest of the evening. No deep and meaningful conversations – just light, fun, sexy banter. So, I gave myself a pass card for the night. I let myself forget about everything from the past and just lived in the moment, with Ky.

He told me about his favourite destinations around the world – he'd been almost everywhere, and I told him about the kids I'd been teaching back in the US. We talked for hours and hours and it felt like time stood still... and when I fell asleep in his arms that night, I finally felt like maybe I was right where I was meant to be.

19

Ky

I WOKE up with my boner poking her in the ass.

"I know, man, I know," I muttered to myself. My dick was ready to go, but he was going to have to calm the hell down – I had a plan to surprise Blake and I wasn't going to fuck it up by letting my hormones take the wheel.

Sensing I was awake, she stirred, before rolling over and yawning. "Happy New Year's Eve," I greeted her.

"That's not a thing," she replied sleepily.

"Don't care."

"Well you should."

"You going to make me care, blondie?"

Little did she know, she'd already made me care, not about talking shit, but about her, about *everything*… about things I'd never even considered before she came along.

"Maybe I will," she replied half-heartedly around another yawn.

"Go back to sleep." I kissed her forehead. "I've got a few things to organise anyway."

She blinked a few times, already looking like she could drift off again. "You sure? I feel bad."

I chuckled. She was a liar, and not a very good one.

"I'm sure, get some sleep."

Her eyes drifted closed and I sat there, watching her sleep for a few minutes before sliding out of bed, coaching my dick to relax the whole time.

"Your time will come, buddy," I muttered, "have a little faith."

I showered, dressed and went in search of food.

Chance was in the kitchen, blending something obnoxiously loud given the reasonably early hour. "Mate! Morning, I was wondering when you were going to drag your ass out of bed."

Knowing Chance and his never-ending energy, he'd probably landscaped a garden already this morning, or sheared a sheep or some shit.

If I was full of energy, then he was a fully charged, megawatt battery – always ready to go and up for just about anything.

He poured two glasses of some type of smoothie and handed me one.

"It's only nine."

"Day started three hours ago."

I wasn't sure if I'd been living the cruisy life of travelling too long, or if he was not quite right in the head, but as far as I was concerned, six was not morning.

"Where's your crotch spawn? I've got a bone to pick with CJ. The little shit put soap on my toothbrush last night."

That was a not so pleasant surprise before I went to bed last night.

Chance laughed loudly. "I did warn you not to teach him our old tricks."

"I might repay him with a short-sheeted bed. Is he up yet?"

"Aubrey's already taken them to our sitter – they're friends of ours with kids the same age. The kids have been hounding to get going all morning. They're staying the night. First New Year's Eve since we became parents that we might actually make it to midnight."

"How times have changed."

He ran his hand through his hair. "I tell you what, mate, having kids is the most challenging shit I've ever taken on, but I wouldn't have it any other way. Bree is showing signs of putting her mother's sassy attitude to shame, and CJ is so much like me, I'm terrified to think of what's going to go down when he's fifteen, but fuck, they're my whole life."

"They're good kids, you and Aubrey are nailing the parenting."

Being a dad suited him. He was patient, fair and fun. He was what a dad should have been, and I hoped that one day, when the time came for me, that I'd be even half the father he was – it would still be more than twice the father mine was.

Blake's face flashed through my head when I thought about my future children – which if it were any other woman, especially one I'd just met, would have caused me to panic, but when it was blondie I could see growing round with our child... holding our baby, it wasn't so scary.

I knew I needed to get a grip on this. Here I was, practically naming our children and we hadn't even slept together.

I was hoping that would change tonight.

"You think you could help me with something?" I asked Chance.

"Of course." He nodded without even asking what it was I wanted help with.

That was Chance for you – he'd give you the shirt off his back without thinking twice about it. He'd give you a hard time afterwards, but he'd do it anyway.

It took us the next two hours, two trips into town and more than a few cuss words to get it all together, but when it was done, it was perfect.

Blake was going to love it.

"Never picked you for the romantic type." Chance smirked as we admired our handy work.

"You're one to talk. I've seen you picking flowers from the garden for Aubrey."

He held up his hands in defence. "I'm so whipped it's not funny, but we're not talking about me, we're talking about *you*."

I walked out of the barn and closed the door behind him when he followed me, not saying a word. I knew when I was being baited and this was one of those moments.

Chance chuckled. "I'm going to take your silence as confirmation."

"Whatever works for you, man."

We walked side by side towards the house, shoulder checking each other every so often, just like we used to do when we were younger, trying to see who could make the other lose their balance first.

"Looks like your girl's finally up."

My girl.

My eyes searched for her, finding her on the porch, leaning against the balustrade, sipping from a cup I knew would contain coffee, and watching us, a smile playing on her pouty lips.

I jogged away from Chance, closing the distance between us quickly. I'd been right next to her only a couple of hours ago, but my body missed hers. It was like a piece of me was missing when she wasn't near.

"Hey, sparky."

"Morning, blondie."

"Sorry I slept so late."

"You did warn me you needed your eight hours."

She'd been asleep for more like twelve, but I figured I still owed her from our flight.

"What are you boys doing out here?"

"Morning, little lady," Chance interrupted, tipping the ridiculous hat he'd been wearing all morning at her.

"What on earth is on your head?" she demanded, and I chuckled.

"You never seen a hat before?"

"Oh, I've seen a hat, but *that*..." she pointed an accusing finger at Chance's head, "is *not* a hat. It's an eye sore."

"Oh c'mon." He grinned. "It's an Australian classic."

He looked like a cliché Australian outback movie had barfed on his head. He was wearing a ridiculous bucket hat with corks hanging off it that shook every time he moved.

"It's ridiculous," Aubrey's voice came from behind us.

"Don't be like that, princess. I thought you liked how Australian I was?"

"I liked your *accent*, not your dress sense. And besides, now that we're living here, that accent is a dime a dozen."

"You wound me, Aubrey." I didn't miss the way he enunciated her name to sound even more Australian. AH-BREE.

Dude was shameless – taught me everything I knew.

Aubrey rolled her eyes and disappeared back into the house, Chance following after her rattling off ridiculous Aussie phrases like, 'throw another shrimp on the barbie' and 'stone the flamin' crows'.

Blake shook her head, her eyes alight with amusement. "You know, it's really a testament to her self-control that he isn't missing any fingers."

"For once, I agree with you."

Now that it was just the two of us, I stepped closer, tugging her against me. "How'd you sleep?"

"Like a baby."

I leaned down and brushed her lips with mine. She tasted of coffee and sunshine.

"I missed you."

She laughed; her cheeks lightly blushing. "You're a sweet talker. Do you think you can just whisper a few sweet words in my ear and win me over?"

I shrugged. "You tell me, blondie, is it working?"

She tugged her bottom lip between her lips, her eyes glued to mine. "*Maybe*. Maybe I like your dirty words better."

Shit, I could work with that.

I skimmed my knuckles down the side of her face and she leaned into my touch. That simple movement told me all I needed to know.

She might have wanted to throat punch me half the time, but what I was doing... it *was* working.

"So, what's on the agenda tonight?"

"We're going to a party."

"What kind of party?"

Truthfully, I had no idea.

"Dress nice."

Her lips turned up in a sly grin. "Last time you told me to 'dress nice', you told me off for doing it."

A woman like Blake was never going to look merely 'nice', she had two settings; *hot* and *smokin' fucking hot*.

"No white dress. My self-control can't take it," I growled.

She sat down her cup and ran her hands up my chest, over my shoulders and around my neck, her fingers playing with the hair at the back of my head.

"Are you going to dress up for me?" she purred.

"I might."

"I'll let you in on a little secret, sparky." She leant in to speak into my ear. "I've got a weakness for a man in a suit."

Tingles ran up and down my spine. Fuck me, a suit it was then.

"That can be arranged." My voice was hoarse.

"What are *your* weaknesses, sparky?"

When I looked into those eyes of hers, one blue, one green, there was only one answer in the world.

"*You.*"

20

Blake

Dear Ida,

I'm falling for him and I don't know how to make it stop. I haven't told him everything and I'm scared. It's New Year's Eve and I have a feeling that tonight is going to be 'the night'. Help, what do I do? Should I stay? Should I run?

-Completely Screwed, Down Under.

I sat my phone down on the bed next to me and held my head in my hands.

I was already dressed, face made up, hair tamed into soft curls. I was ready to go. Ky was waiting for me, but all of a sudden, I couldn't get enough air into my lungs.

I was a terrible person. I was meant to be somewhere else right now, but instead I was here, and there was nothing I could do to change that, not that I would have if I was given a choice anyway, which only made me *more* of a terrible person. I was hurting people.

"What the fuck am I doing?" I whispered to myself.

I liked Ky – I *more* than liked him – and that was the problem. I had no right. I wasn't in a position to share my life with anyone, yet here I was, doing it anyway.

When I looked out the window earlier today and saw him walking that damn goat around on its lead, that was all it took for me to fall even deeper for him.

I'd only had him for three days, I couldn't even fathom how strongly I could feel about him after three weeks, three months, three years... hell, even three decades.

My phone vibrated with an incoming email, and I grabbed it off the bed.

Dear Completely Screwed,

You're from the future. Trippy. Are there flying cars there?

If you're going to run, can I suggest comfortable shoes, I tried to run in heels once – didn't go well. Oh, and pace yourself, I hear it's a long way from Australia.

S x

I groaned. Fucking Soraya. I should have known that she was much better at sarcastic comments then she was actual advice.

She knew damn well I wasn't going to run. She was mocking me.

I tossed the phone and stood tall. She might have been about as helpful as a hole in the head, but she made some good points. The first being, I didn't have any comfortable shoes, and the second, I *was* in Australia, in the middle of nowhere. I didn't really have a choice in the matter. I was staying whether it was the right thing to do or not.

I glanced in the mirror and vowed that I'd talk to Ky – tell him the truth before anything more happened between us – I owed him that.

"Blondie?" There was a knock on the door before it opened, and Ky walked in without waiting for an answer.

The breath got stolen right out of my lungs.

Holy shit.

I didn't know why he ever wore anything else. Ky Bateman filled out a suit like a king. His broad shoulders were covered in a white button-down shirt and black jacket, a black tie tied neatly around his neck.

He was the sexiest man I'd ever laid eyes on, and he was looking at me like the sun shone out of me.

This can't be wrong.

I decided right then and there to just enjoy myself. I'd talk to Ky later, but first, I was going to let this gorgeous man take me out on a date.

"Fucking hell, blondie. You could have warned me that the black dress was hotter than the white one." His expression was pained, as though he was fighting to keep his composure.

Fuck composure. I didn't want control, I wanted him to lose his mind.

"This old thing?" I twirled slowly, showing off.

He groaned. "You have a phenomenal ass."

I huffed out a laugh. "That might be the highest compliment it's ever received."

He prowled towards me, pulling me roughly against him. "I doubt that, most guys are probably too chicken shit to say how they really feel to your face."

I gripped his biceps. "And you're so big and brave?"

"Sure am." His murmur was at my ear, sending shivers through my body.

The things this man could do to me were crazy. I was on a knife's edge whenever he was near.

"We're going to be late."

"We'd better go then," I whispered.

He glanced at the bed, then back to me and then back to the bed. It was comical really. I knew how he felt. It would be so easy to say fuck it, lock ourselves away in this room and spend the night between the sheets, but that would have meant telling Ky everything right now, and I was going to need some serious liquid courage before I went down that path.

"Later, sparky," I promised. "First you owe me a date."

He smiled, a full, megawatt grin. He was too much, too handsome – too captivating.

"That I do."

He stepped away and I took what felt like my first full breath since he walked through the door.

We rode with Aubrey and Chance down to the beach where a huge marquee was set up on the grass right near the sand.

It was a stunning setting. Pretty Beach sure did a good job of living up to its name.

Chance swung open his door. "C'mon, princess, time to get inside you."

"What did you say?" Aubrey called after him.

"I said, time to go inside," he replied, the picture of innocence.

I bit back my laugh. He was such a little shit.

Ky smirked at me and climbed out. He held my hand as we approached the marquee, right on sunset.

I tugged on his arm as he went to follow Chance and Aubrey in. "Can we just appreciate the view for a minute?"

He nodded.

We stood, hand in hand, watching as the sun slowly disappeared from sight.

I sighed. I was going to miss this place when I had to leave – because reality was, the time would come. I couldn't stay in this little bubble of fantasy life forever, no matter how much I might have wanted to.

"Ready, blondie?"

"As I'll ever be."

He chuckled.

We were handed a glass of champagne each as we entered the huge tent, before being stopped for a photo.

"Type your email here and I'll send you the picture," the young woman photographer told me.

I tapped in my email address and handed her back the tablet.

Ky took my hand again and led me across the room to where Chance and Aubrey were talking to a group of people.

Introductions were made, conversations were had, cigars were smoked, and far too many drinks were consumed as the hours slipped by effortlessly.

I was surprised how at home I felt here, surrounded by strangers, with Ky – who was basically a stranger too – at my side. It was too easy to imagine the life I could have here. It felt natural, *easy*, whilst also feeling wild and free.

"It's almost midnight, blondie," Ky whispered in my ear.

I turned my body into his, a little unsteady on my heels, but confident that he'd never let me fall. "Is that so, sparky?"

He nodded, leading me out onto the dance floor. "Dance with me."

We swayed slowly side to side, well out of time to the upbeat song, but not giving a shit. It was just me and him again.

He gripped my chin as the countdown to the new year began, and as everyone around us chanted, "Happy new year!", he kissed me, his skilled mouth moving with mine in a way that it never had before.

This wasn't just a kiss, it was *everything*.

Ky Bateman tasted of whiskey, tobacco and reckless decisions. And nothing had ever tasted so good.

A drunk guy pounded on his chest like he

thought he was Tarzan and then tripped, stumbling into my side.

I turned to glare at him, but before I could school my expression, Ky had shoved him roughly away.

"Watch where the fuck you're going." He glared at the guy, his expression murderous.

Mr. 'I drunk my body weight in beers' stumbled back.

"Hey." I pulled on Ky's arm when he went to take a threatening step towards him. "Chill. I'm fine, I don't need you to protect me. I'm not some weak woman."

I'd never seen him so aggressive.

His eyes flew from the man, back to my face and softened. "I'd *never* protect you because I thought you were weak, Blake." He stepped close to cup my face between his hands, our drunk friend forgotten. "I'll protect you because you're *important*. Maybe the most important out of anyone, ever."

I couldn't look away, no matter how much his confession scared me. "Don't say things like that," I whispered.

"You want me to lie to you, blondie?"

Yes.

No.

Maybe.

I shook my head. I was doing enough lying for the both of us.

"Are you ready to get out of here?" He nuzzled my neck.

I'd be ready for just about anything as long as he was at my side.

I nodded.

"Good. I've got a surprise for you back at the house."

He met my stare, the gold in his eyes burning brighter than I'd ever seen it. He didn't wait for a reply – he didn't even bother saying goodbye to Chance and Aubrey. He just led me out, into a waiting cab.

The short trip back was made in silence, one filled with sexual tension, stolen glances and soft touches.

I couldn't deny how badly my body wanted his – I wasn't even in control of it anymore – he held that power in his hands.

He led me out of the cab, but rather than going towards the house – and the bed – we went around back, heading for the barn.

"Are we visiting the pigs?"

He smirked at me over his shoulder but didn't say a word.

He slid open the big door and I gasped.

There were fairy lights strung up around the place and some of the hay bales had been arranged in a cosy little semi-circle, with blankets laid down on top. In the very middle was the goat.

"Oh, for fuck's sake," Ky muttered.

Pixy bleated.

I covered my mouth as he rushed inside, trying to shoo the goat off his makeshift bed.

"Get out of here, ya bugger."

Ky got him out the door and turned to me sheepishly. "Not exactly how I imagined that going."

I flung my arms around his neck and brought my mouth to his, kissing him fervently.

"It's perfect."

"Yeah?"

"Yeah, *McKay – still not a name*, it's the sweetest thing anyone has ever done for me."

He chuckled. "It's going to be like that is it? I give you romance, and you take the piss out of me?"

I nodded.

I shrieked as he scooped me up into his arms and carried me across the barn to the blankets.

Our eyes locked and I couldn't look away. He had the most expressive eyes... right now they were filled with lust, want, desire; I think I might have even seen a flash of love.

He lowered us to the blanket until he was sitting, with me straddling him. My dress was pushed up around my waist and I could already feel his hard dick pressing against my core.

He was ready, I was ready... there was only one thing holding me back.

"Ky, I... I need to tell you something about why I left America."

He placed soft kisses to my neck and my head fell back.

"Tell me later."

His mouth continued along my collar bone and down to the swell of my breasts.

"I need to tell you *now*," I breathed.

He brought his face back up level with mine and pressed a finger to my lips to silence me. "I don't want to think about anything but you and me tonight, can we just have the night? I'm not going anywhere, Blake, you can tell me anything you want in the morning."

I nodded slowly. "Okay."

I knew it was wrong, but I wanted the same thing he did – one night that was just for the two of us before reality came knocking.

I could give him that.

His mouth found my skin again and I moaned.

I'll tell him in the morning.

21

Ky

ABSOLUTE FUCKING PERFECTION.

That's what she was. I'd never seen something so beautiful in my whole damn life.

Her long, golden hair fell in waves over her shoulders and down her back as I kissed every bare inch of skin I could get to.

Her soft, breathy moans only egged me on further until I couldn't take it anymore. I needed to be inside her so badly I could barely think straight.

That little black dress might have been sexy as fuck, but its time was up – I was dying to see what was underneath.

"Zip," she murmured as I slid the straps down her arms.

I lowered the zip at her back painfully slow, revelling in the way her skin broke out in goosebumps from my touch. It was nothing she didn't do to me in return. She drove me crazy, from zero to the point of insanity with just a single touch.

I lowered her dress to pool around her waist and took my time raking my eyes over her see-through black lacy bra.

Perky tits looked back at me, her nipples peaking under my gaze.

"You've got no idea how many times I've thought about you like this."

Her hands threaded into my hair and tugged. "I think I might."

"I'm so hard for you, blondie."

She pulled on my hair, forcing my face up to hers. "Have me then."

I didn't need to be told twice. I wasn't sure I needed to be told at all. I was going to have her – this dance between us had built past the point of no return.

Her eyes burnt bright with desire as I pulled down the cups of her bra and dipped my mouth to suck on one of her hard nipples.

Her head fell back as I lapped, licked and sucked before moving onto the other.

"*Ky*," she breathed, her hands sliding over my shoulders and shedding me of my jacket before making quick work of the buttons on my shirt.

She dragged her nails over my abs, and I shuddered.

I couldn't hold on any longer. I gently laid her down on the blanket and reached for her dress, sliding it from her body.

"*Fuck*, blondie."

I wished I could take a picture – not that I was ever going to forget the sight in front of me, it was going to be burned into my memory for the rest of my life. No other woman could ever come close to this, I knew that. If this thing didn't work out between us, she was about to singlehandedly ruin me for any women to come after her.

I tossed my shirt and tie to the side and tugged at the button on my pants, desperate to rid myself of them.

Her eyes never left my body as I stripped myself of everything I was wearing, until I was completely naked and kneeling before her.

She swallowed hard as her gaze fell on my rock-hard length.

"See what you do to me?" I growled as I stroked myself from base to tip.

She licked her lips. Fucking hell, I was going to have to have those lips wrapped around my cock before the night was done.

I snagged a condom from my pants pocket and tore the foil packet open, the sound the only noise in the room. She watched me eagerly – *hungrily* as I rolled it on.

"Please, Ky..." she begged, and I snapped, the last of my restraint evacuating the building.

I tugged the scrap of lace from between her legs

and threw it across the barn. Her legs parted for me, and I slid between them like the space was made specifically for me.

I was frenzied, wild, totally and completely out of control.

I gripped her ankle, bringing it to my shoulder and kissed roughly down the length of her calf, up her thigh to the spot I'd been dreaming about non-stop since the first time her eyes met mine.

I ran my thumb from one end of her opening to the other and she gasped.

"Do you want me to touch you, Blake?"

"Yes," she panted. "Jesus, *please*, Ky..."

I smirked. It probably made me an asshole, but I liked hearing her beg. I wanted my name on her lips as I made her come undone.

I slid my thumb into her heat and sucked on her clit simultaneously.

Her hips bucked and her fingers tugged my hair to the point of pain. Fuck, I'd never been this turned on in my life.

"I've been dying to know how sweet you'd taste," I murmured before plunging my tongue into the space my thumb had just vacated.

She writhed beneath me, breathless as I teased her, bringing her to the brink and then easing off.

"I want all of you." She moaned, her hands dragging me upwards.

I gave in, giving her what she wanted, because it was all I wanted too – to be buried deep inside her perfect pussy until I couldn't remember my own fucking name.

I crawled up her body and claimed her mouth. She moaned as she tasted herself on my lips, her tongue plunging into my mouth.

I pulled back and took a minute to really look at her, the flush of her cheeks, the wild look in her eyes, the way her sexy lips were parted.

"I need you, Ky."

"So impatient, blondie."

"Fuck off," she bit back.

Her legs wrapped around my waist, lining me up with her centre, and I pushed inside her, hissing as I felt her grip every inch of me for the very first time.

She let out a load moan as she adjusted to my size.

I eased in slowly, my movements far more restrained than I thought I was capable of, before pushing in hard, right to the hilt.

I felt my eyes roll back in my head as her slick heat squeezed me.

Blake moaned loudly as I began thrusting into her, over and over again, taking every bit of pleasure from her body and giving her the same in return.

Her nails sunk into my back, deep enough to leave a mark, and I growled, loving the idea of her scoring my skin.

We found a rhythm instantly, both of us shaking with pent-up tension.

I stared into her eyes as I picked up the pace,

sliding deeper into her until we both came undone, one after the other.

My whole body shook with my release as Blake trembled beneath me, her body twitching with my every movement.

I lowered my face to hers and kissed her sweetly when she stilled, my cock still buried deep inside her.

There was only silence between us for a few long beats as we both fought to catch our breath.

"Good surprise?" I murmured.

"Best surprise of my life."

I chuckled. "Mine too, blondie."

Her eyes searched mine and I saw vulnerability in them. I knew she had something she wanted to say, but it would still be there in the morning. I wasn't risking tonight. Tonight was ours, no interruptions.

No past bullshit, no goat, no cockblocking three-year-old – just me and the woman I had fallen in love with.

"I'm really glad you lost that bet."

She laughed and I felt myself starting to harden again inside her, the movement of her body getting me going.

"If you're not ready to go another round, you might want to stay still," I warned her.

"And what if I am ready?" she purred, her tone seductive.

God damn woman of my dreams.

"Blake, I think I'm –"

Her eyes widened and she lifted her head to crash her lips to mine.

I kissed her back, letting her take what she wanted from me. I knew what she was doing, she was scared about what I was going to tell her – she was using her body to try and distract me.

"Careful, blondie, I might start to think you're trying to shut me up," I murmured when she finally released me.

Colour rushed to her cheeks.

"No."

"No?"

She shook her head. "I just think I might know what you're going to say."

"You do, huh?"

The playful spark in her eyes dulled and she tugged her bottom lip into her mouth. "I'm certain."

I swept a few rogue strands of hair from her face. "Any reason in particular you want me to turn mute?"

She ran her finger across my jaw. "If you're going to tell me something important, I want it to be when the sun's up, we're sober, and your dick isn't still inside me. Okay?"

I chuckled. "Fair enough."

I could wait. Another few hours which was only going to cement my feelings further, not change them. They might have been famous last words, but I doubted there was anything in the world that could at this point.

"What if I die in my sleep?"

She rolled her eyes. "Dramatic much?"

"I might only have a day left, blondie." I grinned.

"You got somewhere better to be?"

I shook my head and kissed the corner of her mouth. "*No*. Even if I only had twenty-four hours, I'd still want to spend every last one of them with you."

22

Blake

I WOKE, completely sated, to the feeling of warm sun on my back and the sound of someone pounding on the door of the barn.

"Ky, mate, open up!"

I yawned, stretched my arms above my head and grinned as I thought about why my whole body felt like it was made of jelly.

I'd never had so many orgasms in my life.

"Ky! If you don't open up, I'm coming in!"

I shook Ky's shoulder. "Sparky, Chance is calling out for you."

He grunted but didn't move. We'd been up most of the night. I was exhausted, but I'd never been so happy to give up a good night's sleep.

"Ky." I giggled as his hand pressed against my

stomach and dragged my ass against his crotch. Which by some miracle, was sporting a raging hard-on.

"You're insatiable," I teased.

"Only when it comes to you," he rasped against my ear.

My heart thumped in my chest from the sound of his voice alone. I was terrified of my growing feelings, but I couldn't wait to hear him tell me how he felt about me in *that* voice.

I just had to hope that after I told him what I'd kept from him, he'd still feel the same way he did last night. That he'd still tell me he was falling in love with me. He didn't say the words last night, but I saw it in his eyes anyway – felt it in his touch.

I knew how he felt, because I felt the same way.

"Ky! For fuck's sake!" Chance pounded his fist against the door again.

"What?!" Ky yelled as his hand continued on its descent downwards. "I'm fucking busy!"

"I need to talk to you."

I gasped as Ky's deft fingers made contact with my clit.

"Can't it wait?" he called back.

"No, mate, it *can't*."

We both stilled, each of us hearing something in Chance's voice that told us this was serious.

"Is something wrong? The kids? Aubrey?" Ky asked as he leapt out of our makeshift bed and grabbed his pants.

"They're fine, mate, just... you and Blake need to come out here."

My eyes widened when I heard my name.

Me? I couldn't imagine a single scenario that would require my presence.

Ky's eyes moved from the door to me as he did up the button on his pants and snagged my underwear off the floor. He tossed them to me, quickly followed by his white button-up shirt.

I dressed as quickly as I could and followed after Ky towards the door. I wasn't exactly dressed appropriately for company, but the sense of urgency I felt outweighed my need for modesty.

Ky slid open the door and Chance's eyes bounced between Ky and me.

"What is it?" Ky demanded, running his hand through his hair. "Where's the fire?"

Chance's expression turned into one of sympathy as he looked at his cousin and then his attention shifted to me.

His next words confused the hell out of me. "Blake, there's someone here to see you."

"*Me?*" I balked.

He nodded.

"*Who?*"

No one except my sister knew where I was, and there was no way she was here. I doubted she would have bothered coming over if I lived a few minutes away, let alone making a three-hour trip to get down here.

Chance glanced at Ky again, still not answering me.

"*Chance*, who is here to see me?" I stepped forward and *that* was the moment my entire world collapsed. *Again*.

I caught sight of movement around the side of the house, Aubrey was walking towards us and next to her was the very last person I ever expected to see.

"Julian," Chance said his name quietly. "Julian is here to see you."

Sweet Jesus.

This couldn't be happening. I blinked a solid three times, just in case I was seeing things. Maybe I was dreaming. That had to be the explanation for this – my brain was playing tricks on me.

There was no way that *Julian* could be *here*, except that he was. *Right here*. In Australia. In Pretty Beach, walking towards me, while I stood dead still, with *Ky* at my side.

Fuck. Fuckity, fuck, fuck, fuck.

His blue eyes swept over me, his face a mask of hurt and embarrassment as he took in my half-dressed body, clothed only in another man's shirt.

I felt Ky's hand close around my arm, but I couldn't look at him. I couldn't speak, I couldn't even move as Julian got closer and closer.

I swear I saw my life flash before my eyes. Maybe I was dying. I probably wouldn't have complained if the ground had swallowed me whole right now.

"*Blondie*." Ky shook my arm and snapped me from my trance.

It all happened in slow motion. Julian stopped in front of us, and I turned to look at the man who I knew I was about to hurt. "I'm so sorry," I whispered to Ky.

"Hello, Blake," Julian said. I turned back to the blond-haired man before me.

I could feel Ky's eyes on my face, watching me, his face no doubt a mask of confusion as he tried to figure out what was going on.

I felt tears spring to my eyes. I'd really done it this time. My biggest fuck-up to date.

"What are you doing here, Julian?" I whispered.

"I came here for you, angel." His American accent was harsh compared to Ky's Australian one. It had never bothered me before, but it sounded wrong to my ears now.

"Sorry, but what am I missing here?" Ky barked, his hand wrapping further around my arm. "I don't mean to be rude, but who the hell are *you*?"

Julian looked at me for a few beats, his handsome face set in a frown as he glanced between Ky and I. "I'm Julian Knoll." He extended his hand to Ky – he was always so polite; it broke my heart.

"Ky," Ky replied gruffly. "And you know Blake from..." he prompted.

"I ah... I'm her fiancé."

The three words hung in the air between the five of us, crashing down on every good memory I'd created here with these people, killing the feelings I'd stupidly let blossom and breaking Ky's heart in one foul swoop.

"*What*?" he breathed. "You're her *what*?"

Julian shifted his weight from foot to foot awkwardly, unspeaking as I struggled to breathe. God, he was good to the core – even now, when I'd wronged him the way I had, he still didn't want to make things worse for me.

"Blake, what the fuck?" Ky demanded, tugging on my arm so I was facing him. "Is it true?"

I couldn't meet his gaze. I already knew what I'd find in those dark eyes – hurt, betrayal, sadness, anger, disbelief.

"I tried to tell you," I said, my words coming out quiet, barely a whisper. "I'm so sorry... I wanted to... last night, I should have –"

He stepped back as I tried to reach for him, shrugging off my touch, and I finally lifted my eyes to his.

I wasn't prepared for what I saw on his face. Tears overflowed from my eyes as I looked at what I'd done – as I looked at the beautiful man I'd just singlehandedly destroyed.

Every fibre of my being was telling me that he was the one... that I'd made a huge mistake by not being honest from the start... that this decision was going to affect me for the rest of my life.

"*Ky*." I begged, "Please, just listen to me."

His chest rose and fell, his breaths deep, heaving. "I can't believe this. You're engaged?" His eyes darted to my left hand, no doubt searching for a ring.

"Ky, I can explain."

He laughed bitterly, not an ounce of humour in it.

"Nothing good *ever* follows that sentence." He turned and stalked back into the barn, hurt radiating from him.

"*Blake*," Julian whispered, but I couldn't meet his eyes.

"We'll just give you a minute," Aubrey said quietly.

I couldn't look at her either. I'd grown to really like her these past few days, I considered us friends, but I'd kept this from her too – I was an awful person.

Chance and Aubrey left and then it was just me, standing before the man I'd promised to marry, with another man's scent on my skin.

Every part of me wanted to go after Ky, but I couldn't just walk away from Julian without thought again either – I did it once and if recent events were anything to go by, it hadn't worked out well for anyone involved.

"Julian, I... I don't know what to say. Why... *why* are you here?"

"Why do you think I'm here, angel? I needed to see you. You took off without a real explanation." His voice cracked. "I thought if I gave you some space... I assumed you'd be back, but when I called your sister and she told me where you were, I knew you weren't going to make the wedding. You weren't ever coming back, were you?"

I cringed as he said the word 'wedding'. I was meant to have married this man on New Year's Eve – probably right now in US time, but in classic Blake fashion, I messed it up.

"I'm sorry." My voice cracked. "I... I told you I couldn't do it. I didn't expect you to wait. I never thought you'd come after me."

His eyes softened and I hated myself even more for the kindness he was showing me. He was a smart man, an incredibly smart man, but even if he were an idiot, it wouldn't have taken much to connect the dots between Ky and I – we were each wearing half of an outfit for crying out loud.

Julian stood before me, knowing that I'd been with someone else, and he still didn't raise his voice. He didn't scream or throw his fists.

"Blake, I know you've had a hard few months, but we're good together. You love me."

He was right, I did love him. He was a good man, but it wasn't enough.

I knew that when I left the US. I didn't know what I was craving when I walked out on Julian, but I knew now. It was what I had with Ky.

"Come home with me, angel, we can try again, pretend this never happened."

I could have done that. It would have been easy – nothing had ever been easier than my relationship with Julian, but I wanted more. I wanted fire, I wanted someone to push back... I wanted chemistry.

More tears slipped from my eyes and ran down my cheeks. "I... I have to go after him."

He swallowed hard, his eyes glassing over. He nodded.

Fuck, I was ripping people apart left, right and centre today.

"I'm so sorry, Julian, just... just give me a minute, okay? We can talk. I just need a few minutes first."

He nodded again, his gaze falling to the ground and his hands sliding into his pockets.

I turned, took a deep breath and slipped back into the barn, pulling the door shut behind me.

23

Ky

I HEARD HER COME IN, but I didn't turn, instead throwing another hay bale from one side of the barn to the other as forcefully as my arms would allow.

"Ky."

I still didn't turn. Another bale went sailing into the tin wall.

Lift.

Throw.

Crash.

Repeat.

"Ky," she repeated after I threw another five bales, her voice a sob. "*Please.*"

I dropped the bale I was holding, my shoulders slumping forward.

I turned, agonisingly slow, desperately trying to

delay seeing her, because I knew once I did, it was all going to fall apart.

I didn't know how to do this – lose her. I'd only just found her, and she was already being ripped away from me.

She was going to give me some bullshit excuse and then she was going to leave me for her Ken doll fiancé. I could see it coming like a flashing neon sign on a dark street.

Just rip it off like a band aid.

You have to, man.

I lifted my eyes and there she was, wearing my shirt, her makeup smudged under her eyes and her hair a mess from our night together, but she was still so mind-numbingly beautiful, it hurt my heart – fucking broke it.

"Ky, I'm *so* sorry." She swiped at the tears streaming down her face, and it took every last ounce of sheer will I had in me to stop myself from crossing the distance between us and pulling her into my arms.

I might have hated everything she stood for in this moment, but the woman I'd just spent three days with – I *loved* her. I hurt when she hurt. It pained me to look at her in this state, but I had to be selfish now. I had to protect myself. Blake had the ability to crush me, and I couldn't let that happen.

"I should have told you. I should have been honest, but I can explain, please just let me explain." She was begging me again, but this wasn't like last night – I hated hearing her plead for this.

"What's left to explain?" I didn't even recognise my own voice; it was hollow, empty – void of any and all emotion.

"Everything," she breathed, taking a step towards me. "You deserve to know the truth."

"Now?" I rasped. "*Now* you think I'm owed the truth?"

The silence stretched between us.

"It's all I can give you."

I huffed out a humorous laugh. "You should have told me, Blake!" My voice thundered around the barn, echoing off the walls. "You should have told me that another man was going to make you his wife!"

"He's... we're... I..." she stuttered. "I don't know what to say."

"Did you agree to marry him?" I demanded, my voice going from full of rage, to airily calm in the space of a few short seconds.

"I... Ky, I –"

"*Did you*?" I cut her off.

"I did."

"He got down on one knee? Gave you a ring?" I barked the question.

She nodded, and I swear I felt my chest crack wide open. Only an hour ago, I could have seen myself putting a ring on her finger one day in the future, but I knew better now – someone else already had.

"When's the big day?" I asked bitterly.

"It was meant to be New Year's Eve," she whispered.

That confused me, but I didn't let it show. Now wasn't the time for hesitation. It wasn't the time for questions either – not when I wouldn't trust the answers.

"Well, he's here now, maybe you can swing by a courthouse on the way back to the airport."

Bitter. I was so fucking bitter.

"Ky, I never meant to hurt you – *Jesus*, I never even meant to *meet* you. You don't understand what the past few months have been like for me, my –"

"I talked to you about honesty," I cut her off, "I told you how important it was – you heard what it did to Chance and Aubrey, how it tore them apart." I shook my head, disgusted with her. "I *told* you."

"I know." Her lip quivered as she replied. "I don't know how to explain how sorry I am."

"What are you going to do now, Blake? Huh? You going to run off back home to your husband?"

"He's not – *I'm* not... I don't know." She raked her hands over her face. "No matter what I do, I'm hurting someone."

"What did you think was going to happen?"

My chest heaved; my breathing ragged as we stood in a silent stand off – each of us staring at the other.

I couldn't figure her out. I knew she was an enigma – a puzzle I couldn't quite solve, but I never, not in a million years would have expected this from her.

"I left him before I came here."

"Does *he* know that?" I jabbed my finger towards

the door that her fiancé stood on the other side of. "Because he talked in present tense, Blake, not past."

"It's complicated." Her voice, her eyes, they were begging me to understand, but I couldn't.

She was *mine*; at least that's what I'd thought. Turned out I was wrong. She wasn't mine at all. She was his.

"It doesn't seem all that complicated to me, Blake, in fact, it seems pretty fucking simple. He asked you to marry him. You said yes. It's as clear cut as crystal."

She sobbed as I pushed back my shoulders, straightening my spine, and my resolve.

"I think you should go."

She stepped forward again, her hand reaching for me as though there wasn't feet of thin air between us. "Please don't do this."

"Go," I repeated. "I never should have brought you here in the first place."

Those eyes, the ones that already plagued my dreams, went dull. She swiped at the moisture on her cheeks. "Okay. If that's what you want. I'll go."

No.

Stay.

Don't go.

I love you.

I nodded once – a short, sharp bob of my head. This was the way it had to be.

She swallowed deeply. "Alright."

I hated myself in that moment.

Hated the pride that kept me from begging her to stay.

Hated the feelings I'd caught.

Hated that I'd finally met someone I was willing to give my heart to, only to have it rejected.

This was why I didn't do love.

Our eyes stayed locked for a long, long time before she turned and walked back towards the barn door.

I watched her every move like a hawk. This was the last time I was ever going to see her – I could feel it deep inside me.

Her small hand came to rest on the door, and she paused, her back to me. "I truly am sorry, Ky. Everything between us, it was all real. I just wanted you to know that."

My fists balled at my sides, but I didn't get a chance to respond before she slipped out the door and out of my life.

"Motherfucker!" I roared, grabbing the closest hay bale and sending it flying at the door she just disappeared from before dropping to my knees – the pain too much to bear standing.

I felt like I'd just watched my whole future walk away from me.

A sob wracked through my body, tearing up my chest and out my mouth.

Fuck, nothing had ever hurt the way this did.

I stayed on the floor of that barn for what felt like hours thinking of nothing but her – the way she smiled, the sparkle in her eyes, her breathy moans as I made her come, the way she said my name...

Fuck.

I didn't hear the door open, but I felt it when a set of arms wrapped around my shoulders. It was only then that I realised I was sobbing. My whole entire body was shaking – I felt dizzy, lightheaded.

"Ky, mate, you need to breathe."

Chance.

"In and out. Nice, deep breaths, mate, I've got you."

He was kneeling on the ground next to me.

I did what he said, focused on getting oxygen into my body and out again instead of thinking about the crushing pain in my chest.

"That's it, just like that."

I took another dozen or so calming breaths until my chest stopped heaving and my limbs stopped shaking.

"You alright?"

I rolled back, off my knees and onto my ass and rubbed my hands over my face.

Chance studied me carefully, searching my expression. Probably trying to decide if I was about to lose my shit again or not.

"Is she gone?"

He looked at me in sympathy. "They left about a half hour ago."

They. Her and him. *Together.*

"He's taking her home, Ky, back to the US."

I nodded numbly.

That was what I told her to do. *Leave. Go.* But now that she had, I wished I'd never said the words.

As stupid as it made me, I still loved her. I still

wanted her. But the reality was I couldn't have her. I got a little part of her and that was going to have to be enough to last me a lifetime.

"Did she say anything?"

"She spoke to Aubrey, but she was pretty upset, mate, I don't think there was much sense to it."

"She's gone?" I questioned again, hoping I'd somehow heard wrong, yet at the same time, praying she really had left. I wasn't sure I was strong enough to see her again without being able to keep her.

"Afraid so." Chance nodded.

"I... I, fuck... I..." I stammered, unable to find the words.

I'd never been much of a talker when it came to feelings, and apparently that hadn't changed.

"I know." He nodded, hearing what I was trying to say without me even having to say it.

He sat down next to me, not saying a word, but not leaving me alone either, and I was grateful for that.

"Sorry about the mess," I muttered after a long silence.

"Who gives a shit?" was his reply.

More silence.

"She was the one," I admitted out loud.

"You sure?"

I already knew it when we got off that plane – she was the one for me. Fifteen hours was all it took to know that she'd have my heart forever.

"Yup."

"What makes you think that?"

"Because when I looked at her, I saw the rest of my life, and now that's gone, because *she's* gone."

I could see him nodding out of the corner of my eye. He knew. He had Aubrey. "Well *fuck*. This is one time I would have been happy to be wrong, mate."

I nodded in agreement.

"You never know, mate, maybe one day –"

"Don't give me that *one day* bullshit. I know it worked out for you and Aubrey, but it's not like that for everyone. You two are the exception, not the god damn rule. It's over. It's over before it even started."

I jumped to my feet and stormed towards the door, fuelled by anger.

"Ky!" Chance called after me, but I was done talking. All I could do now was act.

I needed air. I needed to get on my bike and ride.

I rushed through the house, collecting all my crap and throwing it into a bag.

I almost broke down again in the bedroom when I saw my white shirt carefully laid out on the bed – the one Blake had been wearing, but I didn't allow myself the release, instead I shoved it deep into the bag and slung it over my shoulder.

I was out of the house and on my bike before I could even think through where I might go.

I didn't care. I just needed to go. Somewhere, *anywhere*. Just not here. I couldn't be here.

I tore out of the driveway as Aubrey ran out of the house, calling my name.

24

Blake

I RAN out of tears somewhere across the Pacific Ocean.

Julian had offered me nothing but support, just passed me tissue after tissue as I mourned the loss of another man.

I couldn't imagine any woman in the world being worthy of this level of kindness, patience and understanding – I certainly wasn't. I didn't even deserve to breathe the same air as Julian Knoll. He was *the guy* – the one you dreamed about when you were a little girl.

He was the boy next door they painted the perfect picture of in movies and music videos. He was the ultimate book boyfriend come to life.

Handsome, smart, funny, kind and caring. He was

a true gentleman; he was sweet and considerate. He opened doors for me and spoiled me with gifts. He smiled when I walked into a room and he made me feel like I was the only woman on the planet that was worthy of those smiles.

He was perfect. But he wasn't Ky.

That had been my last thought before I'd drifted off.

My body had called a time out on me, forcing me to sleep, and when I woke again, my head was on Julian's shoulder as I sat upright in the crammed plane seats.

He'd been about to buy first-class tickets, but I'd thrown a fit at the check-in counter and refused to sit anywhere but economy. I didn't need the memories of me and Ky. It was actually a wonder they'd let a woman so deranged onto the plane after that outburst.

Julian, like the absolute sweetheart he was, had purchased the cheaper tickets without even asking for an explanation.

I lifted my head off his shoulder and glanced at the remaining flight time on the small screen in front of me.

We were only an hour from landing in LA. I was thousands of miles from Ky Bateman and his cocky smirk. It felt so final.

"Welcome back." Julian spoke softly.

"Hi," I whispered as I looked up at him.

"Are you feeling any better?"

I nodded, even though I was anything but better. I was a mess.

He gave me a sad smile and leaned in, pressing his lips to my forehead.

"I'm so sorry, Julian. You don't deserve this. I bet you wish you never met me."

His baby-blue eyes looked right into mine. "I'd *never* wish to not have met you, Blake. You're the best thing that ever happened to me."

"How?" I breathed. "I've done nothing but hurt you."

"Two years, angel. We've been together two years and you've made *one* mistake. Cut yourself some slack."

"*One* mistake? I've made *one hundred* mistakes."

He didn't argue, or agree, so I continued.

"I ran out on our wedding day, our honeymoon. All that money on the wedding... all your friends, they must hate me. I just walked out on *everything*."

There was more, so much more, but I didn't want to hurt him more than I already had by bringing up the fact that I'd slept with someone else such a short time after I ran out on him. He was already well aware.

"It's only money, I've got plenty more. And my friends don't hate you, Blake, but even if they did, it wouldn't stop me from loving you anyway."

"You still love me?" I felt tears prick my eyes again, but I blinked them back – I'd cried enough.

He cupped my face in his hands. "Of course, I love you. I want to marry you, angel. I want things to go back to the way they were before your dad passed away. I just want my Blake back."

His words punched a hole through my chest.

Before my dad passed away.

That was where it all started to unravel.

If I was being honest with myself, I'd never felt like Julian and I were quite right together – my heart didn't race when he got down on one knee and asked me to be his wife, but I *did* love him, and love was love, so I smiled and said yes – told myself that a different kind of love only existed in movies and books. He'd given me more than I could ever dream of wanting or needing and he cared for me. That was what being in love felt like – or so I'd thought.

We'd been doing okay, but when my father died, the wheels slowly started coming off.

I didn't go back home to Sydney when he passed. His instructions were clear; I was to stay in California. He didn't want a funeral. He didn't want a burial. He didn't want anything.

No fuss, no muss. That's what he always said.

He hated the idea of a bunch of people gathered around, crying while they talked about his life and listened to depressing music. It wasn't what he wanted. The idea of not giving him a proper send-off made me sad, but I was okay with it. I respected his wishes. I stayed in California. It wasn't until I thought about the song I was going to walk down the aisle to, that it all finally fell apart.

My dad had planned to walk me down the aisle. He was my dad – it was his right.

I knew when he got sick that his time was going be limited, but I never thought he'd go so quickly. I thought he would have years, not months, but just like that, he was gone.

One month after he passed, I walked out of Julian's penthouse apartment and never came back. He was away on business at the time, and like the coward I was – I left only a note with my ring.

I didn't answer his calls, or his texts, not even his emails.

I ran, I tried to grieve. I justified my behaviour with shitty excuses. I *failed*.

I hid out at hotels and bed and breakfasts, trying to decide what the hell I was going to do with my life.

My dad's death left a gaping hole in my chest – one that couldn't be filled, but it was more than that between Julian and I. Dad dying woke a part of me up. Something was missing in my life.

Julian and I weren't trying for a baby, but we weren't using protection either. He wanted to start a family as soon as possible, and I'd thought I wanted that too. What I wanted was for him to be happy, so I went along with it, but a baby wasn't what was missing. It was passion. It was being *in* love.

I loved him, but I wasn't *in love* with him.

It had all hit me standing in the lobby of some overpriced hotel. I needed to go.

California was beautiful, but it wasn't home.

I booked a ticket to Sydney for the very next day. I had no plans but to go home and figure it out once I got there. Dad's ashes were at my sister's and while I didn't feel like I needed to see them, I wanted to be close to where he was.

That was when I met Ky, and *everything* changed.

"Julian... we can't just pretend this didn't happen."

"Then we won't pretend it didn't happen. I just want to move forward. With *you*. We're good together, Blake, I don't want to let you go. I know everything is all fucked up and it would probably be easier to just walk away but walking away doesn't give me *you*."

I opened my mouth to protest but he silenced me by pressing a finger to my lips. "Just come home with me. All your stuff is still where you left it, we can take it day by day. See how it feels. If you want your own space, I'll get you a place. I'll get you anything you want, angel, just say we can try and save what we had."

I had less than zero faith that we could salvage a relationship between us, but I owed it to him to at least come home.

He was right. All my stuff was there. I had responsibilities. I was an adult. I needed to act like one.

I had to be sure that my father dying hadn't messed with my head badly enough that I was going to throw away something worth having. I owed it to him and to myself to do what I should have done in the first place and be sure.

I trusted Julian – he wouldn't pressure me, he wouldn't try and sway me to do something I didn't want to do. All he was asking for was a chance.

I could give him a chance after everything he'd given me.

"Okay," I whispered. "I'll come home."

"Thank you." He kissed my forehead again and I felt like the world's biggest fraud.

"I'm going to stretch my legs before we start to descend, are you okay here for a bit?"

I nodded, struck again with how heartless I was. He really was the perfect man.

I watched as he strolled up towards the front of the plane, turning more than a few female heads as he went.

What is wrong with me?

Julian was the perfect package. All wrapped up with a pretty bow – problem was, I wasn't sure that particular package was addressed to me.

I took a deep breath and did what I always did when I was in a moment of crisis – pulled out my phone and sent an email. I needed a good virtual slap across the face and there was no one better at it than Soraya.

Dear Ida,

Well, I did it. I finally fucked things up beyond repair. My worlds collided. Julian came to Australia. I'm on a plane with him right now, heading back to the US. I hurt Ky so badly I know he could never forgive me. There's something wrong with me. Why do I hurt the people I care most about?

-Complete Bitch, Miles High.

Her reply didn't come until we'd got off the plane, been through customs and were in the black SUV that Julian drove, heading back to his penthouse.

I glanced at him before checking her reply and he gave me a sweet smile that only made me feel even worse.

Dear Complete Bitch,

I'm sorry, can you repeat that? I think I just had a seizure or something because I thought you said you'd left hot airport guy to go back home with hot ex-fiancé guy?

Look, I get that they're both gorgeous, but this isn't musical chairs. Sit your ass down on a seat and stay there.

S x

She was right. The music had stopped, my ass was on a chair and I wasn't getting up again anytime soon.

25

PART TWO

Blake

Two months later

THE TWO NARROW pink lines that stared back at me were taunting me. Mocking me for my bad decisions.

Positive.

I was pregnant. I hadn't peed on a lot of these things in my life, and I'd never had one come back positive, but those double lines had shown up so quickly I was confident it was no mistake.

I glanced around the modest bathroom of my apartment and bit back tears.

Nothing was right. Nothing felt okay.

I'd messed up every good thing. Julian was still here, as patient as ever, but it was never going to last between us. I think deep down, we both knew that. Our relationship was never going to work, hell, I wasn't even convinced it could be called a relation-ship anymore.

I lived in my own apartment, he lived in his. We lived our own lives. We were more like friends in my eyes. We only saw each other a few times a week and he deserved more. He deserved someone who could give him back the same love he gave... someone who could offer him their whole heart.

I had to end things with him, I knew that, but it broke my heart.

I figured if I gave it time, I'd learn to love him – be *in* love with him – but if anything, time had only made what I already knew, more obvious.

We weren't right for each other.

He had expensive taste, he liked fine wine. He was a businessman, successful, driven and high flying. I was a kindergarten teacher who liked cheap whiskey and knock-off handbags. Our worlds were different. What we wanted was different.

My gaze returned to the test in my hand and I groaned. This only made things more complicated.

I couldn't even recall the last time I had a period.

I'd been stressed ever since my dad died, my emotions had been all over the show, that hadn't changed since I returned from Australia, and my periods had always been irregular, so I didn't think much of it. A baby had been the furthest thing from my mind until I'd caught sight of how many tampons I'd accumulated.

I was probably over four months pregnant by now – given that Julian and I hadn't slept together since I got back – and I'd had no idea the entire time. I'd drunk alcohol. I'd eaten dodgy deli ham and binged on soft cheese. I'd gone to a martial arts class. I may as well have saddled up a horse and ridden it to go and get myself some drugs, given how many rules I'd already broken.

A nagging, somewhat hopeful thought in the back of my brain reminded me that I *had* had sex in the past four months, but I silenced that thought as quickly as it came. Julian and I hadn't been using protection. We weren't trying to get pregnant, but we'd certainly done it enough times for this to be the outcome.

Ky had worn a condom. I might have been high on life and a little bit tipsy that night, but I could still hear the sound of the foil packet tearing when I closed my eyes in bed.

I'd slept with Ky while I carried Julian's baby.

If I wasn't already destined for hell for my past fuck ups, that little snippet of information would have sealed the deal.

I groaned as I dropped the test in the sink and sat down on the toilet, my head in my hands. What a screw up of epic proportions.

Here I was, in a sort-of relationship with a man I knew wasn't right for me – while I was pregnant with his child *and* to top it all off, I was pretty confident I was in love with a different man.

I let my mind wander to Ky, even though I knew it wouldn't do me any good. I was never going to see him again. He was in Australia and I was here. He hated me – there was no going back.

Part of me knew that whatever we'd had was over, but the other part of me – the naive, stupid part – still held onto hope, that maybe one day we'd cross paths again and things would be different.

I woke up every morning from dreams filled with him. I'd dream that I'd get on a plane, fly back to Sydney and find him. He'd pull me into those strong arms, hold me tight and tell me that he loved me – that he wished I'd never left.

The ones like that made me cry harder than the ones that relived him telling me to go – they seemed so real. I could smell his cologne, I could feel his broad shoulders under my palms, I could feel the butterflies in my stomach that only took flight when he was near.

I blinked back tears.

I needed to get a grip and get over myself. I needed to try and get over *him*.

My hand came to rest on my stomach. It wasn't just about me now. I had a baby to think about.

Julian was going to be so happy. He'd always talked about how much he wanted children, how excited he was about the idea of being a dad.

He'd be a great father. He'd give this baby every-thing it could possibly need.

He was going to be a hell of a lot better parent than I could ever be. My morals were questionable at best, my decision-making was reckless, and I followed my heart when I should have followed my head.

What kind of role model would I ever be?

"I'm sorry, peanut," I whispered to my still-flat stomach. "You're not even born yet and I'm already doing a shitty job."

A tear slipped down my cheek and landed on the tiles near my feet.

I knew what I needed to do – I had to go and tell Julian that we were expecting.

I also needed to think long and hard about what this meant for us as a couple.

I knew he wanted me to move back in with him, he was only going to be more insistent about the idea now that I was pregnant, but the idea terrified me. I wasn't sure what I wanted.

Actually, that was a lie, I wanted Ky... but I couldn't have him. Not now, not ever. So that left me in a state of limbo.

I knew Julian deserved better than to be anyone's second choice, but maybe I could do it. Maybe we could be a real family. Together. Happy.

I hated myself for considering it, but I had to. For my baby and for me.

Julian was incredible, and I *did* love him; it was something, but I wasn't convinced it would ever be enough.

I pulled into the underground parking garage of

his flashy building and parked in the spot he still kept reserved for me.

I still had a key to his penthouse and he always kept me up-to-date with the access codes for the elevators.

That alone caused a pang of guilt to rush through me. He was so sweet, so considerate. The perfect partner.

That was the thing about perfection, though – beauty was in the eye of the beholder – and while Julian was practically flawless, he wasn't my kind of perfect.

His biggest flaw was *me*. I was his weakness. He loved me beyond reason, and I felt horrible for it.

I rode the elevator up to the top floor and knocked rather than use my key. Julian had told me time and time again that I was always welcome, that I could come and go as I pleased from my former home, but I didn't feel like I deserved that, so whenever I came over, I knocked like the visitor I was.

I heard his footsteps approach the door – he was bound to already know it was me – not just anyone could access this floor.

The door swung open and Julian stood before me with only a white towel wrapped around his waist, his arms above his head as he dried his blonde hair with another towel.

"Hey, angel." He smiled.

I swallowed deeply. I might have had reservations about our future, but I wasn't blind, and Julian was in *incredible* shape.

He spent countless hours in the gym, and his efforts were definitely having the desired effect.

"Hey," I replied quietly. "Can I come in?"

"Of course, you know you don't need to ask."

He held the door open wider for me and then closed it behind me.

I walked into the room cautiously. He stopped next to me and kissed my cheek. "Make yourself at home, I'll just go throw on some clothes."

I nodded as I watched him leave the room, his defined back and broad shoulders glistening with water.

He was so handsome, but I didn't have that desire to jump him that I'd felt with Ky. One look into the cocky asshole's brown eyes and I was all hot and bothered.

Julian was gorgeous, but he didn't light my fire.

He came back into the room, his blue shirt making his eyes look vibrant and alive.

He came towards me again, this time softly kissing my lips. "This is a nice surprise, angel."

I wrung my hands together nervously. "Yeah... I ah... I wanted to come by and talk about something with you."

He gestured for me to sit on the couch and I gratefully took him up on the offer. My knees were shaking – I was so nervous.

He glanced at my hands which had taken over the shaking now that I was sitting.

"Blake, are you okay? You seem kind of nervous, is everything alright?"

I shook my head, the words getting caught in my throat. "I... I..."

He took my hands in his and squeezed them reassuringly.

"You can tell me anything, Blake, you know that."

Tears welled in my eyes. I knew I could. I could tell him anything in the world and he'd probably still love me anyway.

"Just take a deep breath," he encouraged.

I did what he told me and sucked a big breath of air into my lungs. "I'm pregnant," I whispered on the exhale.

I watched as the words hit his ears and he processed them.

"You're pregnant?"

I waited with bated breath for his response – for him to ask if it was his, for him to question me on the whole thing, but that never came.

His face broke out into a smile and he pulled me into his arms. "We're having a baby?"

I nodded against his shoulder.

He pulled back, holding me at arm's length so he could look at my face. "Are you sure?"

I nodded. "I peed on a stick."

He laughed. "How far along?"

I shrugged my shoulders. "I have no idea."

He grinned wider. "We need to see an obstetrician. An old buddy of mine from college is the best there is, I'll call him and get you in for a scan."

I couldn't believe that he was reacting like this – actually I could – he was reacting exactly how I always imagined he would when we eventually had children, but that was *before* everything that happened. Before I slept with another man.

Isn't he curious?

I knew that Ky and I had used protection, but Julian didn't.

Judging by the smile on his face, he didn't care either. He was over the moon, and I was... I was more confused than ever.

He laid his hand so gently on my stomach that it brought a fresh wave of tears to my eyes. "She's going to be so beautiful, angel, just like her mummy."

I sniffed back my emotions. "She?"

He nodded, his bright blue eyes scorching mine. "I bet she's a girl."

I'd always imagined myself with a daughter – but I didn't want to get too far ahead of myself. There was a long way to go between a positive pregnancy test and an actual baby. Anything could happen in the months that were to come.

"It's all going to be okay, Blake. You and me, we can figure this out," he promised me.

I nodded, not trusting myself to speak, but when I looked into his eyes – I almost believed him.

He leaned in and kissed me again, and this time I closed my eyes and kissed him back.

There was definitely a special place in hell reserved just for me, because when his lips brushed mine, I wished he was someone else.

26

Ky

I STARED at the screen of my phone and watched as it
rang over and over again.

I'd give my cousin one thing – he was persistent.

Every day for the past couple of months he called
me. Every. Single. Day.

I'd only answered him twice during that time,
once because he'd begun texting me non-stop telling
me that if I didn't let him know I wasn't dead in a
ditch somewhere, he was going to report me to police
as a missing person.

He'd tried to bring up Blake with me, but I shut
him down quickly. Hearing her name hurt me badly
enough – I wasn't sure I could handle actually
speaking about her.

The second time we spoke, the bastard played

me. He used his children to get me on the phone.

He knew I had a soft spot for those kids, and I was already feeling guilty for running out on them without saying goodbye, so I'd spent the better part of two hours on the phone with CJ and Bree. CJ showing me how much the pigs had grown and telling me I looked like crap – no doubt relaying his father's words, and little Bree made me say hi to every single one of her damn dolls as she hosted a tea party.

It was fine, until Bree asked me where Blake was. I barely made it off the call before I broke down.

That was a few weeks ago and I'd been dodging any and all calls since then.

I'd always been a tough guy – hard – not showing much in the way of emotions, but lately I was a mess.

I couldn't think straight. I could barely eat. I was off my game.

Drinking too much – trying to forget my sorrows at the bottom of a bottle. It wasn't going well for me. I doubted there was a brew in the world strong enough to rid Blake Vincent from my mind.

No, she was burned into my memory forever. Everything about her went around in circles on repeat in my mind. Her smile, her laugh, her sexy ass, her breathy moans.

I ran my hand through my hair, dropped my phone onto the counter and picked up the sledge-hammer I'd been using to demolish the kitchen.

This was about the only thing that could calm my mind right now – work. I'd thrown myself into this job, a renovation project. Unsurprisingly, breaking shit apart with my hands was great therapy.

I was no builder, but I wasn't afraid of a hard day's work. So here I was, day after day, pulling things apart before putting them back together, better than before.

I smashed through cabinets, benchtops and walls until my shoulders couldn't physically bear the weight of the hammer any longer... until my thoughts were void of her.

I dropped it to the floor and slid down one of the walls I hadn't made crumble to the ground.

I breathed hard, my chest rising and falling rapidly as I wiped the sweat off my brow.

I needed to cool off.

I stripped my shirt over my head and walked out of the house – not bothering to lock anything up. Here in this little community, locks weren't really a requirement.

The beach was only a short walk across the grass and down onto the sand.

It was a prime location.

Blake would love it here.

I cursed myself for thinking about her again. I don't even know why I bothered hating myself for it – she was constantly on my mind, trying to say otherwise would have been a blatant lie.

I thought about her more than was in any way healthy. I didn't know how to move on.

It had been months, but I still had no real closure.

Even though I knew she'd got on the plane with

her fiancé and gone back to California, I didn't know what she was doing now. *Did she get married? Did she leave him?*

I'd even got rip-roaring drunk one night and looked her up on social media, but it was fruitless. She had no Facebook account and her Instagram was private.

It had been like a punch to the gut seeing her smiling face on the tiny Instagram profile picture, and I'd vowed in that moment to never type her name into a search bar ever again. If just seeing a tiny picture of her face was enough to rip my wounds clean open, then I couldn't imagine what it would have done to me if I'd found a photo of her in a wedding dress, smiling with another man.

I was better off not knowing, I'd decided.

Only problem was that was a lie. I wasn't better off at all, because I didn't have her.

I reached the water's edge and dived in, the cool water working wonders on my sweaty, overheated skin.

I stood, flicking my too-long hair from my eyes. I'd let myself go. I needed a haircut and a shave, but I just couldn't find it in myself to give a shit.

Nothing had purpose now. I was a shell of my former self.

I knew I should pick up the phone and talk to Chance when he called. More than anyone else, he probably understood what it was like to lose the woman you loved, but his story was different. He got his happy ending. He and Aubrey had each other. His pain was long gone while mine was still so raw I sometimes struggled to breathe.

I dived under a few more times then turned to make my way back up the beach.

There was a woman sitting on the sand, her cropped black hair blowing in the gentle sea breeze. I recognised her from the house next door to the one I was working on – I'd seen her around a few times.

I made my way into the shallows and she got to her feet to greet me.

"Hey." She smiled brightly. "I'm Sarah – I'm staying there for the week." She pointed down the beach. "I thought I'd just come and introduce myself."

"Ky," I replied simply.

I didn't miss the way she let her eyes quickly sweep me over from head to toe.

She was a beautiful woman; tall, curvy, pretty face, but she held no appeal for me. She was the wrong kind of beautiful.

"Sounds like you've been pretty busy in there." She slung her thumb over her shoulder towards the house I was slowly pulling apart.

"Shit, sorry, I should probably keep the noise down."

She smiled. "It's all good. I'm an early riser."

I nodded.

She cleared her throat nervously. "Anyway, I was just going to let you know that a few of the neighbours are coming over for a drink later tonight, you're more than welcome to join us.

No.

Hell no.

Company was the absolute last thing I wanted.

"I'm not very good company right now."

She batted her lashes at me. "Well the offer is there if you change your mind, I'd really love to see you."

"I'll think about it."

She took a few steps backwards before giving me a flirty smile and spinning around, heading back in the direction of her place.

I blew out a deep breath, my heart racing.

Jesus, what the hell was wrong with me? A beautiful woman invited me over for a drink and I was on the verge of hyperventilating.

Losing Blake had really done a number on me.

I knew she'd screwed me, big time, but I couldn't just turn off my feelings. I was still madly in love with her. I wanted her so badly it actually made my chest ache, and as angry as I was at her for lying to me, I was livid with myself for letting her go – for not fighting for her when I still had the chance.

I should have told her how I felt. I should have asked her to choose me. I should have given myself a shot at keeping her, but instead I'd let my hurt and my pride get in the way.

I'd lost.

I realised I was still standing on the sand, dripping wet. I shook my hair out and headed back up to the house, needing to break something all over again.

27

Blake

I SAT QUIETLY in the front seat of Julian's black SUV, the black leather sticking to my skin. I was so nervous I was sweating.

I didn't know what to expect, but the polite receptionist on the phone had told me that all I needed to bring was myself and a full bladder.

The full bladder part wasn't exactly comfortable, but as long as I didn't pee myself, it would be okay.

Julian informed me that it was necessary so that they could get a better look at the baby on the ultrasound.

I didn't know how he knew that, and I was too scared to ask. He'd probably already read half a dozen baby books or been scouring the web for hours on end – that's the type of dedicated man he was.

It had only been a few days since I found out I was pregnant, and while I was still freaking out, Julian had already started looking at houses out of the city and considering which schools were the best options – things I hadn't even considered.

He'd begged me to move in with him again, and while I hadn't said yes, I'd stayed over the last two nights.

I still didn't know what I wanted to do... About *him*, about *us*.

I knew I should just let go and enjoy what we had. Julian could make me happy; he already did make me happy. There was nothing wrong with a comfortable, peaceful life. That was what my head told me, but my heart... that was singing a completely different tune. In fact, my heart was still back on a white sandy beach, watching the waves roll in.

"You nervous?" Julian asked, interrupting my thoughts.

I nodded. "Are you?"

He chuckled. "I'm excited."

We were going to find out what date the baby was due today and that scared me. It was bound to make this all feel very real. I wasn't showing yet, and I'd had no symptoms. No nausea or vomiting, no bloating or indigestion... *nothing*. It was easy to just carry on with my day-to-day and not think about it, but I had a feeling that when I saw that little peanut on the screen and heard my baby's heartbeat – that was all going to change.

"I'm glad that Rich could fit us in on such short notice, I'm not sure I'd trust anyone else."

I nodded in agreement. I'd only met Rich once or twice, and honestly, I wasn't particularly bothered about who got the honours of looking at my vagina, but if it made Julian happy to go with him, then that was what we'd do.

He pulled into the carpark, grinned at me and rounded the front of the car to open my door for me. I took a few deep breaths as I waited.

Breathe.

Relax.

You've got this.

Julian held my hand as we entered the building. Ever the doting partner, he sat me down on an armchair and went to take care of the paperwork on my behalf.

Part of me wished he'd let me do it myself – I needed to take my mind off the reality of my life, but no such luck.

I needed a distraction, and fast, before I had a full-blown meltdown.

I took my phone out of my pocket and began flicking aimlessly through the old emails in my account from before I'd left Julian.

Dear Ida,

Do you think it's possible to love someone without being 'in love' with them?

Confused, Los Angeles.

Her response was there too.

Dear Confused,

I think there would be a lot of people getting it on with their brothers and sisters if it wasn't.

S x

I had to smile at that.

Another one caught my eye. It was from Soraya, right after my dad died.

I clicked it and slid the screen down to see what she'd written in response to my question.

Dear Ida,

My father passed away yesterday and I'm hurting. Does losing someone ever get easier?

Heart Broken, California.

Her reply had hurt but helped at the same time. It was probably the only time she'd ever refrained from her usual quick-witted reply.

Dear Heart Broken,

I'm so sorry to hear that. No, I don't think it does get easier, but you adapt, you adjust, you learn to live with it. Chin up beautiful, you've got this.

S x

I blinked back a few tears and scrolled on to the next conversation.

Dear Ida,

I think I might have made a mistake. Julian is perfect. I love him, but... there's something missing. We're meant to be getting married and I don't know if I can do it.

Cold Feet, California.

Her response followed.

Dear Cold Feet,

I could send you some socks, but I think you already know you shouldn't need them.

S x

I scrolled faster.

Dear Ida,

My dad won't be there to walk me down the aisle. I don't think I can do this without him. Is it a sign I shouldn't get married?

Freaking Out, Los Angeles.

Her response made a tear slip from my eye.

Dear Freaking Out,

Nothing would have stopped me from marrying Graham on my wedding day. Nothing. Not a sign. Not divine intervention. Hell, not even that bitch Mother Nature.

Read that again. Think about it. You already know the answer.

S x

I did know the answer. I'd already made the decision to leave by the time I got her reply.

I glanced up at Julian who was still dutifully filling in forms.

I opened a new email and began typing.

Dear Ida,

Motherhood is something you'd recommend, right?

Knocked Up, Los Angeles.

I took a few deep breaths and hit send.

"Blake?" Julian said softly. My head snapped up to see him standing before me. "You ready?"

I nodded and he held out his hand for me to take.

I took another calming breath, slipped my phone into my pocket and placed my palm in his.

He led me to the waiting nurse who showed us down a small corridor and into a room with a dentist-type chair in the middle of it.

"Dr. Malcolm won't be too far away, if you'd like to just slip off your lower half and pop on the gown, he should be with you shortly.

I nodded at her.

She left the room, pulling the door shut behind her.

I reached for the gown and looked it over.

Julian cleared his throat. "I'm just going to find a drink of water. Would you like one?"

I shook my head. "I think if I drink any more, my bladder might explode."

He grinned. "Alright, well I'll be back in a few."

I nodded at him as he left the room. I knew what he was doing, and I was grateful for the privacy.

I might have stayed over the past couple of nights, and a handful over the time since we got back, but Julian hadn't seen me with my clothes off in months.

I stripped off my shoes, jeans and underwear. It was hot in the room, so I stripped my top half down to my blouse while I was at it. I pulled the hideous gown over my head and climbed up onto the seat, making sure I wasn't going to flash my bits to anyone that walked in the door.

I took a few deep breaths as I waited for Julian to come back. The minutes ticked by and I found my gaze wandering from the door to the pictures on the walls.

There were all the usual things you'd expect to see in an obstetrician's office, like pictures of babies curled up tight in a woman's uterus which made me cringe. It all looked so cramped.

I stroked my stomach as my eyes travelled further around the room to a poster with some cute baby animals on it. Puppies, kittens, sheep and goats.

My heart rate spiked, and my throat went dry as I stared at the picture of the goat kid with the full-grown goat.

It looked just like Pixy. The same spots and everything.

I gasped for air as it all finally hit me, complete clarity about the mistake I'd made.

I *never* should have left Ky.

I loved him. I loved him so much it physically hurt me to be away from him.

Other than the baby in my belly, I wanted nothing more than I wanted Ky Bateman.

Everything was so messed up, yet nothing had ever been clearer to me than it was in that moment. I had to try. I had to find out if there was a future for me with Ky.

I knew I was going to hurt Julian, and break up our family before it had even got together, but I couldn't live a lie – I'd done that for too long and from now on, I was going to be honest with everyone in my life about everything – starting by being honest with myself.

It was Ky. It always had been.

I was so mad with myself for making such a mess of everything. I'd made mistakes – I'd fucked up. If I were a character in a movie, I'd undoubtably be the villain. But this wasn't a movie, this was real life. I wasn't some Hallmark film, perfect woman. I was real. I was flawed. I'd made these mistakes and now was the time to own them.

There was a soft knock at the door, and I sucked in another breath. Fat tears rolled down my face as my head finally accepted the decision my heart had been sure of all along.

I could do this. I could have a baby with Julian without having to marry him, and I could make sure that I gave it my best shot with Ky. That way, when I was eighty years old and looked back on my life, I'd never have to wonder what might have been if I'd had the strength to go after what I truly wanted.

Julian came into the room, took one look at me and rushed to my side. "Angel. What is it?"

"I'm so sorry," I whispered as he reached for my hand.

They were only three words, but he understood them. His shoulders sagged and a deep sigh left him.

"Knock, Knock, how are we doing in here?" a voice came from behind Julian's back.

He turned and I caught sight of Rich.

"Rich, could we have just a minute?" Julian asked.

Rich glanced between the two of us and offered a reassuring smile. "Of course, I'll just be outside when you're ready."

I was sure he had a schedule to keep, patients that were waiting, but Julian didn't seem to give it another thought as he turned back to me.

He was silent, waiting for me to speak.

"I don't want to hurt you, Julian. You know I love you, but it's not the kind of love that either of us deserve. You deserve someone who puts you first... someone whose eyes light up when you walk into the room. I'm sorry, but I can't give you that."

He still had my hand in his, his thumb stroking the side of mine. He was quiet for several, long, long moments.

"That guy you met in Sydney, you're in love with him."

It wasn't a question, but I still owed him an answer. I owed him so much more than an answer, but I had nothing else to give.

"I am."

His eyes fell to our joined hands. "I wish it could be different."

"I wish that too," I admitted. I'd lain awake countless nights, wishing my feelings would change – that I'd be able to love him the way he deserved, but wishes weren't real... love wasn't easy.

"What are you going to do, angel?" His eyes met mine.

"I don't know, but I want you to understand that I'll never stop you from being in your baby's life. No matter what."

He reached up and wiped a tear from my cheek

with his thumb. He opened his mouth and said the last thing I ever expected. "What if it's not mine?"

He hadn't given me even one indication that he was worried about not being the father of my child. In fact, I'd started to wonder if he really wasn't aware that Ky and I had been intimate. He never once mentioned it. Never questioned me.

"You and I weren't using protection, Julian."

"It just takes one time," he replied.

I shook my head. I wanted to tell him about Ky wearing a condom, but it felt wrong to even bring it up, so I just stared at him while he stared right back.

"I'll go get Rich," he finally said.

I nodded and he went to the door to call the doctor in.

Rich came in, all smiles, apparently oblivious to my tear-streaked face, or just very good at his job.

"It's good to see you both again, and congratulations."

"Thank you," I muttered as Julian came back to take his spot at my side.

"Now, do we have any idea of conception?"

I shook my head. "Should be a few months by now."

He nodded. "Alright, I see that you've been instructed to undress, but if you think you might be a little further along, we can start with an abdominal scan if you'd prefer that to an internal one?"

I nodded furiously and he chuckled.

Julian passed me my underwear and jeans and I

slipped them back on while the men made small talk about baseball and business.

"You can lose the gown too," Rich instructed.

I pulled it off over my head and he reached for a tube of gel. He pushed up my shirt and got me to shimmy down my jeans a fraction so he could have clear access to my uterus.

The gel was freezing as he squirted it on my skin.

I could feel my hands shaking again and I slid them under my butt so that no one could see how afraid I was.

I knew this baby wasn't Ky's, but Julian putting it out there in the universe sparked some tiny little bit of hope inside me.

It was stupid, delusional, and hopeful.

Story of my life.

I didn't want to take this from Julian, but our lives were going to be so complicated. If by some miracle I went to Australia and Ky was willing to give me another chance, Julian and I were going to have a tough time negotiating this co-parenting thing.

"Sorry about that." Rich chuckled as he spread the gel around with a piece of equipment attached to a screen.

He hit a button and turned the monitor, so it was facing me.

I waited, my heart in my throat as a grainy image appeared on the screen, and then shortly after a soft but steady, *whap, whap, whap, whap,* sound filled the room.

"That's your baby's heartbeat," Rich supplied as

he twisted and turned the wand, pressing it firmly against my full bladder.

"And that," he pointed to the screen with his free hand, "is your baby."

I watched on in wonder as the tiny little blip on the screen started to look like a baby.

"Oh my god," I breathed. "It's so tiny."

Julian gripped my hand, but I couldn't take my eyes off the image of my little peanut.

I was in love already; all it took was one look and I loved this baby so fiercely it threatened to consume me.

I was going to be a mum.

I was having a baby.

"Looks like you're not as far along as you thought, about ten weeks by the looks of things."

His words took a moment to register. *Ten weeks*. Ten. Weeks.

The only way that was possible was if...

I gasped.

It was Ky's. My baby was Ky's.

My hand flew up to cover my mouth.

"Are you sure?" I whispered. "The dates... are you sure?"

Rich was busy prodding around my stomach, his eyes on the monitor. "Definitely. I'd say about nine weeks and five days. You'll be due the start of September. Congratulations."

I wanted to cry. I wanted to laugh. I wanted to scream. I wanted to celebrate. I'd never felt so many conflicting emotions in the space of ten seconds.

I turned slowly to face Julian, my heart aching for him. I'd taken everything from him in the space of just a few minutes. I just had to hope that one day he'd see I'd done him a favour. One day when he met *her* – the woman he was meant to be with, he'd be grateful that he didn't marry me, when he had a family of his own – that he'd be grateful that he didn't have another child out there whose time he had to share. I had to hope he'd be okay until that moment came.

"*Julian*," I whispered as I came face to face with him, the man who was the logical path for my life to take.

His blue eyes were full of pain, but somehow, *he* still found a way to comfort *me*. "It's okay, angel, it's okay."

My bottom lip trembled as I told him the only thing I could think of that might have made him feel better in that moment. "You're going to be an amazing dad one day, with someone who looks at you like you're her whole world."

28

Ky

I SAT WATCHING the crashing waves, the half-empty bottle of tequila dangling from my fingers.

No matter what was going on in my life, the sea was my one constant. Nothing stopped the waves rolling in. Sure, some days the sets were big and raging, other days they were small and almost lapped at the shore rather than crashing onto it. The waves were symbolic of my emotions.

I chuckled at myself. I was awfully fucking philosophical when I was pissed.

I took another swig from the bottle and winced as it burned the whole way down. *Fucking tequila.* I hated the shit, but it was about the only thing in the liquor store that didn't remind me of Blake, so I was drinking it anyway.

Blake.

There she was again, running circles 'round my head.

Jesus, I should have looked both ways before I let her cross the street and waltz right into my heart. I should have held up a stop sign. At least a damn give way.

Now it was all broken gravel and road works in there.

Fuck, I wasn't making sense anymore.

I needed another drink, something that wasn't going to make me puke.

I tried to push myself up out of the sand and failed, instead overbalancing and landing on my face.

"Nup," I told myself.

"Ky?" a voice behind me questioned. "Is everything okay?"

"Wut?" My words barely sounded like words as I straightened myself up and held my hands out to the sides to see if I was steady.

I huffed out a laugh.

Nailed it.

"Are you alright?"

She came around the front of me and crouched down to look me in the eye.

Karen. No, Susan... Sophie? Sarah, fucking Sarah.

I tried to give myself a high five and failed.

"Jesus, you're wasted."

"Yup." I nodded.

"Are you alright?"

I shook my head. "Noooo."

"I think maybe you should go back in the house. You probably shouldn't be around water right now."

Wise words, Susan. Susan? Sarah? Fuck it, it doesn't matter.

I fell back into the sand and looked up at the stars.

"Tell me you haven't drunk that bottle yourself."

I felt her pry the bottle of tequila from my hand and I let it go without a fight. Tasted like shit anyway.

"Do you want to talk about it?" she asked.

I lolled my head to the side. She was lying in the sand next to me.

"Bout wut?"

"Whatever's on your mind. A woman, I assume? Never seen a man this drunk about anything else."

I looked back at the dark sky. I could still hear the waves rolling into shore, one after the other.

"Nup."

Yes.

No.

Maybe.

"She break your heart?"

I sighed, the alcohol making me brave, or stupid. I didn't know which. "Maybe."

My head started to spin, the warmth of the tequila mixing with memories of blondie. Thoughts of her always sobered me up quicker than I could drink.

"I bet she regrets it."

I huffed out a disbelieving laugh. "Doubt it."

I ran my hand over the scratchy beard on my face.

I needed to get over myself and shave this fucker off –
I hated it.

"You still love her?"

I let my head roll towards her a second time and
admitted something aloud that I'd barely admitted to
myself. "Yeah."

She gave me one of those 'you poor bastard'
looks.

"Maybe you could still make it work?"

I shook my head. I couldn't have strung together
enough of a sentence to explain the situation even if
I'd wanted to.

"You never know," she replied as she took in the
starry sky. "I was with my Darryl for six years when
he was killed. If he was still here, I wouldn't let
anything stop us from being together."

I swallowed deeply. Here I was being a miserable
bastard because I got dumped, and she'd lived
through an actual tragedy. "Sorry."

I saw her lips curve into a small, sad smile. "It's
okay. It's life I guess."

We lay there in silence for a few minutes before
she spoke again.

"Would you do something for me?"

I nodded slowly.

"Would you kiss me?"

She must have read the surprise on my face
because she quickly spoke again. "Just a kiss? It's
been years since I've felt a man's lips on mine, and
something about you, reminds me of him."

I didn't even think about it for another second. I

rolled towards her, covered in sand and reeking of tequila and covered her mouth with mine, letting her pretend for just a few seconds that I was her dead lover. I wasn't good for much at the moment, but I could be good for that. If there was someone out there who could ease the ache in my chest when I thought about Blake, then I probably would have asked them to kiss me too.

It was probably a shitty kiss, sloppy and loose, but hopefully she got what she needed out of it.

I pulled away, breathless as she smiled sadly up at me. "Thank you."

Her voice was a soft whisper, on the verge of tears.

I fell back to the sand, missing Blake more in that moment than the entire two months without her combined. Kissing a beautiful woman should have made me feel something, *anything*, but all it did was make me think of everything I'd lost.

My eyes started to feel heavy and I let my lids shut.

"If you really do love her, you should fight for her, Ky. You don't want to live with any regret, trust me on that."

I wanted her. I loved her.

I just didn't know what to do about it.

She'd chosen another man and no amount of wanting, fighting or loving was ever going to change that.

"I'll try," I replied.

I drifted off to sleep and when I woke it was in the sand, alone, to the sound of the ocean.

29

Blake

"I'LL GET IT, you shouldn't be lifting anything." Julian rushed over and took the box from my hands.

I rolled my eyes. "It's got pillows in it, not rocks, Julian, I hardly think that's what Rich meant by 'heavy lifting'."

"I don't care. Go sit down and put your feet up or something."

I thought it was stupid, but I did it anyway.

Julian had been helping me pack up my apartment for the past two days. We hadn't really had an in-depth conversation about where I was going or for how long, but we didn't need to – we both knew I was going back to Australia. For good.

I had no idea how to reach Ky, but I'd keep trying until I found a way. I had to.

My ticket to Sydney was booked for tomorrow.

Julian stacked a few more boxes neatly by the door and then sat down on the couch next me to. "I think that's the last of them."

"Thank you. You know you didn't have to help me with all this, I could have managed."

He gave me a small smile. "Don't be silly, of course I'm going to help you."

I might have still been a pretty shitty person, but I was dealing with things like an adult this time. No running, no stupid notes, no excuses.

I took his hand in mine and linked our fingers. "I really am sorry... for everything... for how it all worked out." Tears pooled in my eyes and I breathed out a laugh. "I swear I'm always crying these days... stupid hormones."

"I know you're sorry, but it's not your fault. I don't want you to ever feel guilty for saying how you feel. You deserve to be happy as much as anybody else does, Blake."

"I'm sorry for hurting you."

He shook his head. "I should have seen you weren't happy – I *did* see it – I just didn't want to admit it. You tried to talk to me, and I never let you get it out. I should have. You can't make someone love you back."

"It's not your fault."

"It's just life, angel, not everything works out the way we hope it will."

I let my hand rest on my stomach. "I know I'd told you it was over, but I should have talked to you properly, not just run away... and then everything with Ky... it just happened and I... I'm just sorry."

He took a deep breath. "You know what? I don't like that guy."

I huffed out a laugh. That was the least convincing statement I'd ever heard. Julian liked everyone. I doubted he was capable of anything else. He didn't have a bad bone in his body.

"But only because I know what he has," he added softly. "I hope he knows it too."

"I hurt him."

"If he loves you, he'll get over it."

"You think?"

"He'd be mad not to." He squeezed my hand. "Everything we've been through, all the heartache, the anger, the hurt; it was all worth it, Blake. I wouldn't change a single bit of it, because even though it didn't get me you forever, I got you for a while... and that's better than never having had you at all."

Oh god, my heart. My stupid, broken heart. I wanted it to love *this* man, to beat only for him, but that wasn't my reality. My heart belonged to another.

He leaned in and kissed my forehead. "I should go."

He rose from his seat and crossed the small apartment towards the door. "The movers will be here to take this all to storage in the morning – don't you dare lift a thing."

"Promise."

"And I upgraded your plane ticket for you. I didn't

want you flying all that way in some shitty little seat. Don't bother arguing about it, it's already done."

"Thank you," I whispered.

More tears came; I didn't think I'd ever cried as much in my life as I had the past couple of months.

This was goodbye for us. I might never see him again and as much as it hurt me, I knew it was the right thing.

I wanted to be his friend, but that wouldn't have been fair of me to ask – he'd have said yes, and he'd had suffered for it.

He'd move on this way. A clean break. He'd find someone to love and he'd be happy. He deserved it more than anyone else in the world.

He paused at the door. "Good luck, angel."

I leapt out of my seat and ran across the room to throw myself into his arms. He caught me and held me tight against him, both of us emotionally letting go of the other and closing the chapter of our life together for good.

He pulled away first and I reluctantly let go. "Be happy," I whispered.

His smile reached his eyes for the first time in days, and then he was gone.

I glanced around my empty apartment and sighed. This was it. Tomorrow was a new day for me and my little peanut. I was going to get on a plane to Sydney and then the work would really begin.

I crawled into bed and tried again to search Google for him, even though I knew it wasn't going to turn up anything different than it did yesterday when I tried.

I'd searched, 'Ky', 'McKay', 'Bateman' and every combination of the three possible. All I'd found were some pictures of Chance in his underwear. I grinned as I took in his smiling face. He and Ky were so similar.

I gave up my search and went into my emails.

I'd been avoiding looking at it, but I needed to see it now – the photo of the two of us on New Year's Eve. I sucked in a big breath and blew it back out before clicking the file attached to the email.

I thought I was ready. I *wasn't*. One look at him and my heart felt like it was going to split in two all over again. He was so, *so* gorgeous. His perfect face stared at me through my screen. Those dark eyes, that effortlessly tousled hair...

We looked good together. We looked happy.

I hoped like hell that we could get back to that. I knew it was going to take time, and a lot of effort – if he'd even consider it in the first place – but I wanted it. I'd work for it. I'd do *anything*.

And worse case, if it didn't work out between us the way I hoped it would, I knew I'd have to find a way to have Ky in my life. This baby was his – *ours*. It was half me and half him, and no matter how he might feel about me, I knew he'd be a part of his child's life. I'd seen him with Bree and CJ; he loved those kids unconditionally.

He would be a great dad.

I closed the picture and I giggled as I opened

Soraya's reply to my not-so-subtle pregnancy announcement from the other day.

Dear Knocked Up,

Nope, filthy little critters. All they do is eat, shit and sleep all day. See if it's too late to get a refund.

S x

And five minutes after that, another one.

I told myself I wouldn't ask, but who was I kidding? I HAVE to know... who's the daddy?

We'd emailed back and forth a few more times, discussed the ineffectiveness of condoms, shared a Ross from *Friends* GIF about how they 'should put that on the box', and called it a day.

I'd never met Soraya, but I didn't have a lot of close girlfriends, so I appreciated having someone to talk to about everything I had going on, and the fact that I never had to confront her face to face meant that I wasn't afraid to be honest about the mistakes I'd made. It was a good arrangement.

I tossed my phone onto the mattress and closed my eyes.

Tomorrow was going to be a big day, and I needed some rest.

30

Blake

IT WAS IRONIC REALLY, here I was back in first class, this time without a pesky neighbour, but I still couldn't manage to get a lick of sleep. In fact, I'd been awake so long, I was starting to feel a little bit delirious.

I understood why sleep deprivation was the most effective form of torture right now. I was teetering on the edge of losing the plot.

It was about ten hours in when I really felt myself slip, and I didn't just slip, I fell, head over heels, off the side of the cliff.

Big fat tears rolled down my cheeks and sobs wracked my chest as I tried desperately to be quiet. There was a family of four, a couple and their two children behind me, and the last thing I wanted to do was scare the kids by acting like a crazy person, but I was freaking out.

What if I can't find Ky?

Even worse, what if I found him and he didn't want to know me?

What if he didn't want to know his child?

I knew I was being crazy. Sure, Ky might have hated me and wanted nothing to do with me, but he was a good man under all that cocky bullshit, there was no way he was going to be the type that ditched his kid. But right now, my mind was so far beyond reason. I was in panic mode.

My breathing came in short, sharp pants.

Panic attack. You're having a panic attack.

I wasn't ready to be a single mother. I didn't know how to do this on my own. I needed Ky. I loved him. He *had* to forgive me.

"Breathe," a soft voice commanded from next to me. "Nice and deep."

I forced my eyes up and found the woman from behind me had slipped into the vacant seat next to me.

She reached across and stroked my arm slowly, up and down, up and down.

The rhythm helped me slow my erratic heart rate and brought my breathing down.

"That's it," she encouraged. "In and out. You've got it." She took slow, coaching breaths with me.

I stared into her big blue eyes as I got myself back under control.

She was a lot like me; blonde, petite, maybe a few

years older. But where I was vulnerable and sceptical, she was confident and sure of herself – I could see it in her eyes.

"Good girl." She praised me as I took a large, deep breath and blew it back out.

"Jesus, I'm sorry," I whispered.

"It's fine." Her hand continued to stroke my arm. "Are you okay?"

I should have just said yes and let her get back to her family, but instead I shook my head and said, "No, I don't think I am."

"I'm a pretty good listener," she replied, her Texas accent coming through.

"I'm sure you've got better things to do than listen to my problems."

She glanced back behind her. Their son was asleep, and their daughter was sitting on her father's knee, watching something on the screen. "I really don't," she offered with a smile.

"You have a beautiful family."

"Thank you." Her smiled widened. "We've been visiting friends in LA, now we're going to Sydney to celebrate our wedding anniversary – my husband and I got married there and we wanted to show the kids."

"That's so sweet."

She extended her hand to me. "I'm Kendall."

I shook it. "Blake."

"My husband, Carter, was a pilot when we first met."

"Wow, I bet that scored him some points."

Her eyes sparkled. "I'd be lying if I said it didn't."

We shared a laugh, and I decided I had nothing to lose by talking to this stranger about my problems. Maybe she'd have some advice for me.

"I'm from Sydney originally, but I've been living in California... I recently went back to Sydney, and then back to Cali again, and... look, it's kind of a long story and you'll probably think I'm stupid for chasing a man halfway around the world..."

She made a show of getting comfortable. "I've got nothing but time, and *trust me*, I know more about following a man than you might think."

She was right. We had hours until we'd be landing. We had time.

I tucked my feet up under myself. "Alright... so when I first came to LA, I met this guy..."

I spent the next hour telling her everything. I told her all about meeting Julian – the way he swept me off my feet. I told her about getting engaged, about my dad passing away, I told her about getting cold feet and running away. I told her *everything* about meeting Ky and falling for him.

She sat quietly, listening and asking the odd question as I spilled my guts about Julian coming to Australia, Ky looking at me like I'd crushed him, the pregnancy, the break up that wasn't really a break up because we never really got back together again, and then I was done.

I hadn't realised just how badly I'd needed to get it all off my chest until I was finished.

Kendall looked at me with big, wide eyes. "Well

that's quite the twisted little web you've weaved there."

I huffed out a breath. "I did try to warn you."

"Are you much of a writer? You could write a book about all that."

I shook my head. "Unfortunately, no."

"So does he know you're coming?"

I shook my head. "I know it seems ridiculous, but I never even got his cell phone number, I can't find him on the internet. I have no way of knowing where he is."

"You could try his family."

"They'll be my first stop, but I wouldn't blame them if they turned me away. I probably would if I was in their position."

"I'm sure you'll find him, Blake."

"What if I don't? Or what if I do, and he hates me?"

Anxiety clawed at my chest again, but I did my best to force it back down.

"He's not going to hate you; you love him, it's obvious you shared something special. I bet he loves you too."

"I seem to have a bad habit of hurting the people I love most."

"So, you made a few mistakes; who hasn't?"

"*A few mistakes*. I think I've racked up more than a *few* at this point."

"You didn't almost have a baby just to gain access to your dead Grandfather's millions, so you're doing okay in my book."

My jaw fell open. Kendall had some stories of her own, by the sounds.

"*What*?"

She giggled. "Let's not open that can of worms just yet."

I nodded. "Well, no, I didn't do that, but I did run out on my fiancé and then fall in love with another man not long after, so who am I to throw stones?"

She shrugged. "So what? You don't choose love, it chooses you. You weren't with Julian at the time, and sure, you should have handled it differently, but grief will do some messed up stuff to a person. You've made mistakes, Blake, but nothing that can't be forgiven or fixed."

"I left Ky."

"He told you to go."

"I shouldn't have listened."

"Maybe not, but you're going back now, isn't that what really matters?"

I didn't have a good answer for that.

"You know I'm right."

"I *hope* you're right," I admitted.

"I'm always right, just ask my husband." She grinned.

We both peered through the seats and found her husband watching her, a smirk on his lips. "You talking trash about me, perky?"

"*Never*."

I could tell how in love they were just by one look.

"She okay?" Kendall asked him, inclining her head to the little girl in his arms.

"She wants the song."

Kendall's smile softened. "Then sing it, Captain Clynes."

He rocked his little daughter and softly began singing *Lucy in the Sky with Diamonds*.

It was so sweet – the little girl began drifting off almost instantly.

"*The* song?" I questioned.

"Another long story," Kendall said as I turned away from the daddy-daughter duo.

"They're adorable together."

I wanted that kind of bond for Ky and our baby. I wanted to be there to share every second of it with him.

"They sure are. Best decision I ever made was sharing my life with that man."

"Do you think you'd ever have got over him if it hadn't worked out?"

She shook her head and gave me a sad smile. "No. I don't think I was ever meant to live my life without him. I think it's the same for you and Ky."

"We only had a few days together... what if it's not real?"

She raised a brow at me. "I talked to Carter in an airport bar for fifteen minutes before I got on a plane and followed him to the other side of the world. You're looking at proof that it doesn't have to take years to find the right person."

I laughed, a bit disbelieving, a bit delirious. "He drives me insane."

"You'd be bored if he didn't." She winked at me.

Damn her. She was probably right. I craved his banter, his quick wit, his never-ending stream of energy.

She rested her hand on mine and squeezed. "It'll work out. Have a little faith."

She was right again. I'd trusted Ky enough to get on the back of his motorcycle that day, now I just had to trust him enough to let me back in.

"So, you wanted to know about me producing an heir to my Grandfather's fortune, right?"

I giggled. I sure did. It was exactly the distraction I needed.

31

Blake

I DROVE the car I'd rented at a leisurely pace along the curving coastal roads.

It had taken me twice as long as it took Ky and I on the bike, but I didn't care. I'd managed to get a few hours' sleep after talking to Kendall, but I was still running on little more than empty. I didn't feel like driving the car like I'd stolen it today.

I was getting closer and closer to Pretty Beach and I knew what that meant. At the very least I was going to have to face Chance and Aubrey. I couldn't even let myself think about the possibility that Ky might be there too.

To say I was nervous would have been a vast understatement. I was completely freaking out.

I'd never done something so scary.

I might have had wild younger days, I might have got on the back of a stranger's bike and rode off into the sunset, but nothing had ever terrified me the way that the possibility of losing him for good did.

I pulled into the beach and sat for a long while, just watching the sets roll in from the sea as I tried to find some courage.

What if he's there?

What do I say?

I'd gone over a speech in my head, but I knew damn well that it was all going to go out the window the moment I laid eyes on him. He turned my brain to mush, made my pulse skyrocket and my insides flip, and that was all on a good day. Today was a long way off being a good day.

"Stop being a pussy," I whispered to myself.

I could do this. I had to.

I started the engine and made the short drive up to Chance and Aubrey's – I felt like I could hurl and it had absolutely nothing to do with morning sickness, and everything to do with me being embarrassed with the way I'd handled things.

I tried to remember what Kendall told me on the plane about making mistakes, *and* about deep breaths as I climbed out of the car and slammed the door closed behind me.

I walked on shaky legs up to the front door of the house.

Maybe I'd get lucky and they wouldn't be home.

I shook my head at myself. *Then what? Leave a note?* It's not like I wouldn't come back. I was a chicken shit, but I wasn't about to leave again without trying everything first. I'd learnt my lesson.

Australia was home. Actually, home was wherever Ky was. I'd never been one for geography anyway.

I knocked on the door and wrung my hands together nervously.

All thoughts of getting away without talking to anyone were squashed when I heard footsteps approaching the door.

I held my breath.

I wasn't sure if I was hoping for Chance or Aubrey. I didn't know who would be madder with me. Aubrey was sweet, obviously forgiving, but I thought Chance might have been my best bet – he knew what it was like to screw up and have to grovel to find your way back – he'd walked a mile in my shoes.

The door swung open and Aubrey's green eyes widened as she took me in.

"Hi," I squeaked.

"Blake?" she questioned as she pushed open the screen door and stepped outside. "What are you doing here? I thought you went back to America."

"I did." My gaze fell to my feet. "I... I'm back. I..."

"You're back?" Her tone was puzzled.

I took a deep breath and looked her in the eyes. "I came back for Ky. I never should have left. I love him and I want to make it right."

God, I'd told what felt like one hundred virtual strangers that I was in love with Ky, and I hadn't even been able to tell *him* yet.

A small smile tugged on the corners of her lips. "I knew I wasn't wrong about you."

"What?"

"I told Chance it wasn't over. I told him!" She jumped up and down excitedly.

"I'm confused."

She rushed me and pulled me into her arms, squeezing me tight before letting me go again.

"I was hoping you'd come back. I *knew* you two had unfinished business."

"You *wanted* me to come back, after everything I did?"

"Don't get me wrong, I'm pissed you kept the truth from Ky, *and* from me... but as long as you don't have a fiancé in tow this time, I think we can all let go of the past."

"You don't think I'm a whore?" I asked in disbelief.

"I mean... maybe just a tiny little bit," she teased, holding her thumb and fore finger an inch apart.

"Who is it, princess?" Chance's voice called from inside the house.

She grinned at me and turned over her shoulder. "It's Blake... and you owe me fifty bucks."

"Well, well, little lady, can't say I was expecting to see you here." He sidled up next to Aubrey and slung his arm over her shoulders.

Our eyes locked.

"I needed to see him."

"Alright," he said with a nod.

That was it. Just, *alright*? I didn't know what the

hell to do with that. Why weren't they mad? Why weren't they disappointed in me?

I'd told Aubrey the truth about nearly everything before I'd left with Julian, not that she probably understood any of it through my sobs, but even the truth was no excuse for the way I'd acted – for how badly I'd hurt Ky. They were his family – they loved him. I should have been enemy number one as far as they were concerned.

"Why aren't you mad?"

Chance's brows rose. "Oh, I *am* mad, this is my mad face."

He didn't look mad.

"Okay?" I replied, confused.

His lips twitched and he burst into laughter. "Can't keep a straight face to save my life these days. Look, Blake, I'll level with you, you hurt him and that hurts me. You fucked up... but I'm not in much of a position to be judging other people for their screw ups, and I'm sure you had your reasons. Just make it right with him and we'll be square."

I nodded quickly. "That's why I'm here. I want to fix it. Whatever it takes."

"Well then, good."

Simple as that.

Wow.

"So, can I see him?"

"You can try, and if you track him down, tell the bastard to answer my phone calls. I don't like being ignored."

My heart sank. "He's not here?"

Aubrey spoke next, her brows furrowed. "No. He took off on his bike right after you left, and he hasn't been back. We've managed to get him on the phone a couple of times, but we don't know where he is. He wasn't really up for talking and he hasn't answered in weeks."

I felt my hopes physically deflate. My chest tightened with regret – it was my fault he was avoiding his family.

"He didn't tell you anything about where he might have gone?"

She shook her head sadly. "I'm sorry."

"Don't be," I breathed, "I'm the reason he took off. This is on me and only me. You must have been worried about him."

"We have been," Aubrey answered.

"Nah. Kid can take care of himself, princess," Chance replied.

She gave him a 'what the hell' look. "So that's why you've been calling him like some type of stalker, day in, day out? Because you're *not* worried?" she demanded.

"The kids miss him."

"Bullshit, cocky, you miss him just as much."

He muttered something under his breath.

Aubrey was clearly right. Chance missed his cousin and that was my fault.

"I should go and look for him."

"You're just going to do *what*? Drive around Australia and hope for the best?" she questioned.

I shrugged. "I guess so, what other choice have I got?"

"You could at least get some sleep first; no offence, but you kinda look like crap." Chance eyed me up and down.

Losing the man you love, being knocked up and then flying halfway around the world would probably do that to a person.

"I'll stop for the night somewhere when I need to sleep."

"You can spend the night here if you want?" Aubrey offered.

It was a very generous offer, but it felt wrong without Ky. Even though I knew it was probably going to be pointless, I needed to go out and try things my way. I couldn't just sit around and hope that he might turn up.

"I think I'm going to go for a drive. I know one place he might be. I know I won't be able to sleep until I've looked there anyway."

I thought about the blowhole and how much Ky loved it there – if he was going to go somewhere, my money was on there – even if I was turning out to be a lousy bet.

Aubrey frowned at me. "Just stay one night, I'll cook you –"

"Princess," Chance interrupted her, "she's not going to want to waste time here with us. I know what it's like to go after the person you love. I remember the urgency."

They shared a long lingering glance that made me want to look away and give them some privacy.

"*Fine*." Aubrey finally relented, "but you're leaving a phone number and taking some food."

"Deal," I agreed.

"When you find him, can you tell him I said, 'I told you so'?" Chance smirked.

I frowned at him, not understanding.

"I've been waiting for this moment, don't worry, he'll know what I mean."

I left with the cutest packed lunch, Ky's, Aubrey's and Chance's phone numbers, and an agreement with them that if they heard from Ky, they'd tell him I was here, and if I hadn't found him within the next few days, I'd come back.

32

Ky

I TAPPED the razor against the sink and watched as the scruffy black hair floated around in the water.

I glanced at my half-shaved face in the mirror. I looked like a hobo. And not in that chic, hipster kind of way, but like a legitimate hobo who lived under a bridge and pushed his possessions around in a shopping cart.

I needed to get my shit together. I'd never let myself get this messed up over a chick before, and I hated that I'd let it happen now. I didn't know why.

That was total bullshit, I knew *exactly* why.

Because she's different, my brain screamed at me, telling me what I already knew to be true, but what I was vehemently trying to deny nonetheless.

I could be okay for days at a time, a week even, and then I'd smell something... see something... hear something that reminded me of her, and I'd be right back at square one. Reminders of her seemed to surround me, and I'd started to believe that maybe I was destined to be broken for the rest of forever. Maybe that was the price for loving her – the suffering that followed.

I'd have taken Blake back in a heartbeat. I knew that. It was *fact*. Yes, she'd hurt me, but I still fucking loved her, every sexy, sassy inch of her. I was a fractured man without her. If she walked through the door right now and said, '*surprise, I'm back*', I'd probably fall to my knees and beg her to stay forever. But that wasn't going to happen. She wasn't coming back.

Not to Australia.

Not to me.

That left me with only one choice. Pick myself up and get on with my life. People lived with a lot worse than this every day and they didn't hide away from the world, looking like a bum.

I scraped the razor over my skin again, the prickling noise grated on my nerves. Not quite as much as my cousin's insistent calling, but it was a close second.

The day before yesterday, he'd called, but instead of the phone ringing once and only once, like he usually did, he'd called about fifty times, at which point Aubrey had joined in too.

There were a bunch of texts as well, but I didn't

read any of them. I just shut my phone off and left it on the newly installed kitchen bench.

I had to admit, heartbreak was doing wonders for my work ethic. The bathroom was completed, the bedrooms had their paint stripped and were ready for a fresh coat, and the kitchen was almost finished too. This renovation project was going to be over too soon and then I'd have to move on – find something else to fill my days.

The idea of moving on made me anxious. I liked this spot. I was only about thirty minutes away from Chance and Aubrey – not that they knew that – and it was right by the beach. Whoever wound up living in this place had one hell of a lifestyle ahead of them.

I finished up shaving and I barely recognised my reflection when I was done. I hadn't seen this much of my face for two months. I still needed a haircut, but I wasn't game enough to do that myself – I'd have to get one in town. The shave was a start though.

Fresh shave, fresh start.

I laughed humourlessly. If I spouted that bullshit long enough, maybe I'd actually start to believe it one day. It was unlikely, but worth a shot.

I tugged on a shirt and pulled up my jeans. I didn't feel like being around people, but I was going crazy around here on my own. I needed to get out on the bike for a while and do something that might take my mind off the mess in my life.

There was only one thing that I could think of that might have had the desired effect. Only one place I felt like I could stomach going.

I shrugged on my leather jacket, tossed my still-powered-off phone in my pocket, and headed for my bike.

33

Blake

I WAS STUMPED. Not only that, but I was tired, emotional and just fresh out of decent ideas.

He wasn't in the town with the blow hole.

I'd asked at the campground, and every other accommodation option possible. I'd even sat around down by the lighthouse for the better part of two days, just in case he turned up.

He didn't.

I'd driven up and down the coast, took a second look at every surfer, and still come up empty.

I'd tried his cell a few times, but it went straight to a generated voicemail. I didn't even get to hear his voice.

I'd been checking in with Chance and Aubrey, and they said the same. It appeared Ky had switched off his phone. He didn't want to talk to anyone – because of me.

I pulled into a small, gravel carpark that over-looked the sea and rested my forehead against the steering wheel.

This was fucking useless.

It was totally pointless.

I was *never* going to stumble across him. It was a three-hour trip from Sydney to Pretty Beach, with seemingly endless possibilities for places to turn off and explore. I could have spent a month looking and still not found him – and that was assuming he was even in this area. For all I knew, he'd got on a plane and left the country altogether.

It was like searching for a needle in a haystack.

I blew out a deep breath. I was almost all the way back to Sydney at this point, and I knew Ky wasn't a city boy. It was almost the one place I could guar-antee he *wouldn't* be.

I grabbed my phone and played around on the maps for a while. I googled 'best surf spots around Sydney', but again, there were too many to count. I looked up pictures of little local towns and tried to imagine where I would have gone if I was him.

It was a waste of my time. I was clutching at straws, big time.

I knew what I had to do. I'd run out of options. I was going to have to wait him out, go back to Pretty Beach and wait for him to either call or turn up to see his family.

I knew him; he was bound to be struggling with not seeing or talking to anyone. He'd have to surface one day, and when he did, I would be there waiting for him.

I put the car in reverse and backed out onto the road, heading back the way I came.

I hated that it felt like I was giving up. I would have given anything to find him, to show him that I'd tried, hell, I'd even gone spiritual and been looking for 'signs' everywhere I went – anything to suggest that I was meant to be with him.

Problem was, I'd found none.

Not one fucking sign, and I'd gone all the way down to Bateman's Bay for crying out loud. If I couldn't find a sign in the town that shared his name, I was probably on the wrong path.

I pushed the pedal further into the floor as the kilometres slipped away beneath me, my speed increasing. I was getting pissed off – I was driving like I stole it again.

I was over this. I needed it to stop.

Sure, I'd fucked up and I deserved to pay for that, but I was sick of this state of limbo I'd found myself in.

People did stupid shit when they were in love.

People did stupid shit when they were grieving.

I, apparently, did *really* stupid shit.

I'd lost my dad – the most important man in my life, and I felt like now I was losing the other man that meant something to me.

A sob tore up my throat, catching me off guard.

I'd been so consumed by Ky, it'd been days since I'd really thought about the man who had raised me.

I needed my dad. Now more than ever.

He'd always believed in me. He'd always encouraged me, no matter how bad I screwed up. He'd loved me unconditionally his entire life and I would have given just about anything to hear his voice right now.

Tears blurred my vision and I pulled over to the side of the road, my chest heaving.

I grabbed my phone and angrily swiped at the moisture running down my face, mad at myself for breaking down again.

I'd cried enough. It was beyond a joke how many tears I'd shed these past few weeks, and it got me nowhere.

I'm not even a crier, for fuck's sake.

I might not have been spewing or sporting a bump yet, but I could vouch for my peanut wreaking havoc with my emotions, that was for damn sure.

I pulled up my gallery and found the video I'd only allowed myself to watch once since I received it.

It was of my dad. He looked frail – old. He was dying when he recorded this video, and he sent it to me only a week before he passed.

I hit play.

"Hey, Blakey, it's your dad."

I sniffed a laugh, overjoyed and heartbroken in the same moment.

"I wanted to send you this so that when I'm gone, you never forget just how much I love you. I'll always love you, baby girl, I'll always be with you, even when I'm not around anymore. I need you to be strong – you were always the strong one anyway, but more than that, I need you to be true to yourself. You care too much about other people and not enough about yourself. It's okay to be selfish sometimes, Blake. You deserve to put *you* first every now and again."

He coughed then, the noise a harsh hacking sound. My eyes stayed glued to the small screen.

"I think I'd better wrap this up before I cough up a lung. You're going to do just fine, baby girl. I'll always be with you. I love you."

I cry-laughed as he looked past the camera. "Carmen, is it off? I can still see it going, how do I –."

There was movement, a rustling sound, and then he was gone.

"I love you too, dad," I whispered.

Part of me wanted to go back to Sydney, go to my sister's and be close to where my dad spent the last part of his life, but I knew he wouldn't want that for me. He'd want me to fix things with Carmen, sure, but he'd hate the idea of me moping around, and that's exactly what I would be doing if I went there like this.

"What should I do, Dad?" I asked aloud.

Shockingly, I got no response, so I did the only thing I could do – put the car in drive and got back on the road.

I'd been driving for another twenty minutes or so, when I finally saw something that made me stop and think.

It was a massive billboard, advertising a race meet in the next town over. For *today*.

My heart raced, each thud slamming into my rib cage.

Thwack.

Thwack.

Thwack.

I indicated for the turn off, my pulse racing.

Now *that* was a sign.

The huge lettering said it was the biggest event since the Melbourne Cup. I didn't know squat about horse racing, but even I had heard of the Melbourne Cup – if that didn't catch Ky's attention, then nothing would. If he was in the area, he'd know about this event. He'd be here. He wouldn't able to help himself.

I drove through the centre of town and followed my GPS's instructions out to the racetrack, joining the queue of cars waiting to park.

I drummed my fingers on the steering wheel impatiently. "*C'mon*," I murmured. "Move, dammit."

I was finally directed to a parking spot in the huge paddock and I rushed from the car towards the gates as fast as I could.

There were nicely dressed people *everywhere* as I paid the fee and entered in my cut-off denim shorts. I was massively underdressed, but I didn't care. I wasn't here to win best dressed anyway. I was hoping for a much better prize.

Holy crap. The place was packed.

Even if Ky was here – I doubted I'd ever find him. Hundreds and hundreds of people were in the stands, sprawled out across the lawn and inside the buildings.

I stopped and turned in a slow circle, studying every man my eyes made contact with.

One guy had hair his colour.

One had his broad shoulders.

One guy had a tattoo in the same place.

Another was his height.

But none of them were Ky.

I walked around for half an hour, looking at every possibility, but coming up empty.

He isn't here.

I stumbled forward, desperate for somewhere to sit so I could breathe through the panic attack I felt coming on.

I'd been so sure I'd find him here.

I'd let myself hope.

Each step felt like punishment as I rushed towards a wooden bench and sank down onto it.

A race started, the announcer's voice booming over the arena as people cheered and screamed. I buried my face in my hands and focused on not losing it.

"And *Open Your Eyes* is making a late surge past *Dingo's Baby* and it's *Open Your Eyes* taking the lead, *Open Your Eyes* with half a length, *Open Your Eyes* crossing the line in first!"

God, that dude needed to stop yelling, *Open Your Eyes*, I got it. I looked up, eyes fucking *open*.

My breath got caught in my throat as my gaze caught on the tall, dark-haired man leaning against the fence, silently watching the horses parading before the next race.

My hand flew to my mouth when he turned a fraction and I caught sight of his profile.

Ky.

He *was* here.

I found him.

34

Ky

I COULDN'T HAVE PICKED A FUCKING winner if my life depended on it.

I hadn't been on a losing streak like this one since I was nineteen years old and thought I was invincible.

It was probably because I wasn't making educated bets... no, today, I was mindlessly gambling and doing a fucking shitty job of it too.

Statistically speaking, I should have had at least one winner by now, through nothing more than pure dumb luck, but instead, I was about three thousand down and counting.

I probably should have stopped, but I couldn't.

Every race I found something that reminded me of Blake.

I'd bet unsuccessfully on *Baby Come Back, Don't*

Go Breaking My Heart and *City Girl*. I'd tried picking a jockey with the same blonde hair. I'd even gone as far as picking a horse whose trainer's name was Vincent.

I figured if I bet on one of these horses and it won, then maybe she'd come back to me, some way, somehow.

I really had lost my god damn mind.

I should have put my money on *His Girl*, because that's what she was. *His*. Not mine. I was starting to think that maybe she was never meant to have been mine at all.

I tossed my race book in the bin and raked my hand through my freshly cut hair. I didn't care about the money, but my pride was taking a serious hit right about now.

I leant my elbows down on the rail and watched the horses trot out onto the field.

I'd been sure coming here would make me feel better, but I was wrong, if anything I felt worse. It brought back memories of kissing blondie against a chain link fence, of her placing a bet for me... of the bet I won on the plane...

Fuck. Memories of her seemed to be everywhere I looked.

I'd watch one more race, I decided, and then I was getting the hell out of here. It was time I pulled my head in and made my way back to the real world. I owed Chance and Aubrey an apology – CJ and Bree too. I'd go stay with them for a while.

One more race and then I'm gone.

There was chatter all around me; punters,

couples, groups of friends, the announcer talking about the favourite to win, but one small voice cut through every last bit of that noise.

"Excuse me, I'd like to make a bet."

I froze on the spot, swallowing hard. Maybe I could add hallucinations to my ever-growing list of messed-up conditions, because I would have sworn on my life that I just heard *her* voice.

I stayed frozen, unwilling to turn, because as soon as I did, I'd be nothing but disappointed.

"*Ky?*"

This time there was no mistaking it, no imagining it. That was *her* voice and it was right here behind me.

I spun around and she rocked back on her heels.

Jesus fucking Christ. She was really here. I could see her with my own two eyes. She was so close I could reach out and touch her if I wanted to.

My heart was racing so fast I was worried I was going to go into cardiac arrest. A man could only take so much. I, for one, was at my limit.

She looked tired, *stressed*, she had big bags under her eyes, she looked like she'd lost some weight, but she was still beautiful. *So* fucking beautiful it actually hurt me to look at her.

"A bet?" I breathed the first thing I could think of.

She nodded slowly, those entrancing eyes of hers glued to mine.

"What horse?"

She took a tentative step towards me. My hands twitched with anticipation and want... *longing* – my limbs longed for her of their own accord.

"*Second Chance,*" she whispered, unsure.

Another deep swallow.

"What's the bet?" I questioned.

She shrugged a delicate shoulder. "How about, *my whole life*?"

Her eyes glassed over as her vulnerability seeped through, and I couldn't stand the distance between us a moment longer.

I stepped forward and pulled her into my arms, her body colliding with mine in a way that felt so right, yet so bittersweet.

I needed her to know that I was right here. That I still gave a shit – regardless of why she was back. I heard what she said, I understood what she was implying, but I needed to hear it straight before I could get my hopes up. I was barely surviving losing her once – I had to guard my heart until I knew for sure.

"You're really here," I murmured.

She nodded, her head against my chest.

I pulled back, my hands gripping her shoulders so I could study her face. "Why, Blake? I need to know why, because if you're here to tell me you're happy with that Ken doll dude, I need you to do it now, I can't –"

She lunged forward, throwing herself at me again, our lips finding the others like they knew the way by heart.

She kissed me like she was starved, and I kissed her back like I was desperate for whatever part of her I could get.

"Oh my god, I'm so sorry," she blurted out, her cheeks red as she tried to pull away. "I shouldn't have just assumed it would be like –"

She thinks I don't want her? Fuck that.

I dragged her close and cut her off by crashing our lips together again, she moaned as I swiped my tongue into her mouth, tasting her for the first time in months. I punished her for leaving and treasured her for coming back at the very same time.

"Are you really here?" I whispered, against her lips, my disbelief evident. "Am I dreaming?"

"I can't believe *you're* really here," she replied, her forehead resting against mine. "I've been looking everywhere for you."

I had so many questions, so many things I needed to know, but for right this second, there was nothing more important than holding her in my arms after I thought I'd never get another chance.

She must have felt the same way, because we stayed like that for several long moments.

"My dad died. About six weeks before we met."

"I'm so sorry."

She nodded. "It's no excuse, but I think that's part of the reason I handled everything so badly. I tried to act like I was okay, but I wasn't. I miss him."

I knew how she felt. My mum had been gone for sixteen years and I still missed her every day.

"I bet you do," I murmured. "I wish you'd told me."

"I should have. I should have told you everything."

I wanted to know every little, insignificant thing about her. If she'd let me. I'd spend my life learning those details.

"It's over with him... with Julian..." she said quietly. "It'd been over since before I met you, but I ended it properly this time."

"You didn't marry him?"

My entire life felt like it hinged on this answer.

She shook her head. "How could I, when I'm so desperately in love with you?"

My chest felt like it was full of fireworks, each going off one after the other.

Bang.

Bang.

Bang.

I couldn't think straight, I couldn't think of a time when I'd ever been this happy. I didn't know what to say... what to *do*, so I settled for what I was good at – winding her up.

"I told you you'd fall in love with me, blondie."

A laugh burst from her, filled with emotion. "Don't be an asshole."

I chuckled. "But it's what I do best."

The way we were able to fall back into our old rhythm soothed my soul. We still had a long road ahead, we had a lot to get out in the open between us, but we could do it. I really believed that. She was here and that meant the world. Our banter gave me hope.

She shook her head, disagreeing with me. "*No*, I think loving me might be what you do best."

I couldn't argue with that.

"Pick a horse," I murmured.

"Number five," she replied without missing a beat.

"I'll take number eight."

"What's the bet?" Her eyes fluttered closed, as though she was savouring the familiarity of this feeling between us.

"If I win, you come with me. I want to show you something."

Her soft laughter hit me like a punch square in the chest. I finally felt like I was home. "This again?"

I grinned, nodding.

"Fine, and if *I* win?"

"If you win, blondie, I'll let you take me out to the stables to fool around."

She threw her head back and laughed. I'd been kidding, expecting her to argue, but when she just gave me a look that said, 'bring it', I swear I got hard on sight.

Jumping back into our physical connection right away probably wasn't wise, but I didn't pride myself on being smart. I just wanted her – my need for this woman outweighed all rational thought.

The commentator started talking about the horses before they came flying out of the gates, but neither of us looked away from the other.

Blake was the first to move, walking away from the race, tugging my hand behind her.

"Where are we going?"

"To collect my prize."

"You didn't win yet."

She paused and arched a brow at me. "Are you saying you *don't* want me to collect, sparky?"

Fuck yes, I do. I pulled her hand, tugging her back to me and scooped her up into my arms. She shrieked, and a group of guys cheered at us as I carried her past.

I had a buddy here who trained horses, and he'd shown me around the stables earlier today, so I knew exactly where I was heading.

I walked her right into a vacant stall and slammed the heavy door shut behind us. It wasn't very private, but I had exactly zero fucks to give and even less self-control to exercise.

She backed up as I prowled towards her, until her back hit the block wall at the rear of the shed with a soft thud.

"You look worried, blondie."

She bit down on her lip as her hands tangled in my hair. "What if someone sees?"

"Then I hope they enjoy the show." I growled before dipping my head to attack the skin at her neck.

"*Ky.*" She moaned as I skimmed my hands down her sides to the top of her short, denim shorts.

She smelled just the way I remembered. Her moans sounded even better than my memories could possibly have done justice.

"God, I missed you."

"I wasn't me without you," she replied simply.

Her nails dug into my scalp and spurred me into action.

I undid the button on her shorts and slid them

down her legs, watching as they fell to the hay-covered ground.

She stepped out of them, and I took a minute to appreciate the sight before me. Nothing but a scrap of white lace stood between me and the pussy I'd been so desperate to get another taste of.

I dropped to my knees in front of her and she gasped as my hot, wet mouth made contact with her panties, licking and sucking her through the thin lace.

Her fingers pressed into my head. "Oh my god," she whimpered.

"Watch me," I demanded. "I want to see your eyes while you fuck my face."

Her eyes fell to mine and held. "I don't remember you being so bossy."

"Tell me it doesn't turn you on... I'll wait."

She pressed her lips together firmly and I smirked.

That's my girl.

I pushed her panties aside and slipped two fingers inside her wet heat. Fuck, she was so wet.

She cried out, loudly – her worries about being caught, long gone.

"That's it, baby," I praised as she thrust her hips, taking more from me. "Just like that."

Her moans got louder and louder as I put my mouth back on her sensitive clit, bringing her to the brink.

"Please." She begged, "I want to feel you."

Fuck, if those weren't the sweetest words to ever

leave her mouth. I slid her panties down her legs and she dutifully stepped out of them.

I tugged on my fly and lowered my jeans as I stood, my heavy cock hitting my stomach as I freed it.

Her hands slid from my hair, down to my shoulders, scoring my skin through my shirt as they went.

"I'm so fucking hard for you, blondie."

"Do something about it then," she challenged.

I stroked myself from root to tip, before groaning with the realisation I couldn't go through with it.

"Fuck. I don't have a condom."

Our eyes met.

"I don't care."

I let my head fall back. "You want me to fuck you bareback? *Jesus*, Blake." Now that she'd planted the seed, I couldn't think of anything else. "Are you on the pill, baby? I haven't been with anyone else since you."

I gripped myself tightly again, working myself into a frenzy.

"I haven't either."

I couldn't believe what I was hearing, but I'd unpack that later – right now I had better things to do.

"I've never had sex without a glove," I growled. "Fucking reckless. What if something happens?"

"Ky." My name was weighted.

I snapped my head up, my eyes finding hers.

"I don't think that's going to be a problem."

"Did you miss sex-ed in school?" I continued

stroking myself. "Pretty sure that's how babies are made."

She shook her head, her expression nervous. "No. It won't be a problem... because I'm already pregnant, Ky."

Her words hung between us as I grappled to understand them.

"This isn't how I pictured telling you, but we're having a baby, you and me."

You and me.

We're having a baby.

Already pregnant.

My hand froze.

"A baby?"

She nodded. "I don't know how it happened – we were careful – but I saw it on a scan, I'm about ten weeks."

My mind was spinning.

I was going to be a dad. Blake was going to be a mum. We were going to be parents. *Together.*

Shock.

Panic.

Excitement.

Fear.

Exhilaration.

I felt all that and more in the space of about ten seconds.

"A baby? A real, human baby?"

"Yes."

"You and me?"

"Mmm hmm."

A pain seared my chest and I winced. "Is that why you're here?" I asked, the words tasting like acid on my tongue. "Are you only here, with *me*, because I knocked you up?"

"No." She clutched my face in her hands. "I'd *never*. I'm here for *you*, because you own me, Ky – I knew I wanted you *before* I knew the baby was yours."

Before she knew it was mine.

"You're sure it's not his? Blake, are you one hundred fucking percent sure that this baby is mine?"

She nodded her head, her golden hair falling around her face. "I haven't been with him in months, sparky. This baby is yours. My heart is yours. *I'm* yours."

Her words were like a healing balm to my worries. She might have hid the truth from me before, but she was giving me nothing but honesty now. If the look in her eyes was anything to go by, I'd be willing to bet that she'd never lie to me again.

"A *baby*," I repeated as the reality sank in a bit further.

"Oh my god, are you in shock?" Her palm pressed against my cheek.

"I'm not in shock." I shook my head, while my hand went back to stroking my painfully hard dick.

"You're not?" she asked timidly.

"*No*," I murmured as I leaned down to graze my teeth over the shell of her ear.

She shuddered.

"I'm fucking ecstatic, blondie."

"Really?"

I pressed her firmly against the wall and she gasped.

"*Really*. Because I get *you*," I said by way of explanation.

She moaned as I ran my calloused fingers under her tank top to her ribs. "But a baby is a big deal, Ky..."

I kissed down her neck to the base of her throat. "If you think I'm going to run because you're offering me everything I ever wanted when I looked into your eyes, then you're fucking crazy."

"But it's –"

"It's fast," I interrupted her.

Kiss.

"It's crazy."

Kiss.

"It's *us*."

She sighed, relieved.

I lifted my face from her neck and looked into her eyes. "I love you, Blake. I already love our baby too."

Apparently, those were the words my woman needed to hear. She climbed me like a pole, her legs wrapping tightly around my waist, her entrance lining up with the tip of my cock like she was built specifically for me.

I thrust my hips, pushing into her tight pussy in one stroke, groaning as I buried myself to the hilt.

We didn't speak; no more words were needed. She clung to my shoulders as I dragged myself out of her, painfully slow before slamming back in.

I set a punishing rhythm, thrusting as deep as her

body could take me, bringing her to the brink in no time.

I was barely holding on myself; it had been too long without her.

I slowed my pace and she whimpered as I intentionally stopped her from falling over the edge.

Thrust.

"You *ever* leave me again, and I won't be so quick to welcome you back."

Our eyes locked.

Thrust.

"You ever tell me to go again, and I might not come back," she replied.

That was my girl – always giving back as good as she got.

Thrust.

"Never," I grunted.

Thrust.

"Never," she repeated.

It was a promise.

I sped up, taking her roughly. She screamed my name within seconds, her tight, wet pussy squeezing me so tightly I saw stars. I came hard, hot bursts of cum shooting deep inside her.

"I fucking love you," I breathed, ragged – *spent.*

"I fucking love you too."

35

Blake

KY INSISTED that we return the rental car to the closest branch a couple of towns down the coast so that I could ride with him the rest of the way.

We never did see who won that last bet, but it didn't matter. I would have followed him anywhere – win or lose.

I was beginning to think he was taking me back to Aubrey and Chance's, but he'd turned off about half an hour before Pretty Beach and we'd travelled down a quiet, windy road, heading towards the sea.

I was curious what he was going to show me this time.

I clung on; my arms wrapped tightly around his narrow waist as he navigated the roads with ease.

Bikes had always made me nervous, but when Ky

was the one in control of it, I felt no fear about being on the back.

I trusted him with my life.

He slowed the powerful machine and made another two turns before coming to a stop on the street outside a line of widely spaced houses.

The purr of the engine stopped, and I unwrapped my arms to stretch.

"Here we are, blondie."

He climbed off the bike and I took a few moments to really appreciate his fine physique as he stripped out of his jacket.

His legs were long and lean. His arms were toned and golden brown. That tattoo I loved so much was peeking out the bottom of his t-shirt sleeve.

I saved his face for last, because if I'd started there, I might never have been able to look away.

He smirked at me – the very smirk that did me in each and every time. His heated gaze swept over me and I felt myself blush.

He held out his hand to help me from the bike and I shivered when our skin made contact. His touch was like a warm coat on a cold winter's night.

"Where are we, sparky?"

He gestured towards the house. "I've been working on this place for a couple of months – renovating it."

Our joined hands swung between us as we approached the house.

"I didn't know you could build."

He chuckled. "I can't."

My brows pulled together. "Then how..."

"YouTube. It's got the answer for everything."

My body shook with laughter. "I mean, yeah, sure. That works."

The house was old, but beautiful. A bit of love and care and this old girl would come up amazingly well.

"It's stunning."

"It's a bit of a dump right now."

"Shush. It's got good bones," I argued.

He looked at me curiously as he held the door open and ushered me inside.

I let go of his hand and went ahead of him down the hallway and into a wide, open living space that had a brand-new kitchen. I looked beyond it, out the window.

"Wow. Look at that view."

I went past the construction mess and pressed my hands against the glass.

It was beautiful. Mature trees framed the house with the sand and sea only metres from where the grass ended.

I couldn't imagine what it would be like to wake up and look at that every morning.

"You like it?" Ky asked from behind me.

I glanced over my shoulder at him. "Like it? It's incredible."

His face was unreadable as he watched me.

I stepped away from the glass and walked around the room, noting where he'd removed walls and pulled up old carpets.

I made my way into the kitchen and grazed my fingertips across the benchtop. It was gorgeous.

"You did all this?"

He nodded, his eyes dark, burning into mine.

"I bet the owner is really happy with it, Ky."

"He is."

"You should be proud of what you've done here. I can't wait to see it when it's finished."

I took another look at the view before wandering towards where I saw another hallway, no doubt with the bedrooms coming off it.

"How many rooms?" I asked without turning.

I could feel his eyes on my back. "Five."

"Does he have a family?"

"Not yet."

I nodded. I could imagine bringing up kids here. A kid couldn't ask for a better playground.

"Can I see the bedrooms?" I ask as I took another few steps.

"It's mine."

His words stopped me in my tracks.

"What is?" I turned to face him.

"The house."

"It's *yours*?"

His?

How?

When?

He nodded; his stare intense. "I had some savings. Bought the place on a whim. Thought I'd fix it up and flip it."

"*You* own *this* house?" I asked, still in disbelief. I didn't even own a car, and here he was, a homeowner.

He nodded again.

"And you want to sell it?" My voice rose an octave.

I couldn't imagine having something this incredible and then just selling it – letting someone else have it.

He looked at me for a long moment before shaking his head. "I don't think I do. Not anymore."

I slowly crossed the room towards him. "No?"

He shook his head again. "Not after seeing that look on your face."

Is he saying what I think he's saying?

"Don't fuck with me, Ky Bateman." I growled, "I'm pregnant, hormonal and hungry. Are you saying you want to keep this house?"

"You're hungry?" He frowned.

"I'm always hungry. I'm growing a human that's half you," I snapped.

He chuckled. "Well I know better than to get in the way of a Bateman and their stomach, so yes, I think we should keep this house, blondie. I think we should raise our family here."

Our family.

Just hearing him say those words soothed my heart.

He'd grilled me with questions after we'd finished having sex in the stables; how far along was I? Why wasn't I showing? When was the baby due? How big was it? When could he see a picture... his questions were endless and his excitement was infectious.

I knew he was head over heels in love with his child already but hearing him talk about our family as a unit was exactly the reassurance I needed.

We were going to be okay, him and I.

We were together, we'd figure out the rest as we went.

"I think I could live with that," I said on a whisper.

"I can see our pretty babies running around already."

"Baby," I corrected him. "One baby. It's not twins, trust me, I made him check twice."

"One, for now." He smirked. "But we're having two girls and a boy, remember? At least..."

My breath hitched. He really wanted it. I could see it in his eyes. He wanted a whole life. With *me*.

"Five bedrooms is a lot, sparky."

He lowered his mouth to mine, claiming me. "Lucky we already got a head start then."

The kiss quickly turned into something more as he ground his erection into my hip.

"I *really* want to see those bedrooms," I murmured against his lips as he backed me up.

I knew the way he was kissing me; it was the way that led to clothes on the floor and naked bodies moving together.

"Women, only one thing on their minds." He grinned.

I swatted at his shoulder and pulled back to look at him. "I really do love you."

"I know."

I waited for him to say it back, but he didn't,

instead a smile pulled at his lips as he watched me waiting. The bastard was teasing me.

"Asshole," I muttered, rolling my eyes.

I tried to shove him away, but he refused to budge.

"You know I love you, blondie, think I always have, think I always will."

That was good enough for me.

36

Ky

Two weeks later

THERE WAS nothing you could give a man who already had everything, or so I thought, but Blake was proving me wrong.

We'd spent three nights with Aubrey and Chance so I could make it up to them for ghosting, and so Blake could get the stuff she'd left behind when she first came back to look for me, but now we were home, just the two of us. Alone, in a way we'd never been before.

Home.

Fuck, it still sounded weird. I hadn't had a place to call home in years.

I'd had lots of temporary homes, lots of beds I'd slept in and couches I'd crashed on, but nowhere I really felt like I belonged. No place I'd ever imagined myself staying in for longer than a week.

That had all changed since she came back.

I had a home.

I had something to look forward to.

I had a baby on the way.

I had a woman that I knew would one day be my wife.

And right now, I had that woman's plump lips wrapped around my cock.

Turns out there was something I wanted, after all.

What a way to start the day.

Happy birthday to me.

She tortured me, slipping up and down so slowly it was borderline cruelty.

I tossed the sheet off my body so I could watch the way her cheeks hollowed out as she sucked me.

She looked up at me in surprise, one blue eye, one green, both solely focused on me.

Our gazes locked and I couldn't have looked away if I tried. She swirled her tongue around my tip, and I heard a growl leave my throat.

"Stop teasing me," I grunted.

She grinned at me; her mouth stretched wide around my dick. Fucking blondie, even with my cock in her mouth, she was still showing me she was boss.

I thrust my hips upwards, fucking her mouth, and she hummed in the back of her throat, causing my balls to tighten painfully.

"Jesus, Blake," I moaned.

She wrapped her small hand around the base of my dick and started really working me over.

She had me on the brink of blowing my load in thirty seconds flat.

"I'm going to paint the back of your pretty little throat with my cum, and you're going to swallow every drop of it, understood?"

I might have been able to make her blush on the daily with words far less crass, but my Blake was a dirty girl in the bedroom. She craved my foul mouth.

She nodded, always game.

Her movements quickened, became more frantic; she wanted me to lose control, she wanted to make me blow.

I thrust again and again, taking everything she was willing to give me, and coming hard, white stars dancing across my vision as I poured myself into her.

"Christ," I panted, falling back against the pillows.

She popped off my dick and licked her lips. "Happy birthday, baby."

"Best present I've ever had, blondie. Hands down."

She crawled up the bed and curled herself into my side. "Twenty-nine, how's it feel?"

"Feels like twenty-eight," I replied with a grin.

"How does twenty-eight feel?"

I chuckled. "Like twenty-seven."

She shook her head in amusement.

"What do you want to do today?"

I slid my hand up her thigh and cupped her ass. "I can think of one thing."

"Are you always going to be this insatiable or are you still making up for lost time?"

I chuckled and planted a kiss on her lips.

She snuggled in closer. "It makes me sad to think of all those days we could have had together."

"There's a lot of days left, blondie, we're not missing out on anything." I rolled onto my side and draped my arm around her waist.

I could get used to waking up to this sight every morning. I'd be a happy man.

"You don't wish we'd never been apart?" Her question was filled with curiosity.

"This might be fucked up, but in a way I'm glad you left. I needed those two months to cement the way I felt about you – to learn that I *could* live without you, but I really didn't fucking want to."

"That might be the most real thing I've ever heard come out of your mouth."

"I'm full of surprises." I winked at her.

"You might have learnt a lot in those two months – I did too – but I *never* want a repeat. Okay?"

I pressed my lips to the crease between her eyes.

"I'm never going to let a misunderstanding, or my pride, or your pretty-boy ex-fiancé come between us ever again." I smirked as she narrowed her eyes at me.

"The time for deep and meaningful has expired I see."

"It's my party and I'll do what I want to."

"You're such a brat. Remind me again why I came back for you?"

I pressed my growing erection into her hip. "I think it was because you had a weakness for my cock, blondie."

"You know what? I think you might be right. *For once.*"

I gripped her hip, but she slipped from the bed, her pouty lips grinning at me. "C'mon, sparky, we've got work to do, this place isn't going to renovate itself."

I dropped my head back against the pillows. "You can't force me into manual labour on my birthday. That's barbaric."

"You and I both know I could force you to do anything I wanted, Ky Bateman, so perhaps don't test me."

That got my attention. I loved it when she gave me that no-bullshit attitude. I pushed up on my elbow to watch her dress. She looked so fucking sexy. She was well rested now, the dark circles under her eyes were long gone, and I'd been feeding her up on all her favourite food. She had the slightest of bumps under her bellybutton, and I couldn't wait to see her belly round and full with our child.

"Consider me told."

She snorted out a disbelieving laugh. "Yeah, *right.*"

"That's a hell of a lot of lip for someone who just had my dick down her throat."

She paused in the doorway and arched a brow at me. "Awful lot of backchat for someone who was on his knees with his face between my thighs last night."

Touché.

I rolled over and grabbed her phone off her night-stand to check the time. I grinned when I saw the waiting notification.

"You've got an email."

She huffed out a breath. "You mean, *you* have an email?"

My smile deepened.

At some point during one of our late-night chats, I'd discovered Blake emailed this American chick all the time, asking for advice, so I'd got hold of her phone last night and sent off a few questions of my own.

Dear Ida,

My boyfriend's penis is so big, I can't walk for days after we have sex. Any advice?

Stretched Vagina, Pleasure Town.

Her reply made me chuckle as I read it aloud.

Dear Stretched Vagina,

Yeah, I've got some great advice – change your email password and tell your boyfriend to look up some porn – he won't think his junk is so big after that.

S x

"I don't think you should write to her anymore. She's harsh."

Blake smirked at me.

"She answered both."

Blake had been having a meltdown after reading a baby book that had dilation diagrams in it. I'd had to listen to her whine about how her vagina was never going to be the same for days on end, so I'd turned to Ida.

Dear Ida,

Is giving birth as bad as they say? Everything will just snap back afterwards, right?

Coochie Concerned – Australia, Mate.

"Well, what did she say?" Blake demanded.

I opened the email and grinned. "I think I like her."

Dear Coochie Concerned,

I'm not sure if you want me to lie to you or not so I thought I'd cater for both options.

1. **Of course! You'll be back as good as new, having snug-fitting sex in no time!**
2. **RIP your vagina. That sucker is never going to be the same again.**

S x

I relayed the reply to her, laughing.

"I don't know what you're laughing about, *you're* the one who will be complaining about my ruined vagina."

I chuckled as she walked out, her sexy ass swaying.

My blondie.

My forever.

My perfect fucking match.

Nothing was ever going to be as challenging whilst simultaneously being so effortless, but I was so here for it – ruined vagina or not.

Every last second of it.

EPILOGUE

Blake

Eight months later

"SPARKY, we gotta go, my sister is going to be at our place at two!" I called out in the direction of the barn out back of Chance and Aubrey's place.

Things with Carmen had been going well lately and I didn't want to get back in her bad books. Ever since I had my daughter, I wasn't such a screw up in my sister's eyes. I'd finally managed to get something right. Didn't hurt that she loved my boyfriend either.

But it was nearly twelve, and I had a couple of errands I had to run on the way home, so my streak of good luck was probably going to come to an end if I couldn't get Ky to hurry the hell up.

Luna had managed to shit her way through every onesie we owned, and I was behind on washing. Actually, saying I was merely behind would be a lie, given that four days ago, Ky had decided that he in fact *didn't* like the tiles he'd laid in the laundry room, and had pulled the whole thing to pieces to re-do it.

No washing machine when you had a six-week-old baby wasn't exactly ideal. I had a mountain of dirty clothes waiting for his majesty to find a tile that met the exceptionally high standards he had all of a sudden.

I appreciated his attention to detail when it came to our home, but he'd become borderline OCD about the whole thing. I was officially put off renovating for life.

"Ky!" I yelled again.

"He's in the barn," Bree's voice came from behind me. I turned to find a sweet smile on her face and a cunning glint in her eye.

"I know, sweetie, I need your uncle to hurry up before he makes us late."

He'd disappeared with Luna in his arms about twenty minutes ago and I hadn't seen him since.

She sat her hands on her hips. "Well why don't you go get him then?"

I raised my brows at her. Ever since she'd turned four a few months ago, her sass levels had gone through the roof.

"Where's your daddy?"

She shrugged.

"Your mumma and brother?"

Another shrug.

"Well aren't you just super helpful today?" I tapped the end of her nose with my finger and she giggled.

"If you're going to be late, you should go find him," she told me, eyes wide.

My brow furrowed as I studied her. She was up to something.

"Out to the barn, you reckon?"

She nodded furiously.

"Why does this feel like a trap?"

She covered her mouth as a giggle slipped out. "It's not a trap, Aunt Blake, just go already."

God, it melted my heart every time she called me that. I'd been welcomed into their family with open arms.

"Alright then, I guess I'll just have to trust you."

She gave me a little push out the door, and I glanced at my watch again as I crossed the yard, headed out to the big barn that held so many memories for me – some incredible, some heart-breaking. I didn't have time to relive them all now, we were seriously going to be late, and my sister was going to be pissed. It wasn't wise to get in between her and her time with her niece.

"Ky, we gotta go!" I yelled out again but got no reply.

I could hear Pixy bleating away from somewhere in the paddocks; he was probably trying to get it on with the new rescue goat Aubrey had brought home the other week.

Horny bugger, Chance had called him.

"Ky! Seriously, where are you?"

"In here," he finally answered, his voice coming from inside the barn.

"If we're late because you've been mucking around out here, then *you* can feel the wrath of Carmen, because –" My threat died on my lips as my eyes took him in, dressed in a dark, navy blue suit and white shirt. He stood in the centre of the barn, bunches of wildflowers in mason jars surrounding him.

"Ky?" I questioned as I took a tentative step inside.

He had our daughter in his arms and *my god*, there was just something off the charts attractive about seeing your man holding his little girl like that. Especially when he looked as good as Ky did doing it. I turned to mush at just the sight of them together.

Our daughter was just like her father; dark hair, olive complexion. Thankfully, she had my build and not his, because there was no way I wanted to birth a set of shoulders like he had.

"You looking for me, blondie?"

"Yeah," I breathed, "we're going to be late."

He just looked at me, unspeaking, unmoving.

"What is all this, sparky?"

I slowly crossed the space between us.

"Bree didn't tell you?" he asked, amused.

I shook my head. "She told me it wasn't a trap but I'm starting to think she might have lied."

He chuckled. "It's not a trap. Come here."

I eyed him cautiously as he held out his free hand for me to take.

I closed the distance and clasped his hand between both of mine. Luna was asleep against his shoulder.

"I wanted to talk to you about something."

"Okay..."

He cleared his throat. "I love you, Blake. You're the best thing that ever happened to me."

My pulse whooshed in my ears, making me feel lightheaded.

I knew where this was going. I wasn't stupid. He was surrounded by flowers; he was wearing a suit. He might not have been down on one knee, but he may as well have been.

"*Ky*," I whispered.

"I'm not going to give some big elaborate speech – you already know all the reasons we're so great together... so I'm just going to come out with it... Marry me, blondie."

I swallowed deeply, my heart racing.

He knew how I felt about getting married, we'd talked about it. I was scared I'd never be able to go through with it without my dad to walk me down the aisle, but I also knew I could never say no if he asked me, so that left us at a crossroads. The last thing I wanted was to freak out and run out on another wedding.

It left me with two choices, break my own heart or break his.

"That wasn't a question," I breathed, stalling.

"I know." He smirked. "I figured if I didn't ask a question, you couldn't say no."

"Can't say yes either then," I pointed out.

I wanted to be with him forever, I *did*. I just wasn't sure how to get past this.

My eyes fell to the floor and he brought our joined hands up, under my chin, to force me to look at him.

"We can do it any way you want, Blake. We can go to the courthouse or we can get married at the beach, just the three of us. I don't care who's with us or where we are, I just want to wake up every morning and be able to call you my wife. I know this is hard for you, but I want you to be a Bateman. I want the whole world to know you're mine."

When he put it like that it all seemed so simple.

A casual beach wedding? A trip to the courthouse?

I could give him that. He'd given me everything. I could find a way to do this for him.

"Okay," I whispered, tears springing to my eyes.

How could I say no to this man, after all he'd stood by me through?

I couldn't.

I wouldn't.

Not in a million years.

He was no saint, but he was *mine*.

Those first few months after I came back were anything but easy. We argued constantly and we challenged each other daily. He made me furious and I made him crazy, but it worked for us. We never went to bed angry; we never told the other anything but the truth and neither of us held a grudge. It took us some time to find our rhythm, to settle into sharing our lives with the other – and to this day, we still had a lot to learn about each other, but I was madly in love with him. He was madly in love with me too. That was all we really needed.

I couldn't imagine ever having a life that didn't revolve around him.

A blinding grin lit up his face. "Okay, you'll marry me?"

"Okay, I'll marry you."

"Thank you, blondie." He was so deliriously happy. His smile was so wide, his eyes so bright.

"Can you not give me shit for about thirty seconds so I can do this properly?"

I nodded, the tears that had just been threatening before, now overflowing, spilling down my cheeks.

He dropped to one knee, being careful not to jostle our daughter. "Blake Cameron Vincent, I'm really glad you weren't born a boy."

A laugh bubbled out of me. He let go of my hand and reached into his jacket pocket to pull out a small, black box.

"I love you even when you drive me fucking crazy – shit, didn't mean to swear, sorry baby." He kissed Luna's head. "I love you, Blake, I promise you milk chocolate and summer days. I promise to always answer *no* when you ask me if you look fat. I promise you *everything*... will you be mine forever?"

Those dark eyes were burning bright, the gold slithers the most vibrant I'd ever seen them.

I nodded my head as he flipped open the lid on the ring box, revealing a beautiful gold, princess-cut diamond ring.

"Yes," I choked out.

He was back on his feet in a flash, his mouth pressed to mine in a kiss that was all lips, teeth and tongues, our daughter cradled between us.

He pulled back and grinned. I'd never seen him look so ecstatic, so handsome.

And he's all mine.

"You can come out now," he called over his shoulder.

I looked around and spotted Chance, Aubrey, Bree and CJ as they crept out of their hiding places.

It only made it more perfect that they were here with us to share this moment.

Hugs and congratulations were exchanged. Everyone was so happy for us, and I was happy too, even though I knew the pang of sadness in my stomach would probably never go away completely, but I could live with that. I had Ky, I had Luna, and I knew my dad would be watching over me, smiling.

"Can we talk a minute?" Chance pulled me aside and I looked at him in confusion.

"Is everything okay?"

He went to speak and then paused, clearing his throat nervously. I'd never seen him look so unsure of himself. "I ah... I just wanted to tell you that..." more throat clearing, "I know I could never take your dad's place, but if you want the whole big white wedding, I'd be honoured to walk you down the aisle."

"You'd do that for me?" I whispered, shocked.

He nodded his head and rubbed at the back of his neck. "It would be a privilege, little lady."

I bit back a fresh wave of tears as I looked between each person in the room.

So much love, so much loyalty and at the very centre of it all was the man of my dreams, holding our baby and smiling at me like I lit up the sky... and I was going to be his wife one day soon.

I couldn't have thought of a more perfect day if I'd tried.

The end.

Want to keep up with all of the new releases in Vi

Keeland and Penelope Ward's Cocky Hero Club world? Make sure you sign up for the official Cocky Hero Club newsletter for all the latest on our upcoming books:

https://www.subscribepage.com/CockyHeroClub

Check out other books in the Cocky Hero Club series:
http://www.cockyheroclub.com

THANK YOU!

Thank you for reading Master Manipulator, I hope you enjoyed it.

If you did enjoy it, please consider leaving a review; they give authors valuable feedback, help other readers find new books, and I'd really, really appreciate it!

If you are interested in getting sneak peeks into my work, freebies and giveaways, you can sign up for my newsletter.

If you're into Facebook, please join my reader group, Goodin's Girls.

Please remember:

This book has been written using UK English and may contain euphemisms and slang words that form part of the New Zealand spoken word.

Please remember that the words are not

misspelled. They are slang terms and form part of everyday, New Zealand vernacular.

I.e: I'm from New Zealand and sometimes we say weird things down here... please try and be cool about it.

Thanks again!

OTHER TITLES

Love Like Yours Series

Rushed – Book 1

Pierced – Book 2

Hunted – Book 3

Chased – Book 4

Love like Yours Box Set – Books 1-4

———

Rock Games Novels

Paper, Scissors, Rock: Vol .1

Hide and Seek: Vol. 2

———

My Heart Duet

My Heart Needs

My Heart Wants

Every Last Beat – The Heart Duet Box Set – Books
1 & 2

———

Calendar Boys

Mr. February

Mr. March

Mr. April

Mr. May

Mr. June

Mr. July

Mr. August

Mr. September

Mr. October

Mr. November

Mr. December

Calendar Boys Box Set – Books 1-4

Calendar Boys Box Set – Books 5-8

ACKNOWLEDGMENTS

Yay! I've made it through another book! This one was something different for me, being part of the Cocky Hero Club, which is such a complete honour. I loved weaving my own story in with some of your favourite characters from some of Vi and Penelope's books.

Huge thank you to Vi and Penelope, and their team, especially Dan. It really is such a massive privilege to be part of this project and be allowed to put words into their beloved characters mouths – I hope I've done them justice.

All that's left to say is thank you to everyone who made this possible for me as I've navigated this project.

Special thanks to my girls, Bianca, Stacey and MV, for always having my back, helping me bounce ideas and listening to my whining. I probably couldn't get through this without you girls, and I appreciate your support immensely!

Thank you so much to Stacey and Trina at spellbound for the excellent job on editing, as always!

Also, a special shoutout to Kylee for being so incredibly lovely and supportive of my work, I appreciate you more than you know!

Last but definitely not least, thank you to my readers, new and old, for picking up this book and making it all the way to the end, you're the real MVPs!

Thanks again!

N x

PLAYLIST

Electricity – Silk City, Dua Lipa, Diplo & Mark
Ronson
No One – Alicia Keys
Empty Space – James Arthur
Fire N Gold – Bea Miller
Incredible – James TW
Notice – Thomas Rhett
Don't Check On Me – Chris Brown & Justin Bieber
Trampoline – SHAED & ZAYN
Too Good to Say Goodbye – Bruno Mars
Quite Miss Home – James Arthur
What Am I – Why Don't We
Imagination – Shawn Mendes
I Have Questions – Camila Cabello
Old News – Mitch James
End Game – Taylor Swift & Ed Sheeran
Only Us – Drax Project
better off – Jeremy Zucker
Alone With You – Canyon City

You Are The Reason – Calum Scott

Too Much To Ask (Acoustic) – Niall Horan

Can I Be Him (Acoustic) – James Arthur

I Like Me Better – Lauv

Wild Love (Acoustic) – James Bay

Think Before I Talk – Astrid S

Favourite Ex – Maisie Peters

Worst of You – Maisie Peters

We Don't Have To Take Our Clothes Off – Ella Eyre

Mercy – Shawn Mendes

My Mistake – Gabrielle Aplin

Liar – LEON

Over My Head – The Fray

Rush – Lewis Capaldi & Jessie Reyez

Half A Man – Dean Lewis

Slide – James Bay

Bad – James Bay

Lose You To Love Me – Selena Gomez

You & Me – James TW

Unforgettable – Thomas Rhett

Marry ME – Thomas Rhett

Breakeven – The Script

Thinking Of You – Katy Perry

The Feeling – Justin Bieber & Halsey

Love You Goodbye – One Direction

Why Try – Ariana Grande

The One – Kodaline

One Day – Opshop

Long Gone – SIX60

Ghosts – SIX60

Liar – Camila Cabello

ABOUT THE AUTHOR

NICOLE S. GOODIN is a romance author and mother of two from Taranaki in the North Island of New Zealand.

In mid-2015, she started to write about a group of characters who wouldn't get out of her head. Her first book, Rushed, was published in mid-2016.

Nicole enjoys long walks on the beach, pillow fights and braiding her friends' hair. She dislikes clichés, talking about herself in the third person, and people who don't understand her sense of humour.

Please feel free to contact her either via her website, email, Instagram, Twitter or on her Facebook page, she would love to hear your feedback. If you're feeling really game, you can even sign up for her newsletter.

UPCOMING TITLES

Rock Games Novels

One for the Money